ADVANCED PRAISE FOR *PASQUINADES*

"All roads lead to Rome, where Anthony Di Renzo's narrator (a renowned talking statue) reports on historical and literary events from ancient times to the present. *Pasquinades* is a richly detailed and biting satire, full of warmth and humor."

—Lamar Herrin,
author of *Romancing Spain* and *Fishing the Jumps*

"With deft and rhythmic prose, Anthony Di Renzo brings us vivid portraits of Rome in this exquisite collection of essays voiced by Pasquino, the city's most famous talking statue. We learn about the Eternal City's culture and history and, even more compellingly, its daily life, past and present. Throughout the chapters and the moving epilogue of this excellent collection, Di Renzo shares his passion for the city of his heritage with lively description and compelling commentary."

—Katharyn Howd Machan,
author of *Secret Music: Voices from Redwing, 1888*

"Told from the perspective of Rome's most beloved talking statue, Anthony Di Renzo's *Pasquinades* is a delightful goldmine of stories peppered with information about the Eternal City. Every lover of history and the arts should read this witty, charming, thoroughly entertaining book."

—Tony Ardizzone,
author of *The Evening News* and *In Bruno's Shadow*

"Anthony Di Renzo's *Pasquinades* recounts Rome's history and mythology in a voice both ancient as time and perpetually young. A voice filled with longing, tongue-in-cheek cynicism, and heartfelt affection for everything that is quintessentially Roman. Through centuries of wars and invasions, destruction and reconstruction, hyper-tourism and political upheavals, Rome has always risen anew and will continue to do so forever. It is the Eternal City, and Di Renzo renders it superbly and with great panache."

—Shona Ramaya,
author of *Operation Monsoon*

"Pasquino, in his own words, is 'the Eternal City's enduring monument to sarcasm.' Throughout this book, he crosses timelines to rant against power, unapologetically mocking popes and kings, communists and fascists. Di Renzo's masterful talent for language makes this trip a joyride as he tells the fascinating stories behind Rome's monuments and landmarks but always keeps his eye on the main prize: free speech."

—Maria Lisella,
author of *Thieves in the Family*

"Eccentric, charming, surprising, affectionate, and witty, these essays by Anthony Di Renzo, narrated in the voice of Pasquino (an ancient statue on whose base Romans have written barbed graffiti for centuries) are a fine introduction to the Eternal City. The author's love of Rome is matched by his love of words—a voice full of wit and charm."

—Gail Holst-Warhaft,
author of *Lucky Country* and *Penelope's Confession*

"Nobody, but nobody, tells a story like the erudite and entertaining Anthony Di Renzo. Do you love Rome? From the mouth of Pasquino, a 2,000-year-old battered statue who has been rescued from ruin and for whom Di Renzo is the scribe, you will learn about the wisdom and folly, legends and scandals, dreams and nightmares of the Roman people. Listen to the secrets they whisper in Pasquino's ear and read the messages they post on his pedestal. You will understand how they think and live, and will share their wolfish appetites for fine food and wine. Witty, colorful, and phantasmagoric, these bite-sized, digestible essays about Italy's most fabled city are a delightful feast."

—Julia della Croce,
author of *Roma: Authentic Recipes from in and around the Eternal City*

"I have been to Rome once but am convinced I would have had an even better visit if I had been escorted by Pasquino, Anthony Di Renzo's talking statue, the best tour guide ever."

—Lisa Harris,
author of *Geechee Girl* and *Allegheny Dream*

"Reading Anthony di Renzo's lively essays on Roman culture, history, and personalities is almost as good as a trip to Rome itself—perhaps even better, because Di Renzo gives us an insider's view. He writes like an angel (a somewhat sardonic, mischievous one) and always with an eye for the great narrative, the indispensable detail, the juiciest tidbits from two thousand years of city gossip. This book is a delight, a must-read for anyone interested in European culture, Roman history, and writing as smooth as the finest wine."

—Jeanne Mackin,
author of the *The Beautiful American* and (forthcoming) *Picasso's Lovers*

"What I love most about these charming yet biting reports from Rome—and there's a lot to love—is the sense that I'm in the hands of an author steeped in historical understanding. His accounts are sure to inform and amuse those interested not only in Roman history but also in how that history informs current global events. Pasquino, our narrator, is so endearingly amusing because we perceive him as an authentic barker of satirical truth."

—Cory Brown,
author of *A Long Slow Climb* and *Elisions*

"Part history, part travelogue, and part satire, *Pasquinades* is a passionate love letter to the Eternal City. With erudition, wit, and élan, Anthony Di Renzo guides us masterfully through the centuries. Whether or not you've been to Rome, these essays will leave you longing to go."

—Jack Wang,
author of *We Two Alone*

"Faced with the impermanence of human flesh in a culture distracted by ephemera, readers will enjoy spending time with a marble statue who speaks lasting truths in the Eternal City. Pasquino, Anthony Di

Renzo's eloquent narrator, bears witness to history, offering up his voice for the voiceless long after we're gone."

—Andrei Guruianu,
author of *Portraits of Time*

PASQUINADES

PASQUINADES

ESSAYS FROM ROME'S
FAMOUS TALKING STATUE

ANTHONY DI RENZO

CAYUGA LAKE BOOKS
ITHACA, NY

Cayuga Lake Books

Ithaca, NY USA
cayauglakebooks.com

Pasquinades: Essays from Rome's Famous Talking Statue
by Anthony Di Renzo

First Printing – October 2023
Paperback ISBN: 978-1-68111-531-3
Library of Congress Control Number: 2023947001
Author photo by Russ Baker
Cover photo and book illustrations by Shutterstock

Printed in the USA

0   1   2   3   4

For

SIMONE SCHIAVINATO,
friend and editor

"Rome is human memory, the city that teaches us every morning that life is eternal spring and death a passing cloud. Rome has defeated death, and that is why it is called the Eternal City."

—Amara Lakhous,
Clash of Civilizations Over an Elevator in Piazza Vittorio

TABLE OF CONTENTS

DREAMS OF GLORY

LAST JUDGMENTS

AN APPETITE FOR LIFE

EPILOGUE

INTRODUCTION
Pasquino Speaks

Centuries before Facebook and Twitter, Romans had "talking statues" on which they could post humorous disgruntlements for all to see. Often by cover of night, to avoid arrest and possible execution, citizens graffitied the pedestals of ancient heroic figures with satiric barbs and verses, describing their contemporary leaders in less than heroic terms. Dissolute Renaissance princes, popes dripping with bling, bloated political figures from the Borgias to Berlusconi— all have been smacked in the face with verbal pies by anonymous members of the Roman public.

What all these commentaries had in common were *wit*. They were cleverly written: funny, sarcastic, sometimes obscene but sometimes surprisingly rueful. Though ephemeral—often torn down or sanded away by the authorities soon after their appearance—they displayed the kind of rollicking spontaneity common to public media in every era and locale.

The most famous of these talking statues is a battered old relic popularly called Pasquino, who stands in small square off Piazza Navona, right behind the Museo di Roma. Originally carved in the Third Century BC, he is named after a sharp-tongued tailor who lived in the neighborhood where, after being excavated from a ditch, the statue was re-erected in the early sixteenth century. Even today, Pasquino attracts wiseacres who tape up their gripes to a nearby bulletin board as motor scooters bleat past through rush-hour traffic. In English, a *pasquinade* has come to mean any sarcastic pronouncement made with an amusing turn of phrase.

One man who can turn a phrase with dazzling erudition is Anthony Di Renzo, the author of *Pasqinades,* who claims to be the statue's secretary. His essays—revised, expanded, and collected here for the first time—originally appeared as columns from August 2013 to December 2020 in *L'Italo Americano*, a bilingual newspaper based in Los Angeles with an extensive international readership. Frequently, Di Renzo's pasquinades take savage aim at a wide array of personalities in Italian culture and history. But more often he puts aside his alter ego's satirical perspective and describes with tender affection the daily life, past and present, of one of the world's most fascinating cities.

Di Renzo guides us through side streets festooned with flowers for festival days and entices us with tastes and scents of favorite Italian foods, informing us about their history in the kitchens of emperors and literary figures. He writes of the ways children have celebrated Halloween down through the centuries and of the citizens' love-hate relationship with their city's feral dogs. He explores how modern religious observances have evolved from ancient Roman beliefs and pagan rituals. Di Renzo's Rome is always steeped in history, even when he writes about contemporary music and film goddesses. His Pasquino can turn macabre, as in his mini-biography of a fabled public executioner, or become celebratory to describe the elation with which Romans welcomed the American troops that liberated their city at the end of World War II.

A novelist as well an accomplished essayist, Di Renzo is also a scholar of American and Italian American history and literature and a professor of writing at Ithaca College in Central New York. Used to attracting a wide readership for his columns, he always pens his creative and scholarly work with a light, accessible touch. This master stylist has never met any good descriptive phrases he doesn't like. With the exuberance of Salman Rushdie or Giuseppe di Lampedusa, he artfully tosses them off to describe his historical characters.

Di Renzo clearly loves lively verbs, and enjoys employing them in cascading riffs:

> At dusk, millions of starlings invade Rome.... A cyclone of feathers swallows the sun. The birds scatter and regroup, form a living tidal wave, surge and drown an archipelago of tiles and chimneys, garrets and loggias, domes and spires.

You might think that the birds are here to ornament a pleasant piece of travel writing, but not so: Pasquino recalls Julius Caesar, who laughed at the warning a flock of sparrows gave him as he watched them tear their leader to pieces in midflight; the very next day he was assassinated on the same site. Centuries later, moving through a crowd, Mussolini, too, ignored an avian warning, failing to spot "a bird-like spinster" in a feathered hat who suddenly opened fire on him with a pistol, blowing away part of his nostrils.

For Di Renzo, all things Roman are connected; he can swoop back and forth through the centuries linking ancient monuments to modern eyesores, Renaissance papal intrigues to contemporary Vatican politics, a mob of teenagers gorging on French fries at a

Burger King to an eccentric prince who famously trashed a rival's banquet by leading a cow up the carpeted staircase of her mansion. The author loves colorful eccentrics as well as romantic figures from literature and real-life demagogues with clay feet. It's extraordinary how much history and folklore and culture, high and low, you can absorb while reading his pasquinades.

Anthony Di Renzo's essays are distinguished by an uncurbed enthusiasm for the life of the great metropolis and the people he depicts so vividly. You don't have to love Rome already to enjoy his spirited collection, but you're likely to feel, when you've put the book down, that you'd love to revisit it in person.

EDWARD HOWER
Editor, Cayuga Lake Books

EDITOR'S NOTE

The young man shown on the cover of this book is not, alas, Pasquino. Rome's famous talking statue refuses to be photographed. Not out of modesty—he has none—but because he is painfully aware that he is less than photogenic. Over the centuries, he has lost his limbs as well as part of his nose.

For the cover illustration, Pasquino has chosen his old friend Scongiglio, a merman from a nearby piazza. In Roman dialect, Scongiglio means "Conch." But the two instruments he plays on are auger snail shells, which are easier to shoot water out of if you are sitting in a fountain.

Sometimes, very late at night, Pasquino and Scongiglio visit one another's piazzas and croon ancient songs together in the moonlight.

—E.H.

PROLOGUE

1.

MORE LASTING THAN BRONZE:
Pasquino introduces himself

*B*envenuto a Roma! Welcome to Rome!

If you want to enjoy your visit, shut your guidebook and listen to me, Rome's most famous talking statue. I always tell the truth—with a dash of poetic license, of course—about this beautiful and sometimes brutal city. Cheeky poets and scurvy graffitists might impersonate me, but I am the one and only, the genuine and original PASQUINO!

Everyone knows where to find me: right off Piazza Navona, the most glorious Baroque square in the heart of Rome, at the intersection of two cobblestone streets. The wider and longer street was once a parade route for papal elections and for public executions. Poised on blocks of ancient concrete, I stand at the back of a neoclassical palace housing the Museum of Rome: a battered, limbless torso with a weathered but noble face. I am the Eternal City's enduring monument to sarcasm.

I began as a block of limestone, quarried at Tivoli during the Second Punic War. I yearned to be an arch, an aqueduct, or even a humble milestone, but fate sold me to a provincial magistrate, who had lost his son at the battle of Cannae in 216 BC. A lover of the Iliad, he ordered me carved into a statue of the Spartan king Menelaus cradling the body of the slain young warrior Patroclus. No wonder I have two minds about everything! For seven generations, I remained in the cypress grove at the magistrate's country villa until his last descendant perished in the purges of 43 BC. Octavian Caesar, the future Emperor Augustus, confiscated the estate and brought me to Rome.

The Caesars used me as a punitive white elephant. Whenever a general lost a battle or a governor bilked a colony, a Praetorian Guard delivered me to the offender's estate, accompanied by a brutally ironic thank-you note from the emperor. The recipient usually committed suicide. However, in 81 AD, when the Emperor Domitian became displeased with the entire city, he placed me over the arcade of his new stadium as a warning. Four centuries later, the Vandals toppled me from my niche, smashed my face, lopped off my limbs, and buried me in a ditch.

There I lay for a thousand years . . .

On April 1, 1501, while excavating the foundations of a palazzo, a papal architect found me amid a heap of imperial rubbish. Delighted, he brought me to his patron, a witty cardinal, who placed me on a pedestal facing a cozy square frequented by booksellers and writers. His Eminence invited all Rome to admire me. On St. Mark's Day, he consecrated me to Momus, the Greek god of mockery. The cardinal slipped a carnival mask over my face, draped me in a toga, and decorated my pedestal with Latin epigrams.

Such pranks were common in my neighborhood. As I said, its primary street was a parade route from St. Peter's to the city center. Practically every month a carnival took place, so no one was surprised when anti-clerical squibs, scraps of paper pasted all over my pediment, began to appear. The culprit was a local tailor, Pasquino Mazzocchi, whose tongue was sharper than his needle. Since his trade often took him to the Vatican, Signor Pasquino knew the most delicious gossip.

After his death, I assumed his name. And so I became a bulletin board for anonymous satiric poems, called *pasquinades* in his honor.

Authorities were outraged. Pope Adrian VI, a dour reformer elected in 1522, vowed to throw me into the Tiber, but his advisors dissuaded him. Like a frog, they explained, I would croak only louder in water. Likewise, Charles de Bourbon, whose German mercenaries sacked the city a few years later, threatened to decapitate me. If he tried, military aides warned, some joker would substitute a Jack-o-lantern for my head. Church and state were powerless. Made of stone, I could be neither excommunicated nor executed.

The pagan gods, whose presence remained strong in Christian Rome, protected me. Momus, son of Night and grandson of Chaos, cursed all foes and granted me occult powers. Fully conscious, I discovered that I was clairvoyant. Even now, I can read individual thoughts and project myself into Rome's collective memories. Better still, I can wander the city streets without ever leaving this pedestal. Sometimes I waft about as a disembodied spirit, haunting ruins, museums, libraries, and galleries. At other times, I enter the bodies of unsuspecting passersby here in the Piazza di Pasquino: named, of course, for me.

My hosts vary. Centuries ago, I possessed mendicants, prostitutes, and buskers. Today, I prefer tour guides, journalists, and Uber drivers, people who know every nook and corner of this city and love to hear themselves talk. But my favorite avatar is an old curator at the Museum of Rome, who scorns retirement and belongs to the Free University of Antico Caffè Greco. This club of artists and intellectuals meets each month in Rome's oldest coffeehouse. Thanks to its members, my mind is an attic filled with antique curios and collectible prints.

For almost 525 years, I have been a beloved arbiter. Famous writers, therefore, have presumed to speak in my name: including Pietro Aretino, Giuseppe Gioachino Belli, and Trilussa. But I alone am Rome's tribune of free speech. My motto is *"Pazzia Sapienza."* It means "Crazy Wisdom." As the perennial loyal opposition and a passionate gadfly, I have criticized popes and kings, fascists and communists, conservatives and liberals. I have never betrayed my sacred office. And somehow, I have survived the Four Horsemen of the Apocalypse: War, Urban Renewal, Advertising, and Tourism.

Several years ago, however, Rome's right-wing mayor stripped off my lampoons and scrubbed and bleached me a virginal white. Henceforth, he decreed, all my notices will be posted on a sideboard mounted on a Lucite stand. Supposedly, this edict insures my preservation. Actually, it makes it easier to bowdlerize messages and stifle protest.

How could I work under these conditions? After consulting with the river god Marforio, the colossus Madama Lucrezia, and Rome's other talking statues, I decided to write a series of columns which I am now publishing in this book. I appreciate the willingness of my secretary, Signor Di Renzo, to take dictation from an armless author.

A few years ago, the palazzo I guard was being renovated. Before construction began, workmen erected a plank-board wall around the base of the building, completely covering me. Within days, this wall was slathered in posters and scrawled with graffiti. One notice read:

"You will never silence Pasquino! And you will never silence the people of Rome!"

THE HEART OF ROME

2.

OVERTURE:
Pasquino conducts morning traffic

Whenever I pray to become flesh and blood and to sprout arms and legs, I always ask the gods to make me a *pizzardone*: a Roman traffic cop. Each dawn, I would rise and put on a sexy black uniform, a white British bobby-style helmet, and spotless white gloves. Then I would strut downtown, mount a steel pedestal, and direct morning traffic in the middle of Piazza Venezia.

If all roads lead to Rome, they all intersect at this central hub. The crossroads of Rome's three busiest streets are sandwiched between the huge monument to Italy's first king and the former palazzo of its last dictator, Benito Mussolini. Piazza Venezia feeds traffic towards City Hall, the Italian Parliament, the Presidential Palace, and other vital landmarks. City planners call it the Aorta of the Capital. But to keep things flowing and to prevent fatalities, a good *pizzardone* must be a symphony conductor, not a cardiac surgeon.

Up on the podium, a traffic cop maintains control through elaborate gestures. Although I've never driven a car, for obvious reasons, I know this semaphore by heart. Two outstretched horizontal arms mean "*Go!*" One raised vertical arm means "*Yield!*" Two hands straight out with palms facing motorists mean "*Stop, goddamnit!*" No other maestro could be more expressive—or more exacting about tempi and dynamics.

15

Morning rush hour is the overture to the Roman day, more complex and cacophonous than a tone poem by Respighi. But nothing is scored in Piazza Venezia. At this chaotic jam, anything can go wrong: A Lancia might lose its rear wheel, a delivery truck might spill a load of cantaloupes, or a bus might crush several scooters while executing a reckless U-turn.

But if I were a *pizzardone*, I would face such dangers with pride and confidence. Not only would I belong to the *vigili*—the oldest branch of the municipal police force, founded by Caesar Augustus in the first century BC to supervise night traffic in imperial Rome—but I also would be protected by a friend in high places. No, not the City Traffic Commissioner. I mean Francesca Romana, the patron saint of Roman drivers.

Santa Francesca, born and raised right here in my neighborhood, was the Mother Teresa of fourteenth century Rome. Whenever she traveled at night to help the poor, a torch-bearing angel guided her through the unlit streets. Today, municipal engineers invoke her to upgrade the city's traffic lights. Because Francesca also possessed the gift of bilocation, the ability to be in two places at once, Roman cabbies place her image on their dashboards.

Every March, however, on the Sunday closest to the Ninth (Francesca's feast day), non-commercial drivers flock to her shrine: a Baroque church with a Romanesque bell tower on the eastern end of the Forum. Devout Catholics and proud members of the Automobile Club of Italy, these pilgrims come to have their vehicles blessed by the Pope's prime minister: the Cardinal Secretary of State of His Holiness. I never miss this ceremony because the *pizzardoni* always send an honor guard. One year, however, they showed up in full force to defend their reputation and to teach us Romans a little self-respect.

This happened in March 2018. Rome was nursing a collective black eye. Someone had leaked a forthcoming report from Greenpeace, an environmental group, rating Rome the worst European capital for vehicular traffic, air pollution, and road safety. In fact, the report said, the only city in the world with more severe congestion and worse air quality was Bogotá, Colombia. *Colombia!* The papers wrote fierce editorials, the opposition parties utterly denounced the sitting government, and motorists blamed the Traffic Commissioner and the *pizzardoni*.

I feared the acrimony would spoil the Feast Day ceremony, but everything seemed fine when I arrived in the piazza that morning. Carpenters were finishing a platform for expected dignitaries. Although the street along the Forum was lined with cars, enough space had been cleared for the procession to the Basilica of Saint Frances of Rome.

First, elegant in scarlet, was the Cardinal Secretary of State, who had come from the Vatican in a "pre-blessed" Mercedes-Benz sedan. Next was the Mayor of Rome, Virginia Raggi, wearing a tricolor sash over a black power suit. The Traffic Commissioner followed in a peaked cap and dress uniform. Behind him, in lockstep, were the *pizzardoni,* who sang a military cadence to—and I'm not making this up!—the tune of *The Mickey Mouse Club March.*

Inside the church, where Santa Francesca's remains are buried in a crypt, the Cardinal Secretary of State celebrated a motor-themed mass. The altar was lined with parochial students dressed as crossing guards, holding miniature Stop and Go signs. After communion, the children followed him outside for the blessing. With an aspergillum, the Cardinal Secretary sprinkled holy water on a police van, an ambulance, a fire engine, and a garbage truck parked outside.

"Let the saint intercede to protect our way on the roads!" His Eminence intoned. "And may motorists drive with judgment and prudence!" Reporters smirked. Raising an eyebrow, the cardinal made the sign of the cross, and the faithful responded with a blast of horns and sirens.

Mayor Raggi carefully adjusted her tricolor sash and approached the podium. Everyone expected her to address the Greenpeace scandal, and I could see that she was nervous. "*Sforza*, Virginia!" I said under my breath. "Come on, Virginia! You'll be fine!" At the time, I had a powerful crush on her. Raven-haired and fine-boned, she was not only Rome's first woman mayor but also its youngest. Today, however, she looked haggard.

"Well . . ." the Mayor attempted a little levity, "this isn't going to be easy." She was rewarded with some rueful chuckles and scattered applause. During her election campaign three years ago, she had pledged to solve Rome's traffic problems, so the Greenpeace report was "a personal embarrassment." She took full responsibility, of course, but the challenges had been—

"Maybe we need a new traffic commissioner!" somebody brayed.

A *pizzardone* blew his whistle in fury and pointed at the heckler. The Commissioner, a husky, basset-faced man, who had gallantly risen to stand beside and support Mayor Raggi, snatched the mic at the podium.

"Complaints from the public," he shouted, but with a touch of humor, "should be submitted on our department's website!"

The *pizzardoni* laughed and clapped. Somehow this horseplay relaxed the crowd and emboldened the Commissioner to speak. Everyone loves to blame the government, he said, but the real problem was obvious: Rome had too many cars, and Romans drove them too often.

I didn't need to hear the statistics. I had witnessed the change myself over the century. Before the First World War, Rome had fewer than 200 cars. By 1925, when Pope Pius XI declared Santa Francesca the guardian of drivers, that number had increased twenty-fold. A quarter century later, when Pius XII began the custom of blessing cars on Francesca's feast day, traffic clogged the city—and the flood from the outer suburbs hadn't even begun!

Today, the Traffic Commissioner said, nine out of ten Romans own at least one vehicle. But the city's core, within the old Aurelian Walls, was not designed for motorized transportation. Most of Rome, we all knew, was never planned at all but grew helter-skelter. The historic center, where I live, remains largely a maze of narrow, crooked streets. Its few wide, straight avenues only speed traffic to such bottlenecks as Piazza Venezia.

Strikes, demonstrations, parades, processions, and visiting dignitaries and their corteges increase the congestion, stalling traffic for hours. The exhaust from idling engines suffocates pedestrians and disintegrates monuments. Every year, I disappear a little more. But the fumes also provoke toxic behavior. Drivers speed, cut each other off, and execute daredevil turns. City buses are whales amid schools of rushing, dashing minnows. Kamikaze pedestrians jump off sidewalks and into traffic. Scooters appear from nowhere and weave between honking cars.

"Why, only yesterday," the Mayor, taking over the mic, said in her honeyed voice, "two texters collided at—"

"Then do a better job!" another heckler bellowed.

Once again, a *pizzardone* blew his whistle and pointed. But this time, the Commissioner and his fellow officers addressed the crowd. How could they do a better job if Roman citizens didn't do theirs? What good were traffic laws without common sense and simple decency? Santa Francesca can't protect us if we refuse to help ourselves. We listeners hung our heads in shame and remembered how we had opposed every traffic-calming measure in the past ten years.

When City Hall proposed permanently closing to traffic the four-lane road from Piazza Venezia to the Coliseum, we objected. Why should we commute to work or run errands by threading the narrow, already congested streets behind the Forum? As a compromise, the traffic ban was limited to Sundays and national holidays, but we still complained.

When we clamored for more parking, the city constructed an underground public garage beneath the Janiculum Hill. But almost nobody used it. A fifteen-minute walk to the heart of downtown was too inconvenient for most drivers.

"*Romani,*" said the Traffic Commissioner, "*dobbiamo tutti impegnarci per fare meglio. We must all stive to do better. And with the intercession of Santa Francesca, we will!*"

"We will!" we shouted. And for that moment, we meant it. But resolutions, I thought, rarely last in a city with so many delightful distractions.

The Cardinal Secretary of State beamed and made the sign of the cross. We all cheered. But as a chauffeur whisked His Eminence away, engines revved in the Forum. The church square throbbed, and tires squealed. Mayor Raggi looked to heaven, beseeching Santa Francesca to prevent speeding. It would be a shame to ticket people on such a beautiful Sunday.

When the square was empty, the Commissioner blew his own whistle and the *pizzardoni* assembled in parade formation in their gold-braided dress uniforms. With three short blasts, they began a snappy cadence, the same call and response they had performed before the ceremony.

"For ninety years or more we've all been marching in this squad!"

"Pizzardon', pizzardon'! We're the traffic guard!"

"The pay is pretty awesome, but the work is very hard!"

"Pizzardon', pizzardon'! We're the traffic guard!"

Off they marched, up the Forum—past ruined temples, arches, and columns—jaunty and proud and swinging their arms. And I marched right behind them, if only in my heart.

3.

THE LABOR QUESTION:
Pasquino agitates for workers

Rome considers itself a blue-collar town, even though many Romans either work for the city or national government or dream of securing *un posto*, a cushy bureaucratic job that requires nothing more than punching a keyboard or stamping a form. This paradox, I think, might explain my neighbors' strange ambivalence towards trade unions. Most honor their proletariat roots, but whenever uncollected garbage piles up in Piazza di Pasquino, or a demonstration disrupts traffic in the historic center, or another strike shuts down the hospitals, airports, or train stations, these lower-middle-class Romans will curse organized labor like right-wing industrialists.

Sometimes I'm guilty of the same behavior, I'm ashamed to say. But because so many leftwing flyers cover my pedestal like autumn leaves, I usually sympathize with workers. Despite being glib and cynical, I would never cross a picket line, even if I had legs, and I would never deliberately miss Rome's annual May Day celebration.

Organized by Italy's three biggest unions, all headquartered in the city, this seven-hour rock concert attracts hundreds of thousands of spectators to Piazza San Giovanni in Laterano. Few participants belong to a union, mind you, but all buy T-shirts to support workers' rights.

Watching the 2023 televised concert in a working-class bar, I laughed with patrons. Labor Day, they joked, was becoming as gentrified as their district. Still, it beat the alternative. Between 1923 to 1945, I recalled, the holiday was actually banned.

Who was the Grinch who stole May Day? Benito Mussolini, the renegade leftist turned right-wing dictator, who played cat and mouse with Italian unions.

As a politician, Mussolini flaunted his working-class credentials. I can still see him working the crowd, jutting his jaw and puffing his chest. Wasn't he a blacksmith's son? Weren't his hands as calloused as a bricklayer's? I shook my head in disbelief. Before World War I, he had agitated for labor and edited the Socialist newspaper, *Avanti!* Comrades, however, suspected that he was less interested in advancing the cause than in advancing himself.

After World War I, Mussolini the Socialist, who had organized strikes for workers, became Mussolini the Fascist, who broke strikes for bosses. Fighting in the trenches, he claimed, had taught him that patriotism matters more than class solidarity. Perhaps, but the establishment also offered him status, money, and power to switch sides. Mussolini promised to reconcile capital and labor and restore order.

Shortly after becoming prime minister, Mussolini announced he would visit Rome's Motor Transport Company. If his busy schedule permitted, he added, he would address the men on the assembly line. As if that blowhard could ever resist giving a speech in a factory!

Benito was in rare form that afternoon. Let bureaucrats doze behind their desks, he said. The plant's steering wheel workers, his true colleagues, understood the words of the poet Filippo Tommaso Marinetti, founder of the Futurist movement: *All power to the man behind the wheel!*

Rome, Mussolini maintained, could become an industrial center, but only if she stopped living on memories. The Coliseum and the Forum were glories of the past, but Romans must build the glories of today and tomorrow. They belonged to a generation of builders who, by work and discipline, with hands and brains, yearned to make Italy a nation of producers, not parasites. To achieve this goal, however, workers must put their country before their union.

Mussolini abolished Labor Day and required workers to join the Fascist Party. Easier said than done, I thought. While touring a factory, Giacomo Suardo, Undersecretary of the Ministry of Corporations, asked the foreman about his men's politics.

"One third are Communists," the foreman reported, "one third are Socialists, and the rest belong to several small parties."

Suardo bridled. What?! And how many were Fascists?

"All of them, Your Excellency!" the foreman assured. "All of them!"

Displeased, Mussolini consulted the efficiency expert Frederick Winslow Taylor, another petty tyrant who believed in the one best way to do things. Taylor had revolutionized American industry with stopwatch and slide rule. The Duce established the Italian National Agency for Scientific Management and held the Third International Manager Conference in Rome. No expense was spared to impress participants.

Flags and tapestries decked the Campidoglio, the star-shaped piazza crowning Rome's Capitoline Hill. Soldiers lined the monumental staircase to the Senate Chamber. As a fanfare blared, Mussolini entered, saluted, and lectured bean counters, brass hats, and tycoons on the importance of discipline. Despite five years of Fascism, Italians workers remained "easygoing, skeptical, and individualistic: ill-disposed to take orders." For scientific management to plant deep roots in Italian industry, the soil must be tilled—with a harrow, if necessary.

Speedups and quotas boosted production, but these profitable measures translated into longer hours and falling wages. During the Depression, conditions worsened. Since unions could no longer complain or strike, workers expressed their resentment at a party rally in Piazza Venezia, across from Mussolini's palazzo. Naturally, I attended.

Like other rallies, this one used the standard ritual of call and response. From his balcony, the Duce cried: *"A chi la vittoria? A chi la gloria?* To whom the victory? To whom the glory?" And, as usual, the crowd roared: *"A noi! A noi!* To us! To us!" This time, however, Mussolini also asked: *"A chi il lavoro?* To whom the work? Who will sweat to make Italy great?"

The question was greeted with silence. Mussolini held a granite pose, but his henchmen fidgeted. To save the situation, the Party Secretary, Achille Starace, cried, "Salute the Duce!" and the band in the square played the Fascist hymn, *"Giovinezza."*

Nearly a century later, at Rome's 2023 May Day concert, the crowd chanted slogans and demanded the next act. Instead, a rumpled man in a red windbreaker branded with the letters CDIC, got on stage and took the mic. People booed. Old leftists were scandalized, I'm sure, but young people understandably wanted to hear the Welfare State, a popular band, perform their hit song about the gig economy, not the General Secretary of the Confederation of Labor denounce the Prime Minister of Italy, Giorgia Meloni.

A giant television screen showed a video clip shot before noon. At a press conference, Meloni announced that her right-wing government would loosen rules for short-term contracts and cut welfare benefits.

Such steps were necessary, she claimed, "to protect small businesses and to encourage the able-bodied to look for—"

"*O li o li o la!*" four grannies yodeled in the crowd. With their country accents, black dresses, and muscular calves, they looked like they had spent the morning working in a rice field. They jeered the Prime Minister and began an old protest song. *Miss High and Mighty,* they sang, *close your pride and open your wallet! We workers want our pay!* People clapped and joined in the chorus, until a rock band bounded on stage and deafened the square with amplified music. Three miles away, the vibrations shook the TV set broadcasting the show in my local bar.

Too bad, I thought, shaking my head as I nursed a Campari and soda. The old ladies looked like scarecrows and sang off key, but they were the most authentic act at the concert!

4.

ACROSS THE TIBER:
Pasquino celebrates his favorite neighborhood

Whenever I fear Rome is becoming Milan, whenever another cobblestone street is repaved with asphalt or another Baroque fountain is "restored" by a corporate sponsor, I flee to the most Roman neighborhood I know. Located on the west bank of the Tiber, south of Vatican City, Trastevere is a world apart. "Romans are one thing," residents say, "*Trasteverini* another." Proud and independent, this district dates back twenty-five centuries.

During the Republic (509 BC to 27 BC) Trastevere was disconnected from central Rome, geographically and administratively. Low taxes and light trade regulations attracted Italians from far-flung regions. Sailors and fishermen from Ostia also moved to the neighborhood. Most of Rome's Jews lived here, before the Ghetto was created across the Tiber River in 1526. But despite generations of immigration and crossbreeding, inhabitants of this ancient melting pot call themselves "the only true Romans." Compared to them, I am an interloper.

Locals divide the world into two camps: *noantri* and *voantri*, we others and you others. Or, more colloquially, "us guys and you guys." *Trasteverini* are the Chosen People, and their neighborhood is the Promised Land. Other Romans don't deserve to live in it. Such boasting makes me smile. Crowded and noisy, Trastevere has never exactly flowed with milk and honey. Two thousand years ago, however, it streamed with wine and warehoused potables and condiments. As I recall, a fountain of Minerva spurted olive oil on the same spot where the current fountain in Piazza Santa Maria spouts mere water.

Until the 20th century, the countryside penetrated Trastevere. Vineyards, orchards, gardens, and chicken coops abounded, and artichokes and zucchini grew in hidden courtyards. Jasmine and bougainvillea still bloom in the downspouts and drape over the walls of the old houses. From a maze of narrow streets and weathered cobblestones, rises the Janiculum Hill. When the breeze blows from the southeast, pine and myrtle scent the air.

Partial isolation and a unique subculture give this working-class enclave a bohemian atmosphere. Two college students string lingerie across an alley. A widow smokes Nazionali cigarettes and waters geraniums on a rusted balcony. A fortune teller uses a trained parakeet to predict the future in a tree-shaded square. At the intersection of two narrow lanes, an accordionist plays a mazurka in front of a bar.

I know this melancholy tune. It is a ballad about Regina Coeli: formerly a convent, now a notorious jail. At its stone entrance, there is one last step before the iron door that leads to the cellblocks inside. A Roman is not a Roman, claims the ballad, unless he has "climbed the step." To survive, *Trasteverini* often break the rules. Disdaining middle-class morality, they quote an old proverb: "*Fatta la legge, scoperto l'inganno.*" (You make the law, I find the loophole.) Fortunately, the Madonna forgives. Every July, she is honored at a huge block party called La Festa de' Noantri (The Festival of We Others). The origins of this tradition reveal much about the neighborhood's character.

On July 16, 1535, the Feast of Our Lady of Mount Carmel, a torrential storm nearly drowned some fishermen on the Tiber. Pulling to shore, they found a wooden statue of the Madonna near the mouth of the river. The grateful fishermen donated the statue to the Carmelite friars at the Basilica of San Crisgono. The brothers called her la Madonna dei Carmelitani, after their order, but everyone else called her 'a Madonna Fumarola (the Madonna of the River).

A century later, Cardinal Scipione Borghese transferred the statue to an oratory he had built by the Tiber. A generous but high-handed patron of the arts, Cardinal Scipione had restored the Basilica of San Crisogno with Vatican funds and considered everything in it his personal property. When he commandeered the Madonna's statue, I cursed his arrogance. But those sly *Trasteverini* avenged themselves under camouflage of piety. To subvert His Eminence and to reclaim their rights, they created their own religious festival.

Now housed in the Church of Sant'Agata in Trastevere, the Madonna Fumarola each year returns to her original home. Bejeweled and sumptuously dressed, she is carried through the streets back to San Crisogno, where she stays for eight days before returning by boat on the river. Cheers greet the fireworks from the Orange Garden on the Aventine Hill. Scattering over the Tiber and drifting past the Garibaldi Bridge, the sparks illuminate the statue of Trastevere's other patron saint: Giuseppe Gioachino Belli.

He was born on September 7, 1791, on the eve of the French Revolution. He died on December 21, 1863, seven years before the House of Savoy defeated the Papal States. Liberal friends teased that he had wasted his life in a reactionary backwater during a century of progress. Belli retorted that it was a miracle he had survived at all. Frankly, I never thought the runt would make it.

Dysentery nearly killed Belli in infancy. Because of his family's precarious finances, he was forced to work at an early age. After drudging as a copyist, Belli married a wealthy widow from a noble family. The couple settled in a palazzo by the Trevi Fountain. Leisure allowed Belli to write poetry, but his health was poor. He suffered from stomach cramps and bad nerves. When his wife suddenly died, he sold the furniture to pay their debts.

An accountant and later a censor in the Vatican bureaucracy, Belli belonged to a small but harried middle class, squeezed between an ecclesiastical elite and the masses. He was anything but a man of the people, but in a wild burst of creativity during the 1820s and 30s he wrote some 2,300 sonnets in Romanesco, Rome's rough-and-ready street language of lopped syllables and double consonants. Nearly every day, he would visit me in Piazza di Pasquino and recite his latest poem on gourmandizing pontiffs or masturbating penitents.

Time and routine turned this sly man-about-town, so handsome in cape and cravat, into a pince-nezed civil servant with plastered hair and wispy mutton-chop sideburns. The Revolution of 1848 appalled him, and he repudiated politics. On his deathbed, he begged his confessor to burn his work. Now he stands in Piazza Belli, immortalized in white travertine, wearing a beaver hat and holding a knobbed cane.

Respectability is the kiss of death. Belli is now a monument, and Yuppies, God help us, have gentrified his old neighborhood. But as long we Romans say *bbuono* instead of *buono* and cook *pollo ripieno alla papalina* (stuffed roast chicken fit for a pope) on Sundays, Trastevere will live in our hearts and on our tongues.

5.

WHITE NIGHTS:
Pasquino braves Rome's garish arts-fest

Even statues need sleep. The lucky ones recline on their pediments and snooze in the sun. The rest of us are carthorses, napping on our feet in the wee hours. Thus refreshed, we can better shoulder the burden of time. Sleep is impossible, however, during the Notti Bianche, Rome's garish White Nights.

Each September, this festival draws two to three million visitors. For twenty-four hours, the city's churches, museums, and galleries are open to the public. Their doors and windows blaze like a foundry. Rome glows. Light bulbs decorate the frame of a colossal storage tank. Projectors flash slides of a young Sophia Loren on the Pyramid of Cestius. Floodlights transform the Vittoriano, the massive monument to King Victor Emmanuel II, into a radioactive iceberg.

Power lines crackle and hum, but spectators ignore the stray sparks amid the strobes and disco lights in the old city's central district. The overstrained power grid always threatens to short-circuit during the festival. Rome's first White Night, in fact, coincided with Italy's worst blackout since World War Two.

Goaded by the success of the first Nuit Blanche in Paris, Mayor Walter Veltroni was determined to stage a similar event on the Seven Hills. This cultural binge, to be held on Saturday, September 28, 2003, would be his "token of love" to the Eternal City. The Camera di Commercio (Chamber of Commerce) was delighted.

Such an extravaganza would promote the arts, goose tourism, and generate business.

The overcast sky at the opening ceremony worried the superstitious. "Is this an omen?" reporters asked. Veltroni laughed. "I'm a modern mayor," he replied, "not an ancient aedile." Aediles were the magistrates who administered classical Rome's public buildings and public games. They always consulted the gods before staging a spectacle, but His Honor preferred public relations to augury. A luxury accessories company had supplied the VIPs with free umbrellas. The handmade leather handles were trimmed with garnets and Swarovski crystals.

The festival began well. Veltroni took Paris Mayor Bertrand Delanoe to see Shakespeare's *Romeo and Juliet*, performed in Italian, of course, at the Villa Borghese. Mercutio wore glitter and mascara. Next was a pop version of Puccini's opera, *Tosca*. The singers sounded hoarse and nasal, as if they were auditioning for the Broadway musical *Les Miz*. Drizzle dampened a midnight concert of Nicola Piovani's greatest film hits. The two mayors, however, still dined *al fresco* under awnings at a leading restaurant and toasted each other for the *paparazzi*.

As the cameras flashed, Rome vanished. Streetlamps, traffic signals, and building lights were dead. People blamed the window air conditioners in the housing projects on the city's outskirts. The actual cause was a sudden gale. Toppled pines snapped a major power line. The domino effect crippled Italy's entire grid.

At the Apostolic Palace, Pope John Paul II joked about the Ninth Plague of Egypt. The Director of the Vatican Museums, who had prayed that the White Night would improve attendance, forced a laugh. As His Holiness struggled to light a candle with a palsied hand, the emergency generators flicked on. *Fiat lux*! Light also returned to some hospitals and key government ministries, but darkness ruled the rest of Rome.

The drizzle had turned to rain, the rain into a torrent. Galleries and museums that had kept their doors open were forced to shoo visitors out for security reasons. A ghostly legion of wet and bedraggled revelers was stranded on the streets. Twelve thousand of them found refuge in Rome's subway stations, which had remained open all night for the festival.

The less fortunate panicked. Trapped motorists pounded horns. Shoppers brawled and pedestrians were trampled in the fashion district. A mob breached the barricaded doors of a restaurant in Campo de' Fiori, as the statue of the heretic friar Giordano Bruno looked on grimly. Police abandoned the historic center, but, miraculously, no looting occurred. The only fatalities were three old women who slipped and tumbled down their apartment stairs in the dark.

Rome holds spectacles of light to forget such darkness. This year, ten thousand crystal globes changed colors in the Circus Maximus, the circular park that was once a racetrack. Choreographed lasers formed a kaleidoscope in the Forum. Fire-eaters spewed flames and dervishes twirled torches on the Janiculum Hill. Taillights flowed like lava along the Tiber.

As the city glowed, I thought of Nero. He also promoted the arts. To provide a proper setting for his reenactment of the fall of Troy, he set the Palatine district ablaze. Our White Nights are less destructive than his, but are they less pretentious? Their beauty can't survive the light of day.

Dawn approaches. Dressed in saffron, Aurora tiptoes over the Alban Hills. The morning dew soothes and closes my itchy eyes. Maybe now I will get some sleep.

6.

THE WORLD'S PEOPLE:
Pasquino defends the Roma community

Long before dawn at a Roma camp in the industrial zone east of Italy's capital, my friends Marco and Dacia Spinelli load their rusted VW van with copperware to sell. They rattle past an abandoned penicillin factory, where dozens of Senegalese squatters are exposed to chemical waste and asbestos, and head again for the *centro storico*, Rome's historic center, to set up shop in Campo de' Fiori, the city's biggest marketplace and a magnet for tourists, strollers, and lovers. Unless the police interfere, the couple will work in this crowded square for the next eighteen hours.

To attract customers, Marco and Dacia dress to meet the public's expectations. Marco, squat and dark, wears a fedora trimmed with coins, a long-sleeved shirt, a paisley vest, and stovepipe pants. Dacia, thin and sallow, wears a red headscarf, gold earrings, a V-necked blouse, and a pleated skirt. I know that the couple would never dress this way in private, except for Roma holidays and festivals, but family history has taught them the importance of performance.

The Spinellis' great-grandparents read palms, sharpened knives, and trained horses before becoming buskers in Rome's piazzas. Their grandparents were tumblers and acrobats with the Circo Nazionale Togni, a popular touring circus. Hard times, however, forced the next generation to leave the road for more reliable work as tinkers and crafters in Rome's *borgatte*, the eastern suburbs thrown up between

1950 and 1970 without regard to zoning ordinances or housing regulations. Amid this crazy jumble of industrial parks, apartment blocks, houses, trailers, and shacks, people's tempers fray and ordinary conflicts escalate into violence.

The Spinellis, cousins as well as childhood sweethearts, remember the first time their camp was menaced by *gadjos*, non-Roma neighbors. Marco and Dacia were twelve but already engaged. A gang of boys, barely teens, blocked the railroad tracks near their trailer park and set tires aflame in the trees. "Burn the gypsies!" they cried. But there was more bluster than threat in their tone. Dacia's mother confronted and scolded them. When they sulked, she sang a bawdy song until they joined in the choruses.

This incident, I think, taught Marco and Dacia an important lesson: If you entertain strangers, they are less likely to kill you. This strategy allows them to cope with the hostile working conditions in Campo de' Fiori Market, as if the long hours weren't punishing enough.

Between 6:00 AM to 2:00 PM, they hawk their wares beneath the statue of Giordano Bruno, the Dominican friar burned on this spot in 1600 for the heresy of "cosmic pluralism." A bovine British librarian, chewing a scone from Babington's Tea Room on the Spanish Steps, buys a full set of pots and pans for her cottage back in Devonshire. Inexplicably, this transaction upsets a *Testimono di Geova*, a local Jehovah's Witness, a burly, bearded man in a monkish turtleneck, who spits into a saucepan and leaves a tract. "Gypsies," it reads, "are the children of Cain, cursed to wander the earth and sweat at the forge (Genesis 4:1-16)."

But Roma aren't the children of Cain! Dacia wants to scream. They are the world's people! And they aren't "gypsies!" They originally come not from Egypt but from India. Some Romani, still live there, in Rajasthan, repairing tools and utensils. Dacia's tribe, however, has lived in Italy since 1392, when Roma smiths and canteen keepers sought asylum with Albanian officers and soldiers defeated at the Battle of Kosovo. But the Christians proved more brutal than the Turks. For the next four centuries, Roma were banned from cities, forced to live in camps, and hung for witchcraft and devil worship, despite letters of protection from several popes.

Even when Italy became more enlightened, police always assumed that the Roma were thieves. Romantically inclined artists always assumed they were models. Complaining about injustice, however, is bad for business. Dacia bites her tongue, forces a smile, and sells a copper trivet to a blonde undergraduate from the American University of Rome.

After the market closes and the square is hosed and swept, Marco and Dacia convert their stand into a puppet theater and stage *paramišá*, fairytales, for kids coming home from school. When Dacia gives a straw doll to a six-year-old girl, a nanny drags the child, kicking and squalling, to the far end of the piazza and scrubs her hands in the fountain.

Come evening, the couple entertains patrons from local restaurants, bars, and pubs. Marco plays the accordion, while Dacia dances around Bruno's statue. A tipsy mezzo from the Conservatorio Santa Cecelia asks Marco to accompany her as she sings "*Stride la vampa*" from Verdi's opera *Il Trovatore*. Maybe she has forgotten that this haunting waltz describes the execution of a Roma woman, burned at the stake like Giordano Bruno but for witchcraft rather than heresy.

The Spinellis are familiar with judicial murder. During World War II, their relatives—along with a half-million other Roma—died in Nazi concentration camps because of Benito Mussolini's racial laws. This disgraceful history has not prevented Matteo Salvini, Minister of the Interior, from calling Roma "vermin," and raiding their settlements.

"*Ruspa pronta per gli zingari*! A bulldozer is ready for the Roma!" Salvini posted on Twitter, after a police officer was stoned last Easter at a camp in Rome's Prenestino district. "However," Salvini emphasized, "it is a peaceful and democratic bulldozer." Two months later, the Minister vowed to conduct a census of Roma in Italy, a prelude to expelling those without valid residence permits.

"Unfortunately," Salvini added, sitting at his desk beneath a painting of the Christ Child with the Madonna and Saint Anne, "we must keep the Italian Roma. But others of their tribe, the foreign scum from Serbia, Croatia, and Romania, will have to go."

"All just talk," said Luigi Di Maio, leader of the Five Star Movement, a coalition partner of Salvini's far-right Northern League. "A census based on ethnicity is unconstitutional, so we can't do it." But when politicians blow their whistles, the dogs come barking. TV pundits and talk-show hosts denounced the "Gypsy invasion." Tabloids sensationalized "overcrowding, poor sanitation, petty crime, and drug abuse" in Roma camps. Government and media licensed hatred.

October is always tense. I've seen Halloween punks decked in headscarves, earrings, and vests harass the Roma beggars at the city's largest train station. To commemorate Mussolini's march on Rome, CasaPound—a neofascist political party trending with Italian youth— holds anti-Roma demonstrations in Piazza Venezia. This year, 2019, marks the centennial of Fascism's birth. Fresh from a pilgrimage to Mussolini's birthplace, party members wear black shirts and religious trinkets made from bullet shells. Nothing proclaims one's love of God and country more than a .38-caliber rosary.

Giordano Bruno, condemned for claiming that the earth is not the center of the universe, would have objected. The cosmos, he taught, contains thousands of inhabited worlds, full of billions of souls as human as ours. If that is true, then all of us and none of us are aliens, which is why I say: "Of course, the Roma belong in Rome! Why shouldn't the world's people live in the world's city, particularly in Campo de' Fiori, crossroads of the nations, where fried Italian garlic mingles with toasted Indian turmeric, a pushcart prepares Vietnamese pork *bánh* next to an Umbrian salami shop, and Buddhist and Capuchin monks minister to the homeless?"

Sadly, Bruno's statue, like me, can say nothing when a soccer fan in an A.S. Roma jersey hurls a beer bottle at the Spinellis and yells: "*Gitani!*" Spectators laugh. As the couple packs to leave the square at midnight, it is easy to mistake the dew forming on Bruno's face for tears.

If I had arms, I would chisel these words on his pedestal: "*Once again it is heresy in Rome to defend other worlds, other peoples.*"

7.

O CHRISTMAS TREE:

Pasquino honors the spirit of the holidays

Palazzo Senatorio, the salmon-pink city hall on Rome's Capitoline Hill, broke the news a week before the holidays. Just as I feared, Spelacchio—the woebegone municipal Christmas tree, a 72-foot-tall Norwegian spruce brought from the Dolomites to the capital on a tractor trailer and erected in Piazza Venezia at a cost of €48,000—was dead.

The public outrage amused me. For ten days, the press and social media had ridiculed this poor tree. Now taxpayers vented their grief and demanded an explanation. Who killed Spelacchio? Was it a corrupt trucker paid off by the Mafia, an incompetent arborist who had failed to detect blight, or a pious saboteur ordered to prevent the victim from upstaging the Vatican's rival Christmas tree in St. Peter's Square? It was a whodunit worthy of *Inspector Montalbano*, Italy's favorite TV cop show.

But the Spelacchio affair was also the latest episode in a reality show I call *Degrado*, the shameful degradation of Rome's infrastructure and public services. Uncollected garbage piles up in historic neighborhoods, antiquated buses short-circuit and burst into flames in the city center, and sinkholes swallow cars in the outer districts.

Whatever happens, though, Romans will blame politicians and bureaucrats, even during the Christmas season. We conveniently forget that we're part of the problem. Our self-protective cynicism contributes to Rome's toxic dysfunction. It was no mystery to me, therefore, why Spelacchio was dead. Collective sarcasm killed him.

Poor wooden bastard, I thought. He never had a chance.

The heckling began on the Feast of the Immaculate Conception, after a crane hoisted the sickly tree in front of the monument to Victor Emanuel II, the first king of Italy. The Father of the Fatherland would have objected. When his daughter-in-law, Margherita of Savoy, dedicated Rome's first Christmas tree at the Quirinal Palace in December of 1876 to prove that Italians were as progressive as Anglo Saxons, His Majesty cursed and left the ballroom. His seven-year-old grandson, Victor Emanuel III, bawled under the tree.

Everyone in Piazza Venezia was equally upset, from the guardians of the Tomb of the Unknown Soldier, lancers standing at attention in berets and capes under the eye of the goddess Roma, to the grimacing spectators in their Santa hats and reindeer antlers. A barrel-chested man, wearing a beer-stained sweatshirt, kicked over a steel police barrier.

"*Porco governo!*" he shouted. "Swinish government!"

Spectators agreed. Last year, responding to complaints about severe cutbacks to holiday decorations, Virginia Raggi, Rome's new mayor, the darling of the anti-establishment Five Star Party, had promised the city a better Christmas tree, something worthy of New York's Rockefeller Center or Milan's Piazza del Duomo—not this toilet brush, this plucked chicken, this refugee from a Charlie Brown television special. Because the tree was so *spelacchiato*, so shabby and threadbare, it was nicknamed Lo Spelacchio.

Being a limbless trunk with a ravaged face, I felt for Spelacchio. He reminded me of those maimed Italian soldiers who, every Christmas during and between the two world wars, were herded into the Grand Ballroom of the Quirinal Place. They were posed next to a plush evergreen to receive gifts from King Victor Emanuel III, who was no bigger than an elf. His huge wife, Queen Elena, always wore a Red Cross uniform.

At least the wounded were shielded from public exposure. I can't say the same about Spelacchio. Conspiracy theorists insisted that the tree had been poisoned. Quacks used its image to advertise hair loss remedies. Codacons, a consumer advocacy group, complained about "the grotesque waste of public money" to the National Anti-Corruption Authority, and the Chamber of Commerce suggested using a Chipper Gandini to turn Spelacchio into pencils and toothpicks.

Not all media coverage was bad. With its own Twitter handle and three Facebook accounts, the tree had more followers than branches, but the attention could not slow its decline. Every day, despite its bright lights and colorful bulbs, it turned grayer and shed more and more needles until it became a skeleton.

Rome's Councilor for Environmental Sustainability, who was disliked for letting sheep, goats, and cows graze in the city's long-neglected parks and for banning *botticelle*, horse-drawn buggies from its streets, failed to assure the public. Spelacchio, she explained, was like a Picasso. Highly stylized, it needed time to make a good impression. A few days later, her department announced that the tree was dead. Someone tweeted in faulty Latin: "*Ave*, Virginia, *morituro te salutat*! Hail, Virginia! I am who about to die salute you!"

Mayor Raggi promised an inquest. At a public hearing in Palazzo Senatorio's vaulted and bannered town hall, experts testified between nervous sips of ice water. The President of ADEA (*Amici degli Alberi*, Friends of the Trees), a noted tree historian, said the cause of

Spelacchio's death was "petrified roots." When workers had poured concrete to steady the tree, they killed it. A botany professor at RomaTre University blamed the transport. Journeying 400 miles without a tarp or water, the tree had suffered from exposure and dehydration.

The contradictory testimonies provoked the audience.

Journalists pursed their fingers and wagged their wrists. Auditors frowned and crossed their arms. Two janitors, emptying trash at the back of the hall, stamped their feet and started a chant, one used whenever Italians suspect government complicity in a wrongful death. Slowly, the audience took up the chant until the entire hall echoed with their words:

"*Spelacchio vive! I morti siete voi! Spelacchio vive! I morti siete voi!*"

("Spelacchio lives! *You* all are the dead!")

As ironic sympathy cards flooded City Hall, Mayor Raggi's enemies opened fire. Her most vocal critics, I noticed, were powerful women who considered Raggi a lightweight. The sniping came from across the political spectrum.

"The Five Star Movement can't even manage to get a Christmas tree right," declared an MP from Forza Italia, a center-right populist party. "Imagine how they'd govern the country!" The head of Fratelli d'Italia, a far-right nationalist party, and Italy's future Prime Minister sneered: "Forty-eight thousand Euros to kill a Christmas tree. Well done, Virginia!" A rock star in Italia Viva, a liberal reformist party, who was also the Minister for Constitutional Reforms and Parliamentary Relations, suggested that if *she* had been on the job, Spelacchio would be "a stately baobab on the banks of the Euphrates."

This sorority hazing encouraged vituperative attacks in the press. But when pundits declared that the Spelacchio affair symbolized "the sorry state of the country," Spelacchio himself responded with a diatribe in *La Stampa*, ghosted by the editor-in-chief of the paper's Rome office.

"Look," he said, "you have a dark, chaotic, filthy city. Everything is thrown on the ground, nothing works, and you do nothing but complain. *I'm* not a metaphor for Italy. You are!"

A chastened crowd gathered in Piazza Venezia on the Epiphany to say farewell to Spelacchio. The ceremony was dampened by a cold drizzle and feelings of guilt. Not even the Police Band could brighten the scene. The silver braids and silver epaulettes on their dark uniforms looked tarnished. While a bugler in a cocked hat played *Il Silencio*, the Italian version of "Taps," I shivered and stifled a sob.

"Today," said Rome's environmental councilor, showing off a new perm, "we dismantle a tree that represented so much for our citizens." Spelacchio would be repurposed, cut up and used to build a nursing hut in Villa Borghese where Roman moms could breastfeed in peace. What could be more sustainable?

As city workers turned off the tree's lights, I heard a lone protester cry out: "*Resista*! Resist, Spelacchio! *Vivi per sempre in nosti cuori*! You live forever in our hearts!"

FESTIVALS AND SEASONS

8.

SHOOTING STARS:
Pasquino makes a wish

At the Vatican Observatory in Castel Gandolfo, Jesuit astronomers—the more formal in Roman collars and cassocks, the more casual in polo shirts and chinos—welcome past students from their biennial summer school. These nostalgic thirty-somethings, who have rebooked their old rooms at the nearby Villa Altieri, wish to celebrate the Night of San Lorenzo with their former teachers before flying back to New York on Monday.

The reception takes place between the two wooden domes on the roof of the Apostolic Palace, the observatory's administrative headquarters. I always find the *bruschetta*—toasted bread topped with tomatoes, Parmesan cheese, garlic, and fresh basil—as refreshing as the twilight breeze from Lake Albano. The alumni, a gaggle of astrophysicists, science reporters, and planetarium directors, are impatient to see the shooting stars. For that, they must visit the new facility in the papal gardens.

The Vatican's first in-house observatory, dedicated in 1891 by Leo XIII, was housed on a hilltop in the westernmost tip of Vatican City, where it remained until 1935. When smoke and light pollution made it impossible to study the night sky, Pius XI transferred the observatory to Castel Gandolfo, 16 miles southeast of Rome. Ten years ago, it was moved again to this remodeled monastery, next to the farm that provides His Holiness with fresh vegetables and dairy products.

Brother Guy Consolmagno, Director of the Observatory, apologizes to his guests. Last year, the new moon made viewing conditions perfect. This year's gibbous moon will make star-gazing more difficult, but its glare cannot completely spoil the fireworks from Comet Swift-Tuttle.

Every August, when the Earth plows into its wake, pea-sized bits of debris hit our atmosphere at 132,000 miles per hour, reach temperatures of 3,000 to 10,000 degrees, and streak across the sky. Because they radiate from the constellation named for Perseus, who chopped off the head of the Medusa, the meteors are called the Perseid and rain like sparks from his astral sword. But most Romans, I'm sure, don't need a telescope to appreciate this spectacle. For three thousand years, they have preferred to use their imagination.

Among the portents witnessed after the death of Cleopatra on August 10, 30 BC, the historian Cassius Dio mentions "comet stars," but this annual summer meteor shower already was part of the Roman calendar. The same date honored the god Priapus. A procession of virgins bore an immense erect phallus and sprinkled the fields with a mixture of water, honey, and wine to ensure the land's fertility in a ritual intended to symbolize the primordial ejaculation of creation. At dusk, the heavens echoed this event with a shower of divine seed.

Other deities were celebrated on August 10, including the Etruscan goddess Acca Larentia, mistress of the grain and protectress of the poor. The Early Church coopted her feast when it canonized Saint Lawrence, martyred on the same day in 258 AD.

Lawrence, Archdeacon of Rome under Pope Sixtus II, administered the Christian treasury. When the Emperor Valerian ordered it confiscated, Lawrence brought him the poor, the blind, and the crippled, to whom he had distributed the church's riches as alms. Enraged, Valerian sentenced Lawrence to be roasted to death on a gridiron. Before dying, the archdeacon said: "*Assum est. Versa et manduca.* This side's well done. Turn me over and take a bite."

The real joke is that this legend comes from a faulty transcription. While copying the customary and solemn formula for announcing the death of a martyr, "*passus est*" (he suffered), a scribe accidentally omitted the letter "p" so that it read "*assus est*" (he was roasted). Nevertheless, tradition still insists that the Perseid meteors are the embers from Lawrence's grill.

Romans see what they want to see on the Night of San Lorenzo. At a barbecue on Via del Pigneto, pedestrians munch *porchetta* (roasted pork loin stuffed with garlic, fennel, and breadcrumbs), watch the sparks rise, and dance around the streetlamps. They pretend that the stars nest in the trees. Under lantern-hung arbors in the vineyards of Frascati, wine club members raise fluted glasses and let the stars bubble in their *spumante*. Everyone makes a wish: "*Stella, mia bella stella, desidero che . . .*" ("Star, my beautiful star, grant what I desire . . .")

Only the astronomers at the Vatican Observatory seem to care that these desires are being projected onto a filthy snowball, 16 miles wide and passing the earth every 133 years. But as Father Angelo Secchi, Director of the Observatory at the Pontifical Gregorian University (1853 to 1878) and a pioneer in astronomical spectroscopy, once remarked: "Neither Jesuits nor scientists are immune from illusions." I have been told that even Giovanni Schiaparelli, who discovered that Comet Swift-Tuttle is the source of the Perseids, believed there were canals on Mars.

9.

AUGUST ESCAPE:

Pasquino vacations during Ferragosto

Every year in early August, I witness the exodus from Rome. Factories in the industrial zone grind to a halt. Executives abandon their offices in a corporate complex haunted by Fascist architecture. Shops on Via del Corso and cafés in Piazza Navona shutter their windows and post signs. Surveying the deserted historic center, tourists wonder if they missed a bulletin about some mass evacuation. A *carabiniere* in a sweat-stained, short-sleeved uniform reassures them. The city is not under attack, he explains. It is only on vacation.

I must tell you that *Ferragosto,* the name of this summer escape, has a long history. Back in 18 BC, Caesar Augustus consolidated his power through recreation. After being proclaimed a god, he renamed the eighth month of the Roman calendar after himself and made it a 31-day holiday, the *Feriae Augusti* or Festivals of Augustus, to celebrate his most important victories.

The Pontifical College, which administered Rome's civic religion, objected. The new festival upstaged the *Nemoralia*, honoring the goddess Diana, and the *Vinalia Rustica* and *Consuala*, blessing the harvest and ending months of intense agricultural labor. Augustus smiled at the scowling priests. As Pontifex Maximus, he could combine these existing holidays to provide a longer period of rest called *Augustali*—and he did it quicker than it takes to boil an asparagus.

Rome took a paid month off. Oxen, donkeys, and mules were released from work and decorated with flowers. Aristocrats tipped servants before leaving for their villas in Tivoli and Frascati. Commoners, stuck in the city, were treated to public feasts, gladiator fights, and horse races. Republican senators were apoplectic. "Through the sweetness of leisure," wrote my friend the historian Tacitus, "Augustus seduced one and all."

So did Benito Mussolini, who made summer vacations possible for the masses. During the 1930s, he organized hundreds of popular trips in mid-August through Fascist leisure and recreational organizations. Since this initiative coincided with the Feast of the Assumption, which honored Rome's new virgin goddess, Mary, Mother of Jesus. The Vatican approved.

Tickets for the People's Trains of *Ferragosto,* available at discounted prices, gave the less well-off a chance to visit other cities or to reach seaside and mountain resorts. Limited to August 13, 14, and 15, the offer comprised two options: the One-Day Trip, within a radius of 50-100 km, and the Three-Day Trip, within a radius of 100-200 km. This pattern persisted even after the postwar boom, and strong unions extended the August break to the entire month.

Only affluent Romans can afford to hike in Ortesi, ski at Passo del Tonale, or yacht in Portofino. Working people must endure the indignities of ATAC, Rome's notoriously unreliable mass transit system, or the Fifth Circle of the GRA, the hellish traffic ring surrounding the city, to reach a crowded beach at Ostia or Civitavecchia or a pokey hillside villa near Rieti or Chieti.

Bad trips, I think, are never worth the effort. A concierge, who neglected to fix the ice dispenser, books the wrong dinner reservation.

A poolside *limoncello*, made from frozen concentrate, attracts a squadron of flies. Obese sunbathers, wearing the skimpiest Pucci knockoffs, carpet the entire Adriatic shore.

Good trips, however, always end too soon. The fleeting time makes one desperate to see and do everything. On the last Saturday of *Ferragosto,* vacationers frug the night away at provincial discos. Despite the exhaustion, this is the happiest moment of their trip, when desire takes its last stand against disillusion. Come Sunday morning, they will pack and pray that the boredom of church and the anguish of the long drive home will be extinguished in the anticipated return to the daily grind.

Back in Rome, where I too have stayed behind, of course, marooned residents await the vacationers' return. Like Pope Francis, who prefers the air-conditioned rooms at Casa Santa Marta to the stucco halls of Castel Gandolfo, the papal summer estate above Lake Albano, these humble folk have taken a staycation. For many, it is their first chance to enjoy the city. They have lived in Rome all their lives but, until now, have never attended the film festival on Tiber Island, visited the Pantheon, or picnicked in the Villa Borghese gardens. Instead, they have struggled as clerks and custodians to support their families. Even so, they do not feel deprived, nor do they envy what they cannot have.

"Politicians promise," they say, "but it's all talk. Life is hard, and work is all. Everything else is a dream."

10.

AN ILL WIND:

Pasquino survives the scirocco

When Juno, Queen of Olympus, needed to vent her spleen, she visited Aeolus, god of the winds, on his drafty island off Sicily. I can still hear her storm into his underground palace, a vast cavern carved from granite and obsidian. Always the diva, she sang a rage aria with too many high F's. But who can blame her? The acoustics were perfect.

Juno was outraged that the fugitive Trojan prince Aeneas was destined to found Rome and destroy Carthage, her favorite city. So Aeolus ordered a cyclone to capsize the Trojan fleet. Ever since, Rome has feared southern winds.

If you visit St. Peter's Square, you will see them marked on a wind compass surrounding the Vatican Obelisk. Before the Papal States were blown away, Pius IX noted their names and directions. The *ostro*, the warm and humid south wind, brings summer storms and flash floods. The *libeccio*, the southwest wind from Libya, raises high seas and causes squalls. But the most malevolent is the *scirocco*, the southeast desert wind, a withering blast whose hot and clammy touch hastens death and putrefaction. Every year, I track its progress with dread.

The *scirocco* begins in North Africa, roaring in from the Sahara like a *goum*, or band of wild Bedouins, its burnouse laden with sand. Sharper than a scimitar, it pierces the lungs and shreds the bronchial tubes of consumptives and asthmatics. Algerians and Tunisians barricade doors and windows, stop chimneys and keyholes, and cower in back parlors until the dust storm passes. When all is still, stretcher-bearers remove the dead from the streets.

Crossing the Mediterranean, the flying red desert sand mixes with moisture, and the wind resembles the First Plague of Egypt. In Palermo and Naples, blood seems to rain down. It is only red dust suspended in water droplets, but it still stains monuments and pollutes fountains. Horrified, the superstitious cross themselves, and the old faint. As the wind travels further north, however, it turns more insidious. Scientists cannot explain why, but by the time it reaches Rome, the *scirocco* resembles a cloud of nuclear fallout: invisible, pervasive, and toxic.

Residents know it is blowing even before they open their eyes and glance out the window. Everyone, from the Pope to a pushcart vendor, wakes up with a dull headache. By 8:00 AM, the air is sultry, and low grey clouds fill the sky. A leaden pall hangs over Rome. Nerves fray. Eyes cannot focus. Skin turns to burlap. Lungs gasp. Throats clog. For three days, the dampness liver-spots walls and ceilings and makes mildew blossom everywhere. The grit penetrates bank vaults and scratches machinery. Finally, a cleansing rain dissolves the evil wind and leaves the city's cars with reddish-yellow pockmarks.

The ordeal debilitates and oppresses native Romans, whose history feeds collective anxiety. The *scirocco* of October 1867, I recall, brought cholera and madness. Horses panicked, bolted from carriages, and trampled pedestrians to death.

Visitors, however, seem to be immune, particularly in winter. "I don't find this sort of weather disagreeable," Goethe records in his diary on November 7, 1786. "It is warm all the time, which it never is on rainy days in Germany."

George Augustus Sala, the British journalist, would open his casements and let the *scirocco* fan his cheeks and ventilate his apartment. He likened the wind to "warm milk in a volatilized state." Staying in Rome two weeks before Christmas in 1866 and knowing that London was choked by fog and the mustiness of Fleet Street, he found the "balmy" southeaster "inexpressibly grateful and refreshing."

These imperturbable Anglo Saxons will never understand. Like radiation poisoning, sensitivity to the *scirocco* is cumulative. Prolonged exposure slowly sickens the entire city. The south wind blows 200 days a year in Rome. Over decades, it saps resistance, increases lassitude, and stokes misanthropy, as certain tropical climates, which seemed perfectly tolerable at first, drove early Italian colonialists in Africa to commit atrocities.

When the *scirocco* hits, it blows the lid off Pandora's box. Office workers and sales assistants mope and sulk. Café patrons get dejected or quarrelsome. Waiters scowl and snap. Teachers humiliate students. Doctors mock patients. Suicide rates and traffic accidents spike. If domestic violence occurs, a court may consider the weather an extenuating circumstance, provided the judge has not brained the bailiff with a gavel. The human heart is a whirligig. The worst thing a critic can say about a new book is: "*È scritto in tempo di scirocco.*" It was written during the *scirocco*, which makes it a giddy mess.

The Temple of the Tempestates, the Wind Gods, once stood on the Appian Way. Lucius Cornelius Scipio built it in 259 BC to fulfill a vow. Caught in a storm with his fleet off Corsica, Scipio prayed to the gods for deliverance. We Romans still appease the winds, even though we claim to be Christians. A small anemometer whirls on Bernini's colonnade in St. Peter's Square. This is only fitting, I think. Meteorology is always truer than morality. Mere mortals are seldom better than the weather.

11.

AUTUMN BACCHANAL:
Pasquino savors the Ottobrata

October in Rome is its own season, a fleeting second summer after the first chill of September. During this magical time, when the trees in the Villa Borghese Gardens begin to turn red and yellow, I love to watch the morning mist rise from the Tiber. Moss traces veins in ancient marble, and the pines on the Janiculum Hill become delightfully, sharply pungent. But the most miraculous thing is the light, which intoxicates me in stages.

At noon, the sky is the color of blue Sambuca, an anise-flavored liqueur that forms clouds when served on the rocks. As the shadows lengthen, the light mellows and turns golden until the sky becomes Orvieto, a regional white wine stocked in all Roman restaurants. By dusk, the Eternal City is awash in Vino Santo, an amber-colored dessert wine best used for dunking almond *biscotti*. Bathed in this mellow glow, the Coliseum seems less cruel, Palazzo Montecitorio less pompous, Piazza Guglielmo Marconi less creepy.

October also marks the local grape harvest. The Castelli Romani, the medieval towns located ten miles southeast of Rome at the foot of the Alban Hills and immortalized in the song *'Na gita a li Castelli*, celebrate with various feasts. The most famous, Marino's *La Sagra dell'Uva*, features three wine-spurting fountains. But even this colorful spectacle pales in comparison to the Ottobrata Romana.

During the 18th century, the Ottobrata, the Festival of the Wine Press, was Rome's most joyful holiday. Women trimmed their bonnets with feathers and flowers and wore costume jewelry, silk gowns, velvet jackets, and embroidered stockings. Men peacocked in plug hats, open-necked shirts, bandannas, and britches. The more prosperous rented pumpkin-shaped carriages, hired singers, dancers, musicians, and jugglers, and took their families on a *scampagnata*, a spirited country outing. I hopped for joy (figuratively) whenever the cheering children passed: the boys in black vests and red sashes, the girls in white headdresses with lace edges and black skirts with gold embroidery.

The first stop was Monte Testaccio, located in an area used as a recreational wasteland before the Industrial Revolution. Beneath this mound of ancient pottery shards, Rome's best wine cellar flowed with Trebbiano, Cesanese, and Malvasia. Loaded with bottles, the tipplers headed for the suburbs: out to Flaminio, Parioli, and Tiburtino; up to Monte Mario, Monte Sacro, and Tor di Quinto. Whatever the destination, the goal was always the same: buy out the old vintage from every village tavern to make room for the new, and then picnic in the nearby countryside.

The orchards and vineyards were perfect for setting up a *bocce* court and a swing set. The men competed at *morra*, betting on the number of outstretched fingers in a series of hand throws. The women teased each other at *mosca cieca*, a version of blindman's bluff. The children played *ruzzola*, rolling wheels of Pecorino Romano cheese down a gentle slope. The winded revelers sat in the shade and feasted on gnocchi, capon, tripe, and *abbacchio a scottadito*, grilled marinated lambchops. Then as the musicians strummed guitars, rattled tambourines, and clattered castanets, everyone danced the *saltarello*.

Hands on hips, couples circled each other, tossed their heads, snorted and stamped, swished and laughed, and capered and leapt like goats.

I was sad to see these pagan customs disappear by the mid-19th century. Some blamed the bishops, who were scandalized by the festival's excesses. Students often hung hunchbacks by the waist from lampposts for selling unlucky lottery tickets, and drunken matrons sometimes awoke the next morning to find strange men in their beds. Others blamed the brokers, who built the new stock exchange in the Temple of Hadrian and minted gold coins that outshone the sun. But I blame Giuseppe Mazzini, the prophet of the Risorgimento, a political movement to free Italy from foreign rule and to unite its many squabbling city-states and provinces.

Mazzini was Chief Minister of the Roman Republic, a constitutional democracy established after the temporary overthrow of the Papal States on February 9, 1849. A stern ascetic, Mazzini scolded Romans into abandoning frivolity and mounting the barricades. He even ordered his general, Giuseppe Garibaldi, to place a battery atop Monte Testaccio. During target practice, the blasts rattled and shattered the wine bottles in the cellar. When French imperial troops finally invaded and expelled the republicans, many tavern keepers were relieved and broke open their kegs. Mazzini's sober cause, however, ultimately triumphed. By July 1871, Italy was united, and Rome was its capital. This proved a mixed blessing.

After the Risorgimento, the October sun shone on a different Rome. No longer a city of ruins, landscapes, and museums, it was now the center of a modern democracy. But Rome also had become staid and Victorian. The heroic age was over, I'm afraid. Little remained but a sonorous echo and stilted plaques. Giosuè Carducci, the bard of the

Risorgimento, deplored the electric tram wires in the Corso, but on Sundays in the Pincio Gardens the bank clerks and their prim wives could push their baby carriages without some uncouth revolutionary's Gatling gun disrupting the brass band.

Author and adventurer *par excellence,* Gabrielle D'Annunzio, then a curly-haired gossip columnist from Pescara, loved to ogle young married women as they took the mild October air. A perfumed satyr in a dove-grey frock coat, he stalked them from ten to four. Between their morning mass and their afternoon promenade, these bourgeois Junos—large-eyed, slow-paced, full-figured—would lunch at an *osteria.* Drunk from the October sun, they forgot all propriety. They devoured buttery pasta with cheese and pepper, braised veal shanks smothered in onions, lemony deep-fried artichokes, and honey-soaked figs, all washed down with three or four glasses of Frascati wine. Like dried flowers, these ladies were pressed and preserved in the pages of *Piacere* (*Pleasure*), D'Annunzio's salaciously autobiographical novel and a scrapbook of this elegant but decadent period.

La vita comoda, the easy life, came with a price. Behind these lazy scenes, Rome scrambled to raise its standard of living. Even the aristocracy caught the fever from England and America. Its members renounced centuries of arrogance, pomp, and solitude and professed a new faith in fashion, etiquette, and commerce. Neglecting their traditional duties, they held fewer October concerts in the Teatro Villa Doria Pamphili, fewer October horse-racing tournaments in the Piazza di Siena, the arena in the Villa Borghese Gardens. Instead, they lurked between the Borsa di Roma's Corinthian columns and played at investment. Most ruined themselves, which doesn't surprise me at all.

It takes taste to bid for a Bronzino at an art auction, but it takes brains to pick a commodity on the stock exchange.

October has never recovered. I ask you: How can modern Romans enjoy its sights and sounds when they text from their iPhones and stare at their iPads day and night? Jaded and overworked, they reluctantly drive to the festival in Marino, only to take selfies at the biggest wine fountain or to write snide reviews on Yelp. At Ristorante Pasquino, fifty paces from where I preside over my square, a business party passes around a truffle the size of a man's fist. Nobody sniffs it. Nobody shuts his eyes in ecstasy as if savoring the scent of autumn. Without interrupting their conversations or making eye contact, they return the truffle to the waiter, who shaves slices onto their pasta. The waiter hovers, sighs, and shuffles sadly away.

I feel as if I have witnessed a crime.

12.

WINTER CAPITAL:
Pasquino frolics in the snow

"Rome," I love to say, quoting an old proverb, "is made of heaven, not earth."

The best time to enjoy this city's divine architecture is the low season: midwinter. The sky is less blue in January than in July, but the light is softer and more enchanting. Each afternoon, the low-flying sun turns the historic district into a Baroque stage set. The colors of the bridges, ruins, palaces, and churches—infinite variations of yellows and golds, oranges and reds, ochers and umbers, tans and sierras—deepen and glow until every brick is transfigured. By dusk, the city is an Olympian showroom of dramatically lit ceramic tiles and marble countertops.

Maybe the gods are renovating their bathrooms and kitchens. If so, the weather usually cooperates. Except for the most evanescent flurries, it rarely snows in Rome. Oh, every five to ten years, minor accumulations occur, but for the most part, even during the coldest months, the only place to see snow is from the Janiculum Hill. To the east span the distant white peaks of craggy Monte Gennaro; to the north looms misty and snow-capped Monte Soratte, the Mount Soracte that inspired the poet Horace's classical ode to winter.

But every five to ten centuries, a cosmic disaster forces the gods to abandon their routine home improvement project and to remake the Eternal City from scratch: an epic snowstorm that reduces Rome's bright colors and solid landmarks into a swirling chaos of white atoms. Such was the Great Blizzard of 1985, perhaps the most wondrous experience of my long life.

It began very quietly. After freezing the Danube and postponing a highly publicized trial of six dissidents in Belgrade, a Siberian cold front arrived in Rome on January 6, the morning of Epiphany Sunday. Carved from porous travertine marble, I immediately felt the chill. The pines shivered in the Villa Borghese gardens, and the animals paced in the city zoo. Federico, a bachelor sea lion, dreaming of Alaska in an Art Deco exhibition, awoke, sniffed the frigid air, and clapped his flippers. A pair of female tigers bristled, swished their tails, and growled. Red-faced Japanese macaques huddled in an artificial hot spring and screamed.

As the temperature plummeted twenty degrees in half an hour on the Capitoline Hill, snowflakes fell on the equestrian statue of the Emperor Marcus Aurelius and carpeted the Campidoglio like white petals at a Roman triumph. Sensing danger, the emperor's bronze Sarmatian horse bridled, and the statue of the emperor himself— remembering his long and disastrous winter campaigns in Germania— raised a hand in warning. Too late. The enemy was already inside the gates. Before 10:00 AM, the Campidoglio was six inches deep in snow. Public transportation stalled, and Fiumicino Airport closed. The city soon surrendered.

At first, I doubted the weather bulletins. The last time it snowed almost this heavily was that week in February 1956. Flakes as big as handkerchiefs blanketed the dome of St. Peter's Basilica and froze the locks of the Papal Apartments. An imprisoned and blue-lipped Pius XII read his breviary with steaming breath and chattering teeth as seminarians built snowmen in Piazza di San Pietro. Otherwise, the

Pontifical Gregorian College could find no precedent in its weather records, dating back to 1850, so meteorologists consulted ancient chronicles. They should have asked me. I've witnessed almost every blizzard in Rome's history.

During the winter of 399 BC, badly shaken by its recent war with the Veii, the city was nearly destroyed when a freak storm dumped seven feet of snow in the Forum. Livestock perished, orchards were ruined, buildings collapsed, and citizens froze to death in their homes. On August 5, 358 AD, snow covered the Esquiline Hill on the future site of the Basilica of Santa Maria Maggiore. A double miracle, as I recall. The snow not only fell in the middle of a sweltering summer but also outlined the shape of the entire basilica. The builders placed stakes around the enormous snowbank and measured its dimensions in awe.

But this January blizzard, I soon realized, was more ambitious. It was determined to completely rebuild Rome itself. The storm plastered and stuccoed every windward door and wall and, disregarding all measure and proportion, constructed rival bastions and colonnades. By noon, its wild masonry had replaced the city's warm yellows and soft reds with dazzling whites and slate greys. Stunned, I explored this new winter capital.

Before a now glacial Palazzo di Giustizia, palm trees sagged under the weight of a half foot of snow. The frosted statue of Count Cavour, Italy's first Prime Minister, smiled in a nearby square. Perhaps, I thought, this blizzard makes him less homesick for the sleet and fog of his native Turin. A marble seraph, encased in ice on the Ponte Sant'Angelo, frowned because he couldn't spread his wings. At the far end of Piazza del Popolo, the churches of Santa Maria dei Miracoli and Santa Maria di Montesanto stood like twin igloos.

The Tridente district became the Ice Capades. Christian Brothers, forced to spend winter break at the Collegio San Giuseppe-Instituto de Mérode, swapped their clerical collars for turtlenecks and staged a snowball fight on the Spanish Steps. Antique dealers, anxious about potential theft and weather damage, improvised snowshoes from tennis rackets and inner tubes and waddled to their shops on Via del Babuino. Cross-county skiers glided down the Corso. Muffled lovers tossed chunks of ice in Trevi Fountain.

A mile south, on the slopes surrounding the Circus Maximus, children sledded on trashcan lids. Much closer, Canadian tourists, their flight to Toronto canceled, played hockey with brooms and an old shoe in Piazza Venezia. Snowplow operators puffed on cigars and bet on the blizzard's outcome. Nothing, however, distracted the pilgrims hiking toward the Vatican.

From a window on the fourth floor of the Apostolic Palace, Pope John Paul II greeted the crowd that had braved record-breaking cold to pray the Angelus. "Well, this is a surprise, a rare scene in this city," the Holy Father declared, appearing and disappearing behind a curtain of swirling snow. "But here you are!" he boomed over the speaker system, gazing at the faithful. "Not all Romans are scared of snow, eh? There are some who are courageous!"

The crowd cheered. As the Angelus bell rang, the Pope offered a special blessing for skiers. His Holiness owned a pair of perfectly waxed Head skis and a collection of designer woolen socks with the initials "K.W." in gold thread. One of the few perks of this job, he joked, was being able to escape to Terminillo, twenty miles north of Rome. Of course, its slopes couldn't compare to those of the Tatra Mountains in his native Poland. Still, wasn't it fun to conceal his identity behind scarves and goggles? The Pope's bright smile warmed the spectators and heralded the sun's return.

The storm faded, and Monday morning Rome struggled to dig itself out. Snowplows were not in the city's budget, so trucks were commandeered from the army and hired from private builders. Tons of salt were freighted from Tuscany, but the streets were not cleaned quickly enough to prevent the snow from turning into ice. Commuters were stranded, civil servants played hooky, and public services remained closed. The Ministry of the Interior failed to shelter the homeless. As if things weren't bad enough, Lazio lost a rescheduled soccer match to Milan, 1-0, before 35,000 disappointed and frostbitten fans.

But I was too amazed to complain. Under a bright blue sky, the blizzard had left the city astonished and humbled. Its heavy structures—built deliberately over the ages, stone by stone—could not compete with the wind's frolic architecture of a single day.

It was far lovelier than the mere engineering of men.

13.

GOLDEN THREADS:

Pasquino inaugurates the year with saffron

January is my favorite month in Rome. Consecrated to Janus, the god of beginnings and transitions, it is the best time to recapture the magic those British lords on the Grand Tour must have felt, when they arrived here from the grey north to this golden palimpsest of travertine and snow. Winter in London was never like this!

Rome's January thaw, a season unto itself, sharpens the city's dulled edges and revives its faded colors. Everything seems bigger and brighter. The sky, a grey rag for six weeks, becomes a turquoise canopy fit for a royal wedding. The sun, once veiled by the mists of November and the frosts of December, now shines like a bronze globe in a palace library.

The chill heightens the senses in Rome's historic neighborhoods. In the Borgo, spectators watch the breath steam from the mouths of ice skaters below Castel Sant'Angelo. In the Prati, residents listen to wind chimes tinkle from rooftop gardens. Here in the Parione district, where I have lived for five centuries, pedestrians read the menus of local restaurants with their nostrils.

From the kitchen of Cul de Sac, a popular bar and grill, wafts the smell of saffron. Its sweet and musky perfume, a blend of honey and tobacco, permeates Piazza di Pasquino and intoxicates me. The restaurant's chef, my friend Flavio Santucci, seasons everything with saffron. He comes from a hill town near L'Aquila, which produces the best saffron in Italy. Potent stuff. A single gram can spice and color twelve portions of golden *risotto milanese*.

Flavio prepares Abruzzese dishes: fresh ricotta with honey and saffron; braised fennel with figs and saffron; *spaghetti alla chittara* with minced pancetta and saffron; prawns and squid in saffron sauce. Patrons wolf these specials, a relief from Cul de Sac's usual fare of pâtés, cheeses, and cold cuts. Since I am a statue, I must abstain. But the fragrance of the cooking revives memories of a heady time when saffron corrupted an empire.

Two thousand years ago, saffron was the Mediterranean's most expensive spice. Made from the dried stigmas of the crocus, it came from Cilicia, the remotest province in Asia Minor. Because its production was so labor intensive, it was worth more than its weight in gold. That is still true. No machine can harvest those cupped purple flowers. The work must be done by hand. Back then, the task fell to slave girls or trained monkeys. The delicate red threads were separated from the petals, teased and plucked, and dried over a wood fire until they were steamy and sweet. It took 100,000 crocuses (and 500 hours of labor) to yield one kilo of saffron.

No wonder saffron became a status symbol in ancient Rome. The spice was rarely used in the kitchen except to flavor sauces or to fortify wine. Instead, patricians and wealthy plebeians used it as perfume or make-up. They glazed their wedding cakes with saffron. They dyed their robes in saffron. They flavored their drinks and scented their hair. They also stocked it in their medicine cabinets, but I always suspected the claims about its miraculous powers. Saffron was believed to rejuvenate the skin, restore the liver, relieve coughs and hiccups, and refresh bloodshot eyes. It reputedly cured hangovers but not, alas, megalomania.

Julius Caesar, to please Cleopatra, drank saffron-laced milk to enhance his virility. Whenever Nero returned to Rome from Baiae, a fashionable resort on the Gulf of Naples, the Appian Way was strewn with saffron. The Emperor Heliogabalus—to prove he was an incarnation of the Syrian sun god—bathed in saffron until his skin turned gold. The blasphemy doomed him to assassination, for saffron was sacred to the gods. During religious ceremonies, Romans burned it as an offering in braziers and censed their temple altars and statues with it. Saffron purified public halls, baths, and theaters and was spread along parade routes to bless generals and magistrates. It also inaugurated the New Year.

Between the Kalends and the Ides, the first and thirteenth days of January, saffron spiced the air, enticing Janus, the two-headed janitor of the gods, to unlock the city's shining temples. January also celebrated the election of Rome's consuls, its two chief magistrates, and honored the Capitol *Lares* and *Penates,* guardian spirts of the national hearth and pantry.

Peace and goodwill ruled. Lawyers withdrew suits from the courts. Politicians refrained from disputes in the Forum. Tradesmen stopped cursing on the Aventine. A golden, rosy glow suffused the Seven Hills and reconciled the bitterest enemies. The very air shone with scented flames as saffron crackled on the public hearths. I can picture the scene: the red firelight striking the gilded temples, the flickering radiance reflecting over the rooftops.

Clad in spotless white, a procession ascends the Capitol's peak. Representatives from Rome's three branches of government (legislative, executive, and judicial) assemble in the Temple of Jupiter Optimus Maximus. Preceded by bodyguards armed with axes and rods, the consuls-elect in purple-bordered togas sit in their new chairs of office before a shrine. All bow as virgin priestesses accompany the high priest of the Senate to the altar.

Wearing a saffron-striped robe, the old man performs the rites of Janus, an honor once reserved for Rome's ancient kings. He holds an ivory-handled knife over a brazier and blesses the iron blade. Plump sacrificial bulls seem to offer their throats to be slit.

Saffron incense rises to heaven. From Olympus, Jupiter surveys the Mediterranean. Everything on this porcelain platter belongs to Rome, but the empire's glory is fated to disappear like last fall's crocuses. It will happen like this.

When Alaric, the ruler of the Visigoths, reaches the gates of Rome in late 408 AD, he demands tribute in exchange for not plundering the city. Besides heaps of gold and silver, hides and tunics, the Senate offers him 3,000 pounds of pepper and a cartload of saffron. Alaric accepts the pepper but rejects the saffron, which, to be honest, is not the best quality.

"Such fetid grass," he tells the envoys, "is fit only for Romans."

Two years later, Alaric sacks Rome anyway. I watch the Visigoths raid the city's remaining supply of saffron, gather it in the Campus Martius, and dump it in the Tiber. The reddish gold stain slowly spreads through the river like dye leaking from the hull of a sunken merchant ship.

After this humiliation, Romans lost their taste for saffron. During the Dark Ages and the Renaissance, clerics and princes occasionally stocked it in their pantries, but sixteen centuries would pass before most ordinary people tried it again, thanks to the missionary work of provincial chefs such as Flavio Santucci. Ironically, some of these chefs descend from the Germanic tribes that invaded classical Italy. But despite their efforts, it seems to me, this once familiar spice still seems foreign. This is what happens when shame and guilt, ignorance and cynicism alienate us from our past.

At Cul de Sac in Piazza di Pasquino, waiters emerge from the kitchen with a steaming tureen and serve diners. What do these Romans see when they stare into a bowl of mussels drowning in liquid saffron? A savory treat to warm a chilly evening. But I see below the surface the lost gold of empire, the snapped threads of fate.

HOWLS OF LOVE

14.

A DOG'S LIFE:

Pasquino protests cruelty to animals

This Valentine's Day falls on the full moon. Every dog in Rome's 22 *rioni*, the city's municipal districts, will howl until the Seven Hills echo with their cries. Small packs roam the streets in the wee hours. Some beg scraps from midnight passengers at Termini Station. Others congregate around or splash in the Trevi Fountain, deserted except for the homeless couple wading in and scooping coins from its basin. Still others, bathed in moonlight, chase rats or dig for moles in the Coliseum. Sooner or later, all will relieve themselves on me. But I tolerate this slight because we are fellow outcasts, and because I know how much these poor animals suffer.

Despite the efforts of the Ente Nazionale Protezione Animale (ENPA), Italy's oldest animal protection agency, founded in 1871 by that tender-hearted freedom fighter Giuseppe Garibaldi, Romans are notoriously cruel to dogs, most especially puppies. "Under the tree at Christmas," we joke, "onto the road in August." In fact, most of Rome's 20,000 *randagi* or stray dogs, come from mothers abandoned at *Ferragosto,* the August holiday period when most Italians head for the beach. Many vacationers stop at a discrete service area on the autostrada to fill their tanks, empty their bladders, and shoo poor Fido out of their Fiat 500L, never looking back as they speed away to Terracina. It breaks even my stone heart.

If the orphaned dogs survive hunger or traffic, they limp back to Rome, go into heat, and mate in the crooked and narrow alleys of the *centro storico*, the historic district. Once weaned, their pups run wild and scavenge trash from the cheaper trattorias in the less crowded piazzas. When the owners chase them away, the dogs approach tourists. On the pine-lined trails of the Janiculum Hill, they beg panini from the backpacks of hikers. If they are lucky, they become temporary mascots. For a week they wait every morning in front of the same hotel for a breakfast morsel, a good morning pat, and a word of praise in German or English, until the honeymoon, the business trip, or the academic conference ends, and their transient masters return to Zurich, London, or New York

No wonder these dogs howl for love, and their cries always intensify in February, the month of the Roman Lupercalia. This ancient fertility festival honors the she-wolf that suckled the city's founders, Romulus and Remus, back in 771 BC. On the Ides of February, a crowd gathered on the Palatine Hill at the Lupercal Cave, where legend claims the infant twins had been abandoned. Members of the Luperci, the priestly Brotherhood of the Wolf, butchered three dogs and daubed the blood on each other.

During this ritual, rich young matrons shivered and swooned, but their sham display of delicacy never fooled me. These patrician bitches secretly loved the gore and, for all their airs, were much crueler to their own dogs. Frost-bitten mastiffs accompanied their husbands to the German front in the Cimbrian War. Starving setters guarded their gated villas at Lavinium. Guests stepped on miniature greyhounds at their dinner parties on the Aventine Hill, hence the expression *cave canem* (beware of the dog). If these upper-class women suspected that a lover was seeing another woman, they offered the goddess Hecate nine black puppies to curse their rival.

After a public feast, the Luperci skinned the sacrifices and cut thongs from the membranes. Wearing the dog pelts, nude young men ran round the city walls. Whenever they met nubile girls or newlywed brides, they sniffed and panted, barked and howled, until they struck the blushing and giggling women with their thongs. This frenzied outburst was supposed to prevent sterility and ease the pains of the women's childbirth.

Sterility is hardly a problem for today's dog population. Officials do little to promote spaying and neutering. Most bureaucrats take castration personally. Besides, Rome already invests millions in caring for its 120,000 feral cats, which far outnumber its dogs but promote commerce and tourism. By law, a group of over five cats in a natural urban habitat constitutes a protected feline colony. Dozens of *gattare* or cat ladies keep an eye out for strays. Billboards praise cats for "embodying the spirit of the Eternal City." Visitors and volunteers throng the Torre Argentina Cat Sanctuary. Why can't the children of the She-Wolf love dogs? Poor public relations, I suspect.

Two or three generations ago, most Italians grew up on a farm with a German shepherd named Lupo (Wolf). Their citified grandchildren and great-grandchildren are more fastidious. Cats are clean and kill mice. Dogs are mangy and spread fleas. They also are potentially dangerous. On July 30, 2014, a dog pack mauled a female jogger in Rome's Marcigliana Park. *Il Secolo d'Italia*, Italy's notorious online right-wing newspaper, blamed "a degenerate society that sentimentalizes mongrels" and "a hypocritical government that makes it a crime to kill dogs, even in pounds and kennels." Typical.

Whenever unions strike or public services fail, neofascists bay for canine executions.

Benito Mussolini set this precedent. Before Adolph Hitler's visit in May 1938, Il Duce ordered every stray dog in Rome rounded up and shot. After World War Two, the city government continued to catch strays, lock them up, and after three days gas them. National legislation passed in 1991 ended this practice, and government agencies were formed to protect dogs and to prevent the occurrence of strays. Owners are obliged to register and earmark their pets for identification. All dogs must be reported to the Anagrafa Canina, a central registry. Spaying and neutering are encouraged. Mistreatment and abandonment are punished. Unfortunately, these reforms have not helped and may even have harmed Rome's countless stray dogs.

The city's three public pounds are dangerously overcrowded, thanks to Italy's no-kill laws. Commercialized and unsupervised private shelters not only collect dogs but also large amounts of public money. These funds are rarely used to care for the animals. Instead, the cash disappears into dark channels, while the dogs die of hunger and disease. Because millions of euros are involved, the battle against hidden and corrupt bureaucracies has been futile. *Mondo cane*, as we Romans say. It's a doggish world.

As this Valentine's Night drags on, my four-footed friends still howl for love. May La Lupa, the She-Wolf of Rome, answer their cries. A recent omen gives me hope. After more than a century, wolves have returned to the outskirts of the Eternal City. On September 26, 2017, hidden video cameras recorded a family of four in a nature reserve at Castel di Guido, not far from Fiumicino Airport: a male, a female, and two pups.

Naturalists from Italian Protection of Birds, the wildlife organization running the sanctuary, named the male Numa, after Rome's second king and its first Pontifex Maximus, Chief High Priest of the College of Pontiffs. The female was called Aurelia, who appeared to be a protective but compassionate mother. When a starving feral dog approached her feeding pups, she warned it to keep its distance but then brought it a chunk of wild boar meat. The dog wagged its tail and ate.

15.

MADAMA LUCREZIA:
Pasquino finds love among the ruins

Tucked away in a cobblestoned alley in Rome's historic district is the large marble foot of a woman. For centuries, it stood in the piazza in front of the Collegio Romano, but when Victor Emmanuel II, the first King of Italy, died in January 1878, it was moved here to avoid blocking his funeral procession to the Pantheon. The workers, I recall, whistled at its shapely ankle and placed a red carnation in the crevice between its big and second toes.

About the size of a Fiat 500 subcompact, this marble foot is shod in a Grecian sandal rather than a glass slipper. But every so often, some tipsy Prince Charming—fired by too much grappa from the local bars—vows to track down and propose marriage to its owner. If these louts were serious, I would take them to her. An old friend of mine, she lives in the shadow of the sprawling monument to Victor Emanuel in Piazza Venezia.

Her name is Madama Lucrezia. She and I belong to the Congregation of Wits: a group of five statues used as bulletin boards in downtown Rome. Lucrezia, however, is rarely witty. Instead, she mopes in a corner of the Basilica of San Marco, surveying with a bleak expression the row of bus stops across from the Vittoriano.

Although she is ten feet tall and quite buxom, disembarking passengers ignore Lucrezia as they rush to the Forum or the Capitoline Hill. Heartbroken lovers, however, leave tear-stained notes on her pedestal. They identify with her tragic story. Set in the late Middle Ages, it reads like a tale of unhappy love from Boccaccio's *Decameron*, except this tale happens to be true. Well, true as any tale can be in a deceptive city like Rome.

To celebrate the Great Jubilee of 1450, a year of renewal after decades of schism, Pope Nicholas V repaved Rome's streets, restored its aqueducts, and rebuilt its basilicas. During the reconstruction, fragments of a female colossus were unearthed near the Church of Santa Maria sopra Minerva: the head and trunk, left shoulder and upper arm of a mysterious robed woman. Except for a snub nose, her features were completely eroded, but her gaping mouth seemed to lament her shattered state. When a blacksmith clamped the fragments together, I swear to God, the giant appeared to breathe.

Ogling its swollen chest, a scholar claimed the statue represented the Empress Faustina, the wife of Constantius II. But I insisted it was the Egyptian goddess, Isis. After all, it had been discovered at the former site of the Iseum, her temple in Rome. In addition, the statue's gown, with its double knot secured by an amulet, resembled the robes of Egyptian priestesses. Too busy with other projects to resolve this controversy, Pope Nicholas ordered the statue to be left alone. For the next seven years, it stood in the shadow of Santa Maria sopra Minerva, awaiting the woman fated to claim it.

Lucrezia d'Alagno, the spirited daughter of a poor but noble Amalfian family, was the favorite of Alfonso of Aragon, King of Spain and Naples. They met in Naples on June 23, 1448 at the Festival of St. John's Eve, when Alfonso was 54 years old and Lucretia was eighteen. Riding on horseback in a church procession, the king spotted a girl with sparkling black eyes and a ripe bosom standing on a balcony.

She wore a damask gown and a brimless scarlet cap, and her long tawny hair was plaited in front.

When Alfonso spurred his horse to get a closer look, the young woman smiled and leaned over the balcony, holding a vase of barley between her breasts. All Neapolitan girls, rich or poor, tried to foresee their future loves by cultivating barley on their windowsills.

"I've sown barley thinking of Your Majesty," she said. "Now I expect a present."

Delighted, Alfonso ordered his treasurer to give Lucrezia a bag of gold. She took the bag and fished in it for an *alfonso*, a small coin worth a doubloon.

"One Alfonso is enough for me," she said and tripped away.

Alfonso gawped. I can understand why. For years, the king had lived apart from his cold and sickly wife, Maria of Castile, who had failed to produce children and had stayed behind in Spain to serve as his regent. Even from a distance, her sour and pockmarked face still clouded his heart, until Lucrezia's smile pierced the gloom. It sparkled like sunlight on the Bay of Naples. Alfonso fell in love then and there and made the girl his mistress.

Lucrezia brightened the Neapolitan court. She entertained ambassadors, heard petitions, and inspired the Sicilian poet, Antonio Beccadelli. "*As the King prevails over nobles and the Sun over the Stars,*" he wrote, "*so Lucrezia rules over the nymphs of Campania.*" Sculptors carved her face on the Castel Nuovo's triumphal arch. Bishops praised her virtue from the pulpit because she had declared before witnesses that she would not sleep with the king until his marriage was dissolved. An opportunity arose when Alfonso Borgia, the uncle of Lucrezia's brother-in-law, became Pope Callixtus III.

On October 11, 1457, Lucrezia came to Rome to secure an annulment for the king. Not as a humble suppliant but as the de facto Queen of Naples, accompanied by a retinue of 500 knights and 70 ladies-in-waiting. Romans flocked by the thousands to greet her at Porta Sebastiano, the southern gate of the city facing the Appian Way, where she was received by Callixtus's two nephews: Cardinal Rodrigo Borgia (later Pope Alexander VI) and Pedro Luis, Prefect of Rome. That evening, the Pope assembled a consistory, a solemn council of cardinals, in her honor.

During the torch-lit reception, Lucrezia charmed His Holiness, although I doubt that he believed the claims about her virginity. Like all Borgias, Callixtus appreciated female beauty. He also placed a Mafia-like premium on family loyalty. The next morning, while entering the papal apartments for a private audience, Lucrezia was confident that she would win her case.

But the Pope refused to annul the marriage between Alfonso and his wife, Maria. Although he was related by marriage to Lucrezia and admired Alfonso, his former patron, Callixtus felt personally indebted to Queen Maria, "whom I owe more," he explained, "than the mother who gave me birth." When Lucrezia protested, the Pope, who had excommunicated a comet for disrupting the Christian siege of Belgrade, lowered the boom.

"You're very beautiful, my dear," he said, "but I won't go to hell for you."

Lucrezia was stunned. Until now, her beauty had never failed to conquer older men. Feeling sorry for her, the pope offered her a consolation prize: the female colossus dug up by his predecessor near the Church of Santa Maria sopra Minerva. Perhaps the gift was symbolic: a proclamation, for appearance's sake, that the pope considered Lucrezia more chaste than marble. At any rate, this public gesture shielded her from disgrace.

Lucrezia shrugged. Whatever the outcome of her mission, Alfonso had promised her the island of Ischia. But before leaving Rome, she decided to visit the statue. Like Lucrezia, the marble woman had round breasts and wore her thick hair braided in the front. Staring into her ravaged face, Lucrezia could not have imagined the future. By late June, Alfonso would be dead, and she would flee Naples and return to Rome.

For the next twenty years, Lucrezia languished on the margins of high society. She rented a shabby palazzo near Piazza di San Marco, an unfashionable part of town, and wore costume jewelry and secondhand gowns at audiences. Believe me, it is easier to be a beggar in the streets than a supplicant at court. Slowly, Lucrezia's hope turned to stone. Every day, before entering the Church of Santa Maria sopra Minerva to kneel at the tomb of the painter Fra Angelico, she placed flowers on the statue the Pope had given her. But despite her pain and humiliation, Lucrezia never regretted her affair with King Alfonso.

"Some moments of joy," she said, "are worth a lifetime of grief."

Lucrezia died on February 19, 1479 and was buried in the church where she so often had prayed. A half century later, the marker on her grave disappeared and Cardinal Innocenzo Cibo moved her statue to the Basilica of San Marco, near her old neighborhood. Locals called the broken colossus Madama Lucrezia in her honor, but that doesn't mean they treated it with respect, not when Roman history is such a carnival.

At the Ballo dei Poveretti, staged every May Day, cripples and hunchbacks danced before Lucrezia's statue. Urchins decorated her with garlands of ribbon and lace and necklaces of garlic, onions, and pepperoncini. Prostitutes smeared rouge on her cheeks. During the Napoleonic wars, Jacobins toppled her and broke her nose. A wag then traced this lampoon in charcoal on her back: "I can't stand it anymore!"

Such shenanigans, I'll bet, never occurred in the Temple of Isis.

Isis, they say, retrieved and restored the scattered pieces of her husband Osiris's body in Egypt. Nothing, however, can restore our shattered past, not even the memory of great passion. This sad truth oddly comforts us Romans. In a world of ruins, the ruin of our own happiness seems a natural catastrophe, not a moral failure. Almost tenderly, the Eternal City invites us to rest our weariness upon things that have crumbled for centuries but remain upright. Until Lucrezia's statue collapses into dust, therefore, the brokenhearted will continue to leave notes addressed to their lost loves on her weathered pediment.

16.

THE SAME OLD SONG:
Pasquino raps about love

Ovid, whose book of poems, *The Art of Love*, delighted and scandalized first-century Rome, had intended to write his witty erotica as a proper epic in Latin hexameter form—or so he told me at a private reading at the villa of Julia the Elder, daughter of Caesar Augustus. But as the poet was working, Cupid flew in through his study window and—can you believe it?—with a snicker lopped off one foot from every other line. This amputation, Ovid claimed, strumming his lyre, changed the poem's original rhythm from a grim march to a playful canter. Only fitting, I thought. Sooner or later, every epic becomes a burlesque in the imperial brothels. Roma spelled backwards is Amor: *Love!*

Caesar was not amused and banished Ovid to a distant outpost on the Black Sea. Even so, I still think Ovid was right. Sex is war: fierce but playful hand-to-hand combat at close quarters. At least in Rome. Later at night, behind every bush, against every pillar, under every aqueduct, I've seen couples of all ages wrestle, bite, scratch, and kick. Their snarls of rage turn into sighs of bliss. Passion, I've learned, does not distinguish between pain and pleasure. Both form the eternal counterpoint of desire, the ancient song of *odi et amo*: I hate and love. This is true not only in classical Roman poetry but also in contemporary Roman music.

Love sings a bitter tune here on the Seven Hills. Let Venetians croon barcarolles on the Grand Canal and Neapolitans strum serenades below Vesuvius. We Romans are children of the She-Wolf that nursed Romulus and Remus. Randy, snide, and fierce by nature, we howl spitefully romantic street songs even in St. Peter's Square. These songs are called *stornelli.*

The *stornello* gets its name from the custom of singing *"a storno,"* that is, bouncing the voice from place to place. Born of passing inspiration, these improvised quips were first sung in taverns and trattorias, then spread from balcony to balcony, alley to alley, and prison cell to prison cell in Rome's Trastevere district. Circulated by carters, vendors, and waiters, the rough tunes were adapted and performed by street singers and transcribed and polished by folklorists.

Stornelli romansechi date back to at least the eighteenth century but did not become truly popular until after World War II. Broadcasting and tourism mainstreamed these songs, thanks to such singers as Alvaro Amici, Gabriella Ferri, and Claudio Villa, who introduced elements of cabaret, jazz, and pop into their interpretations. Their recordings still serve as a balm for Roman boomers.

But what exactly is a *stornello?* Giggi Zanazzo, the dialect poet and folklorist, said it best: "a sigh of love, an accent of hatred, a whim of fantasy."

Accompanied by a guitar or an accordion, the singer announces a topic and apostrophizes his or her beloved as a flower. Not a rose or gardenia but something wilder and coarser plucked from the fields, gardens, parks, and greenways near Rome, such as pigweed or sow-thistle. The remaining lyrics, whether traditional or extemporaneous, form an equally pungent and thorny bouquet of double-entendres, complaints, and insults. The effect is funny and provocative but also haunting and heartbreaking.

Gabriella Ferri's throaty voice transports you to a café in Seville or Morocco. Her clear, cutting alto, however tender or playful, is always ready to flow into the ancient Roman sneer, with a laugh like the jets of the Trevi Fountain but with a sigh of melancholy whenever she twists and suffocates a note. Left with a void in your stomach, you hunger for more, even if it means enduring ridicule and abuse.

Stornelli amorosi are often indistinguishable from *stornelli dispetti*, a popular way for Romans to dis each other in public. The basis of this musical rhyming game is to wait until the end of a verse to react and then return the courtesy. Some performances are legendary. In 1973, Italy's national public broadcasting company televised an unforgettable match between La Ferri and Claudio Villa, the king of Roman crooners.

Like gladiators, they circled each other. The willowy Ferri was attired in a red feather boa and a hippie skirt patterned with wheat and poppies. The stubby Villa appeared in a black Stetson and a double-breasted, navy-blue leisure suit. For ten minutes, they improvised insults as a stage band vamped.

"*Ma nun lo vedi quanto sei tappo?*" Ferri sang. "Can't you see what a shrimp you are? Guess your Mamma couldn't waste much on you."

Mentioning mothers is against the rules, but Villa was having too much fun to call foul. Instead, he wagged his finger and belted with mock ardor: "*Tu canti proprio come e 'na sirena!* You sing exactly like a siren. The siren of an ambulance, that is!"

The studio audience whistled and clapped, but the laughter from its shabbily dressed members sounded rueful to me. Like Villa and Ferri, these Romans came from the kind of neighborhoods in which *stornelli* comment on the messy sex lives of the poor. If you doubt me, watch the opening to Pier Paolo Pasolini's scandalous film, *Mamma Roma*.

Mamma Roma, an ex-prostitute played by Anna Magnani, marries off her former pimp Carmine to a county girl named Clementina. The reception is held in a stark banquet hall at a *borgata*, a public housing complex on Rome's periphery. The wedding guests, aware of the *ménage à trois*, ask for a song.

"*Fior de gaggia*!" Mamma Roma begins, leaning against a chair and chuckling softly. "Acacia flower! When I sing, I sing with joy. But if I told all, I'd ruin this party!"

Carmine, mustached and wearing a loose-fitting tux, rises and accepts the challenge.

"*Fiore de sabbia*!" he croons. "Sage flower! You laugh, joke, and play the saint, and all the while rage bursts your chest."

Clementina responds. With a veiled headdress resting on a wild mane of black hair and coarse features better suited for a wrestler than a bride, she is hardly a shrinking violet.

"*Fior de cocuzza*!" she sings. "Squash flower! Once a woman was crazy for this mustache, and now that she's lost him, she makes a stink!"

Mamma Roma brays and wiggles her broad hips.

"*Fiore de merda*!" she spits. "Turd flower! I freed myself from that noose. Now it's another's turn to be his servant!"

Film critics claimed this scene illustrated "the alienation and commodification of desire" in postwar Italy. But Pasolini—whose own love life was often chaotic and sordid, despite his conscious commitment to leftist causes—knew better. Whatever Marxist academics might think, I myself believe that sexual strife has nothing to do with poverty. If it did, my friends Claudio and Flavia would never quarrel in front of me.

Claudio and Flavia, a professional couple from the affluent Parioli district, visit Piazza di Pasquino at least once a week. They dine al fresco at Cul de Sac, a popular wine bar and eatery, always ordering the charcuterie board and a bottle of Valpolicella.

The meal always starts well. Claudio and Flavia rest their chins on their hands and gaze adoringly into each other's eyes. With matching haircuts, blazers, and slacks, they look eerily like twins, so I can understand their mutual fascination. But then something—a momentary lapse of attention, a careless remark, a stray glance at a passing stranger—will set Flavia off.

"*Mortacci tua!*" she screams. May the souls of your dead relatives burn in hell!

Claudio smashes her plate. Flavia throws a glass of ice water in his face.

Since the quarrel is in public, everyone takes sides: the diners, the servers, the pedestrians. But before the situation escalates, the maître d' suggests a *stornello* contest. As somebody plays a guitar, the couple compete to create the most outrageous invective. Every verse is a bullet, every bullet a bird's-eye:

"*You are trash, Flavia, piled in the street. You don't stink unless you get heated!*"

"*You're a ray fish, Claudio, buried in the sand. You won't sting unless I step on you!*"

They continue insulting each other . . . until they kiss and make up.

Why, I wonder, can't Romans express affection without hostility? Why must love and hate be so entangled? Blame the gods! Cupid, the god of erotic attraction, is the son of Venus (the goddess of love) and Mars (the god of war). He was conceived when the adulterous couple was caught *in flagrante* in the net of Venus's husband, Vulcan, and made the laughingstock of Mount Olympus, home of the immortals. Ever since then, the brat has avenged his parents by wounding and humiliating his cousins: us Romans.

Targets of a spiteful archer, we are fated to be snipers in love.

17.

ANNA AND TENN:

Pasquino joins friends for cocktails at eight

"*M'aricordo bbene*. I remember it well . . ."

On September 28, 1973, before the crowd of mourners made parking impossible, a van pulled up to Bellini's Elephant and Obelisk in Piazza della Minerva to deliver twenty dozen roses for the Italian film star Anna Magnani's funeral. As dignitaries gathered inside the Basilica of Santa Maria sopra Minerva, *paparazzi* wondered who had sent the flowers, but I, along with residents of Rome's Pigna district, guessed that it was Tennessee Williams.

I'm sure that Williams' tribute was a coded message. The twenty bouquets meant "*alle venti*," at twenty-hundred hours or 8:00 PM. The American playwright and the Roman actress would meet at this time for cocktails, conversations, and confessions on a rooftop terrace in the *centro storico*. Their friendship, spanning twenty-three years, was a passionate romance.

Williams fell in love with La Magnani when he saw Roberto Rossellini's *Open City*. She played Pina, a pregnant widow whose lover is arrested by the Nazis. When the prison truck drives off, she chases it, howling defiance, but is shot down. Williams was rarely moved by screen performances, "but this woman," he confided to his diary, "has sunk her claws into my heart." He felt inspired, even compelled, to write a play for her.

For three years Williams telegrammed his muse. No reply. Coming to Rome in January 1949 for the Italian premiere of *A Streetcar Named Desire*, he begged the director Luchino Visconti to introduce him. But it was Gore Vidal who arranged a meeting the following August. Magnani kept Williams waiting for an hour before she sent a courier to fetch him.

At Doney, a sidewalk café on Via Veneto, the diva pretended not to speak English—until Williams asked her to play the lead in a new work, *The Rose Tattoo*. Their collaboration began what I believe was the most joyfully productive period of his life.

"Rome is the capitol of my heart," said Williams, who spent springs and summers here in Rome in the 1950s to escape the repression of Eisenhower's America. He and his lover, Frank Merlo, shared a huge matrimonial bed in an apartment on Via Aurora overlooking the Villa Borghese gardens. Nobody better embodied the city's vitality better than Anna Magnani. With her coarse black hair, sharp snout, flashing eyes, and full breasts, she was *La Lupa,* the she-wolf who suckles orphans and outcasts.

After a hard day of writing, I think that Williams needed nursing. Whenever he called, Anna said: "*Ciao,* Tenn! What is the program?" They always met at eight at her penthouse in Palazzo Altieri, large enough for her invalid son and a menagerie of pets. Williams never knew what to expect. Once she greeted him singing and dancing, wearing only a pair of transparent panties. Clothed or naked, she announced: "*Ho la ruzza!*" ("I'm itching for fun!")

They danced at Café de Paris and drank at Rosati. They drove by the aqueducts in the Aniene Valley as Anna's German shepherd raced alongside their car. If they dined in Trastevere, they demanded a huge bag of leftovers and fed the stray cats around the Forum and the Colosseum. Often they were joined by Anna's latest boy toy, whom she impetuously had picked up and soon would discard, who sulked in silence until they returned home.

The rest of the night was spent on Anna's terrace, where they sipped Negronis and admired the view of the Pantheon. For hours, they discussed art, life, and love. Despite a string of unhappy affairs, an addiction to coffee and cigarettes, insomnia, and mood swings, Anna was happy. She was thrilled when people recognized her on the streets or when a cop in the middle of directing traffic shouted: *"Eh! Nannaré!"* With head flung back and hands planted on hips, she released a geyser of mirth from a deep wellspring.

"When Anna laughs," Williams wrote Truman Capote, "all of the questions about the why of everything are addressed more than adequately."

During the 1960s and 1970s, the friends continued to meet, but I could tell the magic was gone. Frank Merlo had died of lung cancer, and times had changed. Increasingly savaged by critics and vilified by editorialists and politicians, Williams struggled to get his plays produced. Magnani, who looked her age and who reminded Italians of struggles that most wished to forget, was offered roles that were beneath her. "In this country," she told Williams, "only the monuments survive."

When she died of pancreatic cancer, Williams was too shattered to attend her funeral. "Age has made it difficult for me to have much faith in things," he remarked, "but the death of Anna Magnani has made it almost impossible. It still seems incomprehensible that the world—my world—can function without her in it."

Words failed him, so he said it with flowers: "*Ci vediamo alle venti.*" See you at eight.

CAFÉ SOCIETY

18.

A PERPETUAL SPREE:
Pasquino carouses with Nikolai Gogol

On a fashionable street in Rome, a brisk Sunday walk from the church at the top of the Spanish Steps, stands a six-storied apartment house. I love this old building for personal reasons. But because its cracked façade of sepia plaster is so shabby compared to the area's gilded shops and marbled offices, most people ignore it. Today was no exception. As usual, the ground-floor bar struggled to attract a matinee crowd from the next-door theater. I, however, had come to gaze at the second-floor apartment above the bar's entrance.

Displayed between its two shuttered windows were a marble plaque, with inscriptions in Russian and Italian, and a bronze relief of a slouched little man with an unruly mop of hair and a large, hooked nose. Nikolai Gogol, the great comic writer, lived here between 1838 and 1842. For this brief period, we were boon companions in what seemed a perpetual spree of high jinks and fine dining. I rekindled Gogol's imagination and restored his confidence to write again after a long depression. Gogol, in turn, reawakened my zest for Rome—an endless banquet of sights and sounds, smells and tastes—at a time when I was disenchanted with it.

I blamed Pope Gregory XVI. Elected in 1832, he was the worst killjoy ever to sit on the Throne of Saint Peter. His repressive edicts, which included banning streetlamps and trains, turned Rome into a dreary backwater. No one posted wisecracks on my pedestal. Young women drooped like underwatered geraniums. Young men slouched like overburdened donkeys. But that all changed when Gogol came to town in March 1837.

Gogol arrived on the eve of Palm Sunday, shortly before his twenty-eighth birthday, and checked into a fleabag hotel off Piazza di Pasquino. This is my turf, so for good luck, at the suggestion of the concierge, he left his bags unpacked in his room, rushed down the block, and introduced himself to me in faulty Italian.

"I am here," he announced, "as a pilgrim, not a tourist. I wish to be reborn in Rome!"

An odd duck, I thought. (Gogol in Russian means "mallard," he told me.) A tow-headed runt with a big beak, he waddled and quacked but demanded respect. He was a baffling mixture of piety and impudence, humility and arrogance. The next week, to my delight and amazement, he crashed Easter service at the Vatican, despite the prohibition against non-Catholics receiving communion at mass. But Gogol, I later realized, had not gone to celebrate Christ's resurrection. No, he had gone to celebrate his own.

Gogol had been buried alive in Russia. According to him, it was the Ninth Circle of Hell: "a pit of slush and ice." St. Petersburg, the cultural capital, had crucified him after the fiasco of *The Inspector General*, his satire on political corruption. Overnight, however, Russia—with its bureaucrats and censors, pedants and critics—had vanished like a bad dream, and Gogol awoke in what he considered the Promised Land.

"*Bella Italia!*" he cried. "I was born for you!"

Gogol's exuberance amused me. It was wonderful seeing Rome through his eyes, beginning with Piazza Navona. "The beating heart of the city," he called it: an oval-shaped public square punctuated by three gushing fountains and hemmed in by churches, palaces, and rust-colored houses, their terraces overflowing with red carnations. Basking in the spray of the Fountain of the Four Rivers, the largest of the three fountains at the very center of the piazza, Gogol watched the sun pulse on its rippling basin.

"This isn't a piazza!" he exclaimed. "It's a countryside, a theater, a fair, a delight!"

Very poetic, I murmured, but only sidewalk painters work on the streets. Gogol needed permanent lodgings. For eighteen months, perhaps for religious reasons, he lived in the shadow of a Franciscan monastery. But in October 1838, he took my advice, moved to the historic center, and rented a room on what was then Via Felice. In English: Happy Street.

The street was aptly named, for the next four years were the happiest in Gogol's tragically short life. He composed the first part of his novel, *Dead Souls*. The plot delighted me. Exploiting loopholes in Russian property law, a sly bureaucrat purchases the rights to dead serfs from their former landlords and amasses a fortune. Despite its foreign subject, I maintain, this epic tale of chicanery could be written only here in Rome: the capital of dreamers and schemers.

Gogol studied both specimens. The Spanish Steps, a brief walk from his apartment, swarmed with poets and artists, beggars and hustlers, charlatans and quacks. After witnessing a couple fleece a plodding English tourist, Gogol was shocked when the crowd cheered the grifters and mocked their victim. Romans, I explained, divide humanity into two categories: *furbi e fessi*, wise guys and patsies. Whatever morality might claim, it is better to be the first than the second.

Such street scenes exhilarated him, but Gogol always retreated to his apartment to write. Ventilated by two high windows, the room was furnished with a tall desk and an antique oil lamp with a beak as pointed as his nose. The mosaic tiles rang whenever he paced the floor, but this exercise was nothing compared to his afternoon constitutionals in the Villa Borghese gardens.

Gogol's nose, I thought, certainly equipped him to take the fresh air. He inhaled deeply. "*Che fresco!*" he sighed, as if a hundred angels had flown into his lungs. "Pasquino," he said, "I feel an irresistible urge to transform myself into an immense nose. No more eyes, arms, or legs. Nothing but a gigantic nose with nostrils as big as buckets to savor the fragrance of spring."

Or the aroma of cooking. When he wasn't writing, Gogol held court in cafés and restaurants. Once a finicky eater, whose delicate stomach could tolerate only boiled milk and rice pudding, he had developed a wolfish appetite in Rome. He never deviated from his routine.

At the city's oldest coffeehouse, Gogol breakfasted on loaf-shaped buns filled with whipped cream, which clung to the tip of his nose, and drank gallons of cappuccino. He lunched on toast and antipasto wherever he could. But he always ate his big evening meal at Falcone's, an elegant trattoria near the Pantheon, where the broiled lamb, he claimed, "surpassed that of the Caucasus." The cherry tart was fresh, but not as fresh as Fabrizio, the maître d, who mock-saluted Gogol as if he were a privy councilor.

"Ser Nicò!" Fabrizio boomed. "Mr. Nick! Here to disgrace yourself again, I hope."

I could see why he teased Gogol. Fabrizio, who exuded pomade, was tall and devilishly handsome. Gogol, who stank like an onion, was practically a dwarf. Even so, Fabrizio liked him. Ser Nicò might look like a Neapolitan coffeepot balancing a bowl of polenta, but he spoke the Roman dialect perfectly. Gogol had learned it by listening to Giuseppe Belli, the vernacular poet, recite his obscene and scatological sonnets and by studying the vulgar slang from Rome's more disreputable markets. Now he could bully Fabrizio's staff like a street tough.

While Gogol barked orders, waiters scurried to fetch cheese, butter, vinegar, mustard, broccoli, onions, and chicory. Gogol, his face glowing, snatched the ingredients from their hands and raised a pyramid of condiments and vegetables. Soon, a covered dish of macaroni arrived and was set before him. When the lid was removed, a thick, odorous steam arose and made his nose quiver. Gogol threw a lump of butter onto the noodles, added the greens, powdered the mound with cheese and dried sage, and seemed to vacuum the meal through his nostrils.

Fabrizio, I fear, encouraged these excesses. Whenever Ser Nicò overindulged, he over-tipped like a big shot. Fabrizio then plied him with wine until the little man picked up every tab in the restaurant. If a guest demurred, Fabrizio winked and quoted a popular proverb: "*Un cojone che viè, le paga tutte.*" ("Sooner or later, some jerk comes along who pays for everyone.")

Gogol avenged himself by snookering the staff at billiards. Despite his shyness, he had developed a disturbing knack for larceny, whether cadging loans from gullible expats or cheating unsuspecting locals at cards or dice. Fabrizio blamed me. After all, I had taught Gogol to emulate the follies and vices of us native Romans. But I defended myself. It was foolish, I said, to expect Ser Nicò to behave. He was simply too cuckoo, as Fabrizio and his staff knew full well.

Sometimes, he sang a Ukrainian folk tune and danced on a table, twirling his umbrella until it flew off its handle. Other times he brooded as if he were Napoleon in exile, holding his stomach and muttering about defeat and betrayal. Like a Russian stacking doll, Gogol contained multiple selves. Which one would dine tonight at Falcone's: the high liver or the ascetic, the preacher or the pool shark? No one could predict, but Fabrizio knew how to handle him.

One evening, Ser Nicò was being more opinionated than usual. Like most reactionaries, he loved Rome because it was frozen in time. It was eternal, he claimed, because it had rejected progress. The city had no trains or streetlamps. Its clocks never agreed. Its residents were immune to the fever of capitalism infecting England, France, and America. True, they were browbeaten by bureaucrats and hounded by the police, but at least they were spared the grim obsession of constantly making—

At this point, Fabrizio twisted Gogol's his nose. "*E và*, Nicò! Come off it Nicò!" he said and huffily cleared the table.

The restaurant' patrons was stunned. How would Gogol react? To his credit, Ser Nicò neither threw a tantrum nor groveled on the floor. Instead, he clasped Fabrizio's hand, looked him in the eye, and apologized. Fabrizio patted Gogol's shoulder and told the waiters to bring more coffee. The matter was forgotten, and everyone resumed their meal. Romans are like that. Call it a tolerance for human frailty, or an acceptance of human contradictions. We praise the bigamist who sends anniversary flowers to both his wives and admire the tax cheat who donates money to the poor.

But as Gogol sipped his coffee and was pampered by the waiters, I had a premonition that he would never be this happy again. Only in Rome could he truly be loved and accepted. When he left for good in September 1842, I feared the worst.

Over the next decade, Gogol slowly succumbed to depression and religious mania. His spiritual director, a twisted fanatic, convinced him that his genius for comedy and passion for food were mortal sins. Gogol burned the second half of *Dead Souls* and subjected himself to punishing fasts. He died of starvation on March 4, 1852.

Rome still remembers my friend. The bar beneath his old apartment advertises itself as Caffé Gogol. His corner table in a fabled coffeehouse is preserved like a shrine, complete with a miniature portrait of the author and a framed autographed letter. A bronze statue, a gift from a Russian sculptor, stands in the Gardens of Villa Borghese. But none of these memorials mean as much to me as the tribute by Trattoria Falcone.

When he learned of Gogol's death, Fabrizio ordered the staff to wear black armbands and to place chrysanthemums on the tables. A customer, allergic to the flowers, complained. Was it right to demand that regular patrons fuss over a dead stranger? Fabrizio showed him the door.

"Ser Nicò," he said, "was one of us."

19.

THE SWEET SMELL OF EXCESS:
Pasquino bottles Gabriele D'Annunzio

A young poet declaims beside my statue in Piazza di Pasquino. The passing crowd ignores his wild words and flamboyant gestures, but a tiny camera on an aluminum tripod records his performance for an online audience. His Woody Woodpecker haircut, thick eyeshadow, glitter makeup, and green fingernails should earn thousands of likes and shares on Facebook.

All the same, I suspect our bard is a fake, a rich kid from Rome's Pariolini district. His black tunic and white capris are too clean and well pressed. He also wears a perfume called Aqua Nunzia, a heady mix of orange, lemon, lavender, rose, jasmine, patchouli, sandalwood, and musk costing €160.00 a bottle. I swoon on my pedestal because the scent reminds me of its namesake: Gabriele D'Annunzio, the fragrant poet who seduced Rome in the late nineteenth century.

Almost nobody reads D'Annunzio today. If he is remembered at all, it is not as a writer but as a philanderer whose myriad lovers included the actress Eleanora Duse, an aviator who lost an eye in World War I, and an agitator who inspired Benito Mussolini. But I prefer to picture him as a young man on the make (like our friend here), a slick opportunist whose marketing and exhibitionism anticipated today's social media.

When D'Annunzio first arrived in Rome in 1881, he was the boy wonder from Pescara, a backwater in the Abruzzo region. His promising verses had earned the attention of leading critics and a scholarship at La Sapienza University. Barely eighteen, Gabriele was a faun: a wildling with pointed ears, curly hair, soulful eyes, and a goaty smell. Utterly provincial, he had no sense of style. On Sundays, wearing a black suit and an open-necked shirt, he resembled a Calvinist pastor honeymooning in Rome but homesick for Geneva. A year later, however, after *La Tribuna* hired the ambitious young hick as a society columnist, Gabriele ingratiated himself with barbers and tailors, borrowed money to buy a new wardrobe, and became an arbiter of style.

Fashionistas adored him, but the makeover damaged his reputation. Great writers were supposed to be shabby. The poets of the older generation—Giosuè Carducci, Mario Rapisardi, Enrico Panzacchi—were *scapiglaturi*, disheveled bohemians, who considered good clothes an insult to intelligence. Gabriele's English ties and impeccable riding coats worn at hunting meets in the Campagna, shocked the literati far more than his sexual escapades. At the height of an extravagant affair with Alessandra Di Rudinì, daughter of the Prime Minister, Gabriele owned a hundred suits. But he and Alessandra slept naked on Persian rugs, next to their horses.

Gabriele's success with women baffled me. Curly-headed when I first met him, he was now balder than a turnip. Gabriele blamed this condition on a duel with a fellow journalist. His considerably taller opponent bested him with a cut to the head. Alarmed by the blood, the attending doctor poured iron perchlorate over the wound, destroying Gabriele's hair follicles and causing him to go bald. This story is no more believable than the claim, included in all his press releases, that D'Annunzio was conceived in an open boat during a storm on the Adriatic.

Fortunately, Gabriele didn't need be seen to impress the ladies. They could smell him coming a block away. Each afternoon and evening, he bathed, redressed, and sprayed himself with scent. He averaged a pint of cologne a day. A bottle of perfume, used more sparingly, might last a week. Shops created customized scents with such names as *Borgia*, *Chypre*, *Mousse de Diane*, and *Tout la Forêt*. When these proved unsatisfactory, he concocted his own formula from jasmine, rosewater, and ambergris. This perfume, he believed, would revolutionize the fragrance industry and finance his luxurious lifestyle.

But manufacturers never responded to his queries, so D'Annunzio never patented the formula. Nevertheless, he distributed free samples whenever he visited Antico Caffè Greco, Rome's oldest and most prestigious coffeehouse.

Still located on Via Condotti near the Spanish Steps, Caffè Greco remains a haven for poets and writers, who commune with the spirits of Casanova and Goldoni, Shelley and Keats, Goethe and Leopardi over cappuccino and dessert. Its hushed inner sanctum—a procession of dimly lit crimson and golden salons, furnished with marble-topped tables, banquettes, antiques, paintings, and etchings—looks exactly as it did when D'Annunzio held court here during the Belle Époque.

The man who can dominate a Roman coffeehouse can dominate the world. Amid the Greco's red damask and gilt mirrors, D'Annunzio behaved like a sultan, summoning the staff by beating on the floor with a marble-headed cane. The black tailcoated waiters always forgave him, however, because the little tyrant had such panache.

Who will forget the time our poet came to the Greco in a straw hat, a double-breasted tweed shooting jacket, flare-hipped riding breeches, and a tricolored bowtie? Accompanying him was a leashed greyhound in a jeweled martingale collar. Patrons stared as the two chose a table. D'Annunzio ordered a *babà*, a Neapolitan sponge cake soaked in rum syrup, filled with custard, and decorated with whipped cream and cherries. When the treat arrived, D'Annunzio set the plate on the floor and let the greyhound lick the topping.

Everyone was amused, except a former mentor. This hardboiled journalist, a fellow Abruzzese, had befriended D'Annunzio when he first came to Rome. Since their last meeting four years ago, D'Annunzio, he believed, had become "a perfumed turd." As the greyhound chewed the *babà*, the journalist stirred a demitasse of espresso and gave our poet the side-eye.

"Go back to Pescara," he growled, "before these excesses ruin your writing."

D'Annunzio's eyes twinkled above his petite handlebar mustache. "Actually," he said, "my tastes are quite simple. All I need to write are 50 inkwells, 500 goose quills, and 50,000 sheets of scented paper from Miliani Fabriano," Milan's deluxe stationery store.

The journalist sipped his coffee. "Considering how much cologne you use," he said, "you should scent the paper yourself."

Patrons laughed but not at the joke. D'Annunzio's greyhound had stolen a meringue from another table. To atone, D'Annunzio signed a soiled napkin, removed his bow tie, pinned the autograph to it, and gave both to the owner for framing. Still fragrant under glass, this souvenir now hangs in Caffè Greco's Gubinelli Salon.

Has the young poet here in Piazza di Pasquino ever sniffed it? I doubt it. He has been taught to consider D'Annunzio a right-wing fop and to believe that the present is more advanced than the past. Both claims may be true, but I don't think that he should feel superior. Our young friend might prefer Starbucks to the Greco and Amazon to Feltrinelli bookstores, but he too seeks attention at any cost. And it looks like his efforts have paid off.

After the poet finishes his set, a middle-aged man in rumpled Panama suit approaches. Doffing a Havana hat, he presents a business card and introduces himself as a critic and editor. Would the young poet like to appear on his podcast? They could discuss it over lunch at Tre Scalini, a nearby restaurant noted for its *cacio e pepe*, an elegant mac and cheese dish.

The young poet hesitates, scanning the older man's lined face and speckled head. Is he interested in the poet's body of work or merely his body? Whichever, the poet beams and flirtatiously tosses his head. His wafting perfume reminds me of an advertising slogan.

Aqua Nunzia, I think. *Nothing is sweeter the smell of success.*

20.

THURSDAY WITH THE QUEEN:
Pasquino crashes a royal salon

When Princess Diana of Wales died on August 31, 1997, Babington's—the British tearoom at the foot of Rome's Spanish Steps—placed a dignified announcement on its door and closed for business. The rest of Rome went mad with grief. It was a Sunday, after all, and there was nothing better to do.

Mourners packed the Piazza di Spagna. Solemn young men with soul patches carried photos and posters of the People's Princess. Sobbing young women dyed and bobbed their hair to better identify with her in death. Bouquets of forget-me-nots, Diana's favorite flower, flooded the Spanish Steps. At a candlelight vigil, an Elton John impersonator sang a bad Italian version of "Candle in the Wind." The spectacle upset me, but I couldn't figure out why until three days later at the Free University of Antico Caffè Greco.

This club of shirt-sleeved intellectuals meets each month in the red-damasked salon of a fabled coffeehouse off the Piazza di Spagna. Naturally, as Rome's most opinionated monument, I am an *ex officio* member. Usually, we discuss the best venues for art exhibits, debate which palazzi should be restored, and ponder which fountains to clean. Today, however, all we could talk about was Princess Diana, whose death had upstaged the passing of Mother Teresa, who had died the same day in Calcutta. Even the atheists among us thought that was wrong.

But what could we do? Diana's tale was a tragedy for our times: a fairy-tale princess hunted down by a wolf pack of *paparazzi*. It was unprecedented. And yet Diana's fatal glamor and the media hysteria it had inspired seemed all-too familiar. They reminded us of Margherita of Savoy: Queen of Italy from 1878 to 1900 and Queen Dowager from 1900 to 1926. Like Diana, Margherita was ignored by her husband, adored by her people. For the bourgeoisie and the patriotic poor, she was a fashion icon and a media star. But her resemblance to Diana ends there. The Princess of Wales loved her fans. The Queen of Italy patronized hers. Her snobbery and pretention tainted Rome's cultural life in the thirty decadent years preceding the First World War and contributed to that calamity.

The real source of this poison, in my opinion, was the Circolo della Regina, the Queen's Circle: a coterie of reactionary highbrows and hacks, nearly all dilettantes. Their toxic influence transformed Margherita from Lady Bountiful to Lady Macbeth, a harpy who encouraged the clubbing of strikers and the massacres of colonial subjects, and who anointed a ruthless dictator. Her self-appointed advisors might as well have served arsenic with her tea.

I remember Margherita's allure in the first years of her reign. She and her husband, Umberto I, assumed the throne in January 1878 after the death of Italy's first king, Victor Emmanuel II. The royal couple were cousins and completely mismatched. Umberto was an oaf with a square head, wide-set eyes, and a walrus mustache. Margherita was in the first bloom of her beauty. Almost thirty, the former Crowned Princess had finally shed the last vestige of an adolescent gawkiness that had veiled her natural grace. She also had an extensive wardrobe.

All too soon, Margherita would become plump as a penguin, but when the poet Giosuè Carducci met her in July 1878, she was tall and stately. With soulful blue eyes and a battering ram of a brow, she was an enchanting blend of gentleness and fierceness, the dove and the eagle. Bewitched, despite his republican sentiments, Carducci compared her to the warrior princess Célanire, daughter of Vitikund, chief of the Saxons.

Propagandists exploited the Queen's beauty to glamorize the House of Savoy, Italy's new regime. I don't blame them. Everything else in Italy was so shabby—not only the parliamentary politics but also the overcoats and caps of the soldiers, the coat of arms of the state, even the government postage. A sepia-colored, thirty-cent stamp, which showed Umberto's stolid and whiskered face, looked like an advertisement for cough drops.

It's impossible to make a silk purse out of a sow's ear, I thought. Umberto lacked culture, preferring his stone hunting lodge to the wooden-paneled Rococo library in the Quirinal Palace. Even the most obsequious lavatory attendant could tell that he would never be a great king. But with a little sleight of hand, Margherita could be passed off as a great queen. Courtiers pretended that she was the second coming of Isabella d'Este: Renaissance woman, patron of the arts, and leader of fashion. In fact, she recited Dante and Petrarch like a schoolgirl in a pageant, barely knew enough Latin to get through a mass, and spelled atrociously.

Ashamed of her ignorance, Margherita collected erudite men of proper rank and opinion. "No other nineteenth century queen," remarked her friend Juliette Adam, the French journalist, "surrounded herself with so many scholars and so few cavalry officers." She craved attention. Umberto, who preferred the company of his mistresses, had stopped sleeping with her after the birth of their only child, Victor Emanuel III.

The Queen's Circle met Thursday afternoons in the Quirinal Palace. If the conversation didn't sparkle, the monocles and the medals certainly did. Beribboned savants taught her Latin and schooled her in autocracy. Democracy, they said, threatened the Kingdom of Italy. Liberals were insufferable: "foolish when they voted, mad when they governed, disgusting when they crashed society." Only unquestioning obedience to the House of Savoy and complete immersion in high culture could redeem the masses. Italy needed fewer trade unions, they claimed, and more Dante societies and string quartets. The palace ministers, however, were more practical. They slyly manipulated the media and turned hapless Margherita into a superstar.

Romans had a word for the craze that swept the country: *Margheritismo*, Maggie Mania. The symbol of this national cult was the marguerite daisy, a pun on the Queen's name. Crates of marguerites were shipped from the Canary Islands. They swamped the flower stands on the Spanish Steps and flooded the florist shops in the city. Chirpy middle-class housewives exhibited daisies in their parlors, using tasteful flower arrangements from the pages of *Margherita*, Italy's most popular fashion magazine.

The Queen taught chic aristocrats to smoke flavored cigarettes, drive fancy racing cars, collect pearl and coral, and keep a menagerie of pug dogs. But to win the love of commoners, she wore regional folk costumes and showed enthusiasm for local customs and traditions. Once, in a carefully staged breach of royal etiquette, she publicly ate a chicken thigh using her hands. This publicity stunt spawned a meme:

114

"Anche la Regina Margherita mangia il pollo con le dita." ("Even Queen Margherita eats chicken with her fingers.") Milanese bakers invented desserts in her honor. Neapolitan chefs named a pizza pie after her. Topped with tomato, mozzarella, and basil, it replicated the red, white, and green of the Italian flag.

But Margherita was still starved for affection. Worse, her hand-picked sages deliberately kept her ignorant in order to make her rely on them. As the years passed, I watched in horror as she became bigoted and cruel. Her adulation of Francesco Crispi, her despotic Prime Minister, and her appetite for colonial expansion caused military defeats in Ethiopia in 1887 and 1896. When protests and strikes erupted at home, she vowed "to cleanse Italians in a purge of blood." After General Fiorenzo Bava Beccaris massacred a crowd at the Milan bread riots of 1898, the Queen blamed the Socialists and justified the violence.

"We're not fighting a political party," she explained to Umberto, parroting her tutors, "but a set of murderers of all contemporary spiritual culture." Umberto apparently believed her. He jailed the protesters and awarded the general the Great Cross of the Order of Savoy. This outrage prompted Gaetano Bresci, an Italian American anarchist from Paterson, New Jersey, to assassinate Umberto on July 29, 1900.

Widowhood proved trying for Margherita. Her son, Victor Emanuel III, was determined not to repeat Umberto's mistakes. He sequestered Margherita in a fake Renaissance palazzo on Via Veneto so that he could collaborate with his Prime Minister and Parliament. Margherita considered this "a betrayal of the Italian monarchy." Although the Queen Mother lacked political power, she still patronized the arts and directed charities. She also insisted on protocol and ceremony. Sitting in a high-backed chair with a red velvet cushion, she became an idol. Her blue eyes hardened into sapphires, and each of the six-hundred-eighty-four pearls in her choker necklace looked soldered into her bust.

Now old, Margherita rarely attended public functions, unless she could steal the spotlight. I'll never forget her appearance at the farewell party I attended for Field Marshall Luigi Cadorna. This was in May 1915, the evening after Italy declared war on the Austro-Hungarian Empire. Dressed in black, the Queen Mother presented Cadorna with a personal copy of Caesar's *Gallic Wars* and placed a daisy in his boutonniere.

Half a million men died in the trenches. After the war, all Italians wore red poppies to honor their memory, even Margherita. Nationalists still adored her because she symbolized the gilded past and seemed to wear mourning for the entire country. But leftists partly blamed her for the carnage. Hadn't she nagged her son into entangling Italy fatally in European affairs?

"God will vindicate me," Margherita declared, "and restore Italy's greatness!"

Her prayers seemed to be answered when Benito Mussolini secretly visited and asked her to bless his coming coup against the liberal government. "Gladly!" she said. She considered Mussolini a *condottiero*, a Renaissance soldier of fortune, who served the royal family.

Mussolini's homage rejuvenated the Queen Mother. Before my astonished eyes, she aged backwards. She lost weight. Her skin became smooth and rosy. Her eyes regained their sparkle. Except for the white hair and silver-tipped cane, she was exactly as she was in her prime. I was shocked, therefore, when she suddenly died on January 4, 1926 at her winter villa in Bordighera, a resort on the Italian Riviera. Mourners mobbed the funeral train as it journeyed to Rome, where her body lay in state in the Pantheon.

Mussolini delivered a fulsome eulogy, praising Margherita's "austere composure in sorrow and fervent love of the Fatherland." *Who the hell is he describing?* I thought. Not the foolish and sometimes vicious woman who had dashed our hopes and broken our hearts.

The catafalque was smothered with daisies. The smell sickened me but not as much as the professional mourners, who shuffled in to pay their respects. "Queen Mother!" they wailed. This farce was interrupted when a one-armed veteran burst into the Pantheon and tossed a bouquet of red poppies onto the bier. Before being ejected, he yelled: "That's for all the men you killed!"

These memories haunted me as I chatted with my clubmates in Antico Caffè Greco. "Democracy must be terribly disappointing," I joked, "if the masses still need royal fairy tales." Princess Diana's funeral would be televised in a few days to two billion people worldwide. Babington's hung a huge screen in its tearoom, but I preferred to watch the service on the tiny set in the Greco's espresso bar. The opening prayer by the Dean of Westminster Abbey moved me.

"As a Princess," he said, *"Diana profoundly influenced this nation and the world. But we especially remember her humane concerns and how she made ordinary people feel significant."*

Not like Margherita, I thought. I raised my demitasse in a toast to Diana. The barista nodded and made the sign of the cross. From the tabernacle of a golden espresso machine, steam rose to heaven like incense.

21.

HEAVEN IN A CUP:

Pasquino worships at his favorite espresso bar

Outside Caffé Sant'Eustachio, my favorite espresso bar in Rome's historic center, students and cabbies, bankers and brokers, pundits and senators sip coffee and mock the news. Starbucks, the U.S. chain with 32,600 locations worldwide (including Milan, God help us), plans to open its first two coffeehouses in the Eternal City: one near the Vatican Museum in the former Manaldi bookstore, another between the Pantheon and the Trevi Fountain in Piazza San Silvestro.

"Blasphemy," pronounces a silver-haired archivist from the Palazzo della Sapienza. He stirs his demitasse and flicks a froth of crema onto the sidewalk. "What next, do you suppose?" He flares the nostrils of his aquiline nose. "Will Starbucks place an inflatable mermaid in the Trevi Fountain to attract customers?"

Everybody brays, except me. Since the Trevi Fountain is already sponsored by Fendi, the Italian fashion house that paid for its 2.2-million-euro restoration, such crass advertising is quite possible. A solemn little priest, dressed in a cassock, raises a hand and restores order. The circular brim of his black felt hat, I notice, resembles the saucer balanced on his lap.

"No mermaid will appear," he assures us. "Keep the faith." And he points to a mosaic paving the café's entrance: a stag's head with a cross between its antlers. Our bar takes its name and emblem from a nearby church dedicated to the first century martyr St. Eustace, patron of hunters. Starbucks may be a $14 billion multinational corporation, but Caffé Sant'Eustachio, Rome's most popular coffeehouse, is a cult.

During the reign of the Emperor Trajan, a Roman general named Placidus often hunted deer in the forests near Tivoli. One day, he saw a cross glowing between the horns of a stag and converted to Christianity. He baptized his entire family, changed his name to Eustace, and adopted the stag and cross as his crest. Too bad he never copyrighted it. His descendants would have made a fortune. This crest is now the café's logo, stamped on all its merch.

Trajan tolerated the converted general's eccentricities until they interfered with his duties. When Eustace refused to offer incense to the pagan gods at a public ceremony, the emperor ordered him to be roasted alive inside a bronze bull. With gruesome aptness, his church in Piazza Sant'Eustachio, the site of his martyrdom, is filled day and night with the incense of burning oak and toasted coffee beans from local espresso bars.

The area boasts many fine cafés. Tazza d'Oro, Sant'Eustachio's biggest rival, rules in summer, thanks to its *granita di caffè*: frozen coffee interlaced with layers of whipped cream. Camillioni, small and unpretentious, serves exquisite chocolate *dolci*. Giolitti, a fashionable ice cream parlor since the Belle Époque, features a golden salon and tunicked servers. But only Sant'Eustachio enshrines a retro coffee culture.

Opened in 1938, the establishment replaced a failing 19th century bar called Caffè e Latte. For a modern look, Alberto Ottolini, the new proprietor, used floor tiles with geometric shapes. The industrial white walls, zinc fixtures, and lack of chairs and tables made the interior resemble a train platform. Streamlined and efficient, the café served 5,000 espresso shots a day. But all innovation becomes tradition.

When Raimondo and Roberto Ricci took over in 1999, they kept the hand-cranked coffee grinders, black-and white photos, Arte Moderne clock, and semicircular bar. The cups and saucers, stamped with the stag and cross, became popular gifts. For caffeinistas, they are neither souvenirs nor status symbols but relics from a temple.

Screens surrounds the bar's espresso machine, like the chancel screens separating the tabernacle from the congregation in early medieval basilicas. Behind them, the high priests of coffee, wearing snappy bow ties and burgundy vests, concoct a sacred brew amid steam and tinkling spoons. Like most believers, I choose not to question the mystery.

Nobody knows the secret of Sant'Eustachio's *Gran Caffè*, a double espresso with a creamy head thick enough to turn a smooth-lipped nun into the Bialetti Man, the mustachioed trademark of a coffee machine company. God knows, I've asked about this enigma. Some people say it is the water from the Aqua Vergine, the aqueduct built by Marcus Vipsanius Agrippa, general and son-in-law of Augustus, which supplies the Pantheon district from a pure spring in the Alban Hills eight miles east of Rome. According to legend, a maiden discovered and led thirsty legionnaires to this site, hence its name Virgin Water.

Others credit the mix. Sant'Eustachio blends the best imported beans from Brazil, the Dominican Republic, Ethiopia, Galapagos, Guatemala, and Saint Helena and roasts them in an 80-year-old, hand-operated, wood-fueled machine. This colossal cylinder resembles the brazen bull in which Trajan tortured St. Eustace. As the beans rotate, crack, and toast, two interns from the American Academy's Rome Sustainable Food Project try to figure out the recipe. Does the barista add powdered milk to the grinds? Does he beat the cream, sugar, and coffee together?

Such vain speculations, fitter for Silicon Valley than the Seven Hills, amuse the Ricci brothers. The Vatican permanently damaged its brand when it substituted Latin with the vernacular and made priests face the congregation. The Riccis will never make the same kind of mistake. Customers prefer ritual and mystery. Although the Church removed Eustace from the liturgical calendar in 1969, the faithful still celebrate his feast every year on September 20. Ideally, with a cup of espresso.

The year Joseph Ratzinger became Benedict XVI, pilgrims from Deggendorf, Germany worshipped at the Basilica of Sant'Eustachio and then stopped at the bar. The guide, a member of the Bavarian Forest Club, removed a bottle of Jägermeister from his backpack, showed the regulars the label with the cross and stag, and poured a shot in his espresso. Delighted, everyone else ordered the same *caffè corretto.* If Ratzinger had partaken of this sacrament, I like to tell the faithful, he might not have resigned.

PAPAL INDULGENCES

22.

COINS AND LENTILS:
Pasquino audits Pope Sylvester

Shortly before midnight, three coltish young women with working-class accents stagger into Piazza di Pasquino, pelt me with confetti, and blow party horns in my face. Have they come from the concert on the Via dei Fori Imperiali, the fireworks at the Circus Maximus, or the disco ball in Palazzo Bracaccio? Even if I could ask, they wouldn't answer a grim monument like me. Instead, they giggle, pop a bottle of cheap prosecco, and fill three plastic flute glasses until they foam and brim over.

"*Buon anno, Pasqui!*" they toast. "*Tanti auguri per duemilaquindici!*" ("Happy New Year, Pasquino! Best wishes for 2015!") Then, before the chimes of Sant'Agnese in Agone strike twelve, they rush back to their flat in the Trastevere district. Once home, I imagine, they will slip into matching red nighties and prepare a traditional bowl of lentils.

Resembling coins, lentils—*lenticchie*—symbolize good luck and are consumed throughout Rome on New Year's Eve. Diners at Ditirambo, a cozy restaurant with stone arches and beamed ceilings near Campo de' Fiori, feast on lentils and *cotechino*, a slowly cooked, highly seasoned pork sausage with a thick rind. Farmers in Viterbo, a medieval town fifty miles north of the capital, prefer lentils and *zampone*, boned pig's trotter stuffed with backfat and spicy ground pork. Rangers in the Aurunci Mountains warm themselves on lentil and escarole soup. Fishermen on Ponza, the largest island in the

Pontine archipelago, caulk their boats while lentils and eels stew in a cast-iron pot.

This custom of eating lentils on New Year's Eve began in classical times. To wish friends and neighbors prosperity, ancient Romans would give a *scarsella*, a leather purse full of lentils, with the hope that they would turn into *aurei* (gold coins). The real alchemy, of course, occurred in the kitchen. Once cooked, the lentils plumped and increased in size, evoking the idea of abundance—particularly when served with fatty pork. Ironically, early Christians would adapt this lip-smacking pagan tradition to honor St. Sylvester and the Donation of Constantine.

Sylvester, whose feast day is December 31, led the Catholic Church between 314 and 331 AD, the first years of its earthly prosperity. As pope, he was both God's vicar and investment banker, which, even I must admit, is an unbeatable combination. Unlike Pope Callixtus, who had embezzled money from a picayune savings and loan company more than a century earlier, Sylvester acquired a huge nest egg that formed the foundation for the Vatican's future wealth. This was his reward for converting Constantine the Great, Rome's first Christian emperor.

Constantine had adopted the cross as his military standard to win the Battle of the Milvian Bridge, which secured his throne in 312, but he never fully accepted the faith until after he was stricken with leprosy. Sylvester ordered him to repent and be baptized. I was not invited to the dunking, but supposedly, when the emperor emerged naked from the pool, his blighted skin was pink and smooth as a newborn babe's.

Grateful, Constantine gave Sylvester a tenth of the Senate treasury and 15,000 square miles in Central Italy that would become the Papal

States. During the Middle Ages, the rents and taxes from this territory transformed the papacy into an aristocratic and feudal institution. While the poor starved, lentils from Umbria and pork from Emilia-Romagna filled the Vatican's larder.

To justify this wealth, popes cited the *Donatio Constantini*, Constantine's imperial edict carefully preserved in the Vatican's archives. The document was a forgery, as Lorenzo Valla, a pugnacious scholar and papal secretary, proved in 1440; but even after the Reformation, the laity cynically accepted it. As long as the popes beautified Rome with basilicas and fountains, the common people not only tolerated but also gloried in the church's worldliness. Personally, I prefer this splendor of Renaissance patronage to the sleaze of modern capitalism.

Everything changed after the final unification of Italy in 1870, which overnight deprived the Vatican of its lands and feudal income. During the next sixty years of financial distress, popes publicly denounced usury while accepting massive loans from the Rothschilds and making their own interest-bearing loans to Italian Catholics. Beginning with Bernardino Nogara in 1929, the Vatican also appointed a series of often shady financial advisers to wheel and deal with many counties around the globe, including Nazi Germany. At Nogara's suggestion, Pope Pius XII in 1942 founded the Institute for Works of Religion, better known as the Vatican Bank.

After that, the church shed the last vestiges of feudal restraint and became a savvy international holding company with a maze of offshore shell corporations. It laundered money for the Mafia and provided slush funds for Italian politicians. The Vatican also associated with such rogue financiers as Roberto Calvi, nicknamed "God's Banker." Calvi, Head of Milan's Banco Ambrosiano, bankrupted that institution and was convicted of illegal exporting currency. When he was found dead in London on June 18, 1982, hanging from the Blackfriars Bridge, this note was posted on my pedestal:

"What's the matter, Calvi? The bridges in Rome not good enough for you?"

It is easy to blame the Donation of Constantine for this mess. Pope Sylvester, the poet Dante argued, should have rejected the emperor's gift to preserve purity of the Gospels. In the Gospels, however, Jesus allows himself to be anointed with expensive oils and perfume, and only Judas Iscariot, the crooked treasurer of the Twelve Apostles (doomed to hang like Roberto Calvi), objected to Jesus' extravagance. The money, he said, could have been saved for the poor. Judas probably wanted to keep the money for himself, but he still had a point. To this day, Christianity's hypocrisy about money remains as bad as its hypocrisy about sex.

If you need an example, visit the Church of San Carlo ai Catinari at the edge of the Roman Ghetto. Suspended above the main altar is a ten-foot-wide gold medallion, golden rays bursting from it as if from a newly minted imperial *aureus* gleaming in the sun. Draped across its middle, a sash spells in golden capital letters "HUMILITAS," humility. The old proverb is true: *"A Roma Iddio nun è trino, ma quattrino."* Roughly translated, it means: "Rome's God isn't the Trinity but the threepenny."

Nevertheless, Romans still prefer a pontiff who spends his own cash. After Pope Francis I was elected on March 13, 2013, he returned the next morning to Piazza delle Cinque Lune and paid his hotel bill at the Domus Internationalis Paulus VI. (A suite there costs €85 a night. Very reasonable for the historic district.) Now he lives in Casa

Santa Marta, a guest house for clergy having business with the Holy See, and takes his meals in a cafeteria.

On this New Year's Eve, however, after the Papal Vespers and Te Deum conclude at St. Peter's Basilica, a Salesian sister brings His Holiness a bowl of hot lentils. Pope Francis smiles but declines. Diverticulitis, he says, makes it difficult for him to digest legumes. Perhaps, but a more likely explanation for his upset stomach, I suspect, is yet another newspaper exposé of misdeeds at the Vatican Bank.

23.

BELLS AT NOON:

Pasquino rings St. Peter's chimes

At noon, a cannon on the Janiculum Hill fires a shot across the Tiber River. The echo reverberates two miles away here in Piazza di Pasquino and makes me vibrate like a tuning fork on my pedestal. Around the corner in a huge public square, the boom startles lunch crowds at outdoor cafés. As an old man drops a tuna and tomato sandwich and turns off his hearing aid, Rome responds with a salvo of church bells.

This daily ritual once synchronized the city's clocks. Now it deposes time and enthrones chaos in the historic center. How I relish the pandemonium! A thousand jangling notes collide, stopping traffic and stunning pedestrians. Gradually, the din subsides, and I slowly recognize the chimes of individual churches.

From its towering belfry, the bells of Saint Mary Major call the tardy home. C# and D, they scold, F# and G. The carillon of Saint John Lateran debates a tedious point in canon law, droning D#, B, D#, B ad infinitum. The most distinct clang, however, is a majestic but slightly muffled E natural from il Campanone, the Great Bell of Saint Peter's.

Hanging in the basilica's western clock tower, il Campanone rings only on special occasions. During the liturgical year, it heralds Christmas, Easter, and the Feast of Saints Peter and Paul, the patrons of the Holy City. It tolls sadly to proclaim the death of one pope, peals jubilantly to announce the election of another. It warned Pius IX to flee revolution and saluted Benedict XVI as he helicoptered from the Vatican to Castel Gandolfo after his resignation.

For some Romans, this bell is the sound of fate. When composer Giacomo Puccini strikes a note of doom in Act III of *Tosca*, his tragic opera set in Rome, a bass chime in the orchestra tolls the low-E from il Campanone. Other Romans, however, are more sentimental.

"*Great Bell of St. Peter's Square,*" a pop song gushes, "*you enchant us with your sound! You are the voice of peace and love for all the world!*" Personally, I will never understand how such a heavy object could inspire such a light tune.

Once the ninth largest bell in the world, il Campanone weighs nine tons. Its massive exterior is girdled with cherubs and apostles, embroidered with crests and keys, and crowned with putti and dolphins. If the rococo scrollwork strikes a false note, it is because its designer was better suited to craft a silver tureen than to cast a bronze bell.

Luigi Valadier, Rome's most fashionable jeweler and goldsmith in the late 18th century, created exquisite tableware, furniture, and altar pieces for noble and ecclesiastical patrons. Everyone visited his workshop, despite the fact that high society considered him an upstart. Valadier's father had been a French immigrant. In contrast, most of his clients came from wealthy families who had lived in Rome for at least seven generations. They paid him well but remained aloof, even when etiquette required inviting him to the weddings and baptisms for which he had fashioned such beautiful objects.

Valadier knew this, I'm sure. He never relaxed in public. At banquets and functions, he looked uncomfortable in his brocade suit. His hands, so steady at the drafting board, shook at the buffet table. His lofty brow and strong chin made a good first impression, but his restless eyes and a slight tic in his right cheek always betrayed him. Whenever a lackey tinkled a tiny silver bell to announce dinner or the next dance, the goldsmith gasped.

Fortunately, the most powerful man in Rome admired Valadier. This was Count Giovanni Angelo Braschi, elected Pope Pius VI in 1775. I used to be his extended family's mascot. In fact, I still guard the rear of what was once their palazzo in Piazza di Pasquino.

The Pope recognized and rewarded talent. He knighted the goldsmith and showered him with commissions. Despite his title, Cavaliere Valadier was overawed by the Vatican, easily distracted by the jingling Sanctus bells from its many side chapels. But the atmosphere was less intimidating in the Pope's private suite, where the two men discussed a mutual hobby: gemology.

"A stone's flaw," the Pope said, smiling significantly, "catches the light and makes it more beautiful." But this very quality, I could have told him, also makes it more vulnerable. Like fine crystal, a gem can split along a hidden fault.

The Pope and the goldsmith became intimate friends. Nevertheless, the city was shocked when His Holiness asked Cavaliere Valadier to forge a new great bell for Saint Peter's Basilica. Even I was a little surprised. Valadier had never attempted such an ambitious project. Would he or the bell crack under the pressure?

The previous great bell had ruptured in February 1780, after thirty-three years of service. It not only needed to be replaced but also moved, with Saint Peter's smaller bells, from the left-hand corner of the basilica's façade. The bells were hung here in 1646, when the first of the church's two planned bell towers had to be demolished. Meant to be only a temporary fix, this awkward location was completely unsuitable because it smothered the sound of the bells.

Work on il Campanone began in June 1785. VIPs came to the studio and observed. The ladies fanned themselves and gossiped, the gentlemen preened and took snuff, but I was too fascinated by the process to be annoyed. First, the crew formed a core in the exact shape of the bell's hollow. Around this, they constructed a prototype.

A wooden frame allowed wax to be poured and spread evenly and precisely over the bell's core. After Valadier himself ornamented its surface with figures and designs, the crew coated the core with clay, braced it with iron bands, and melted the wax to create the actual mold for casting the Great Bell. This required the construction of a special kiln. The mold would be fitted inside a sturdy wooden frame, packed in dirt, and placed in the red-hot furnace. This was the moment of truth. "A dangerous moment," the foreman added. "To make a mold might take two months or two years. To make a bell takes only two minutes."

At this point, the project stalled. Valadier lost confidence and postponed the final stage. Although he understood the basics of casting, the science of acoustics alluded him. A bell's tone, he told me, depends on many factors, including its dimension, the quality of the bronze, and the finishing work. Even the smallest design flaw could ruin a bell's note. He lacked the necessary knowledge and experience, he feared, and convinced himself that he would fail.

Delay brought the project into the red. Too distracted to tend to his regular business, Valadier went into debt. He borrowed money, first from bankers, then from usurers. But the bills still mounted, and creditors still hounded him. Rumors of his impending ruin circulated in Rome. His rivals—disappointed bell-makers who resented that a

French goldsmith had been commissioned to cast il Campanone—gloated. The Cavaliere, so-called, was finished.

On September 1, 1785, Luigi Valadier walked from his workshop to the city's docks and flung himself into the Tiber. Boat workers tried to save him, but he had drowned before they fished him out. His suicide scandalized Rome and should have barred him from Catholic burial, but the Pope intervened and gave him a splendid funeral. He was buried in the French national church in Rome, four blocks from my square.

His son, Giuseppe Valadier, finished the work ten months later. He encased the bell in a wooden scaffold, mounted it on a giant sled, and transported it from the foundry to the Vatican. I will never forget how the winches and mules strained to pull the load, how the hat bands and hairnets of the burly workmen glistened with sweat. As it inched across the city, the bell rang loudly and attracted cheering crowds. At the Holy Door of Saint Peter's, in the presence of the assembled cardinals and nobility, Pope Pius blessed the mighty Campanone.

The Great Bell was hung in the small cupola above the Gregorian Chapel. When it was rung for the first time, it caused a tremendous cacophony inside the basilica. One cardinal went deaf, but the sound failed to carry even to the neighboring Borgo district.

This fiasco perturbed the Curia, the administrative office of the Holy See. At a discordant meeting of the Pontifical Commission for the Cultural Heritage of the Church, it was decided—"with enough inanities to make the dogs howl," according to the Superintendent of Buildings—to return the bell to its original location: the small tower at the far right of the basilica's façade. But the belfry would have to be widened and reinforced to improve its sound and to accommodate the bell's extra weight and motion.

The cardinals worried about the cost and the risks. But after architects confirmed that the renovation had not compromised the tower's structure, il Campanone was finally installed. His Holiness clapped and bounced up and down like a little boy.

"*Campanon' a distessa!*" he told the sexton. "Let the Great Bell peal!"

Sometimes history ends on a note of triumph. The Great Bell rings to this day, startling and delighting the Seven Hills. But for me, even on the most joyous occasion, it seems to toll a requiem for Luigi Valadier.

24.

ROSES IN WINTER:

Pasquino venerates the Madonna, after a fashion

On December 8, 2012, the Feast of the Immaculate Conception, I shake my head as a snow-white *papamobile* or popemobile leads a caravan of black limos from Vatican City to Piazza Mignanelli in Rome's *centro storico*, the historic district. The crowd cheers, oblivious to the ironies of history. A stone's throw from the Spanish Steps, Piazza Mignanelli was once the haunt of upscale prostitutes, who serviced the nearby Embassy of Spain to the Holy See and were thus protected from arrest by diplomatic immunity. Now this square is a shrine to supernatural purity, thanks to the campy monument occupying center stage.

La Colonna del Immocolata, the Column of the Immaculate Conception, stands between the Palace of the Propagation of the Faith and Palazzo Gabrielli-Mignanelli, the corporate headquarters of Valentino S.p.A, Italy's luxury fashion house. A reparational gift from the Kingdom of Naples for abolishing its annual tribute to the Papal States, this 40-foot monument was erected on December 18, 1857, three years and ten days after Pope Pius IX had declared that "the Most Blessed Virgin Mary, from the moment of her conception, was preserved from all stain of Original Sin." I remember how, at the sound of a bugle, 220 city firemen used eleven winches to raise the perpendicular column. However, this is nothing compared to the mental strain of trying to understand a papal bull, or edict.

I doubt if many contemporary Romans still believe in the Immaculate Conception, not with the tabloids printing stories about pedophilic priests and mascaraed seminarians cruising the bars on Monte Caprino. No, the crowd is assembled here to enjoy the spectacle and to get a head start on its holiday shopping. Today, after all, marks the beginning of Rome's Christmas season. But in a city of tangled red tape, everyone admires the bureaucratic neatness of church dogma. As a personal favor, Pius IX had allowed Christ's mother to retroactively receive the sanctifying grace available to ordinary people only in the sacrament of baptism after birth. It was the ultimate loophole and a touching example of divine nepotism. What's the Latin expression? Yes—"*Potuit, decuit, ergo fecit.*" ("It was fitting, it was possible, therefore it was done.")

As the papal cortege enters the square, a parade marshal dressed like a Roman centurion conducts a marching band playing "Immaculate Mary." From the windows of the Palazzo di Spagna, interns hang the Spanish flag and unfurl a banner of Bartolomé Esteban Murillo's painting *La Inmaculada Concepción de los Venerables*. Not to my taste, but Pope Benedict XVI, a connoisseur of schmaltz, beams in his *papamobile*. The Vicar of Christ descends from his vehicle's bulletproof glass booth and blesses the spectators. Among them is the designer Valentino Garavani, now retired and living in Palazzo Gabrielli-Mignanelli with his business partner and lover Giancarlo Giammetti. At a recent papal audience, Valentino complimented the Pope's fashion sense and confessed that his favorite place to window-shop is Gammarelli, the ecclesiastical tailor shop on Via di San Chiara.

For a German, Pope Benedict makes a *bella figura*. Wearing a white cassock and a white *zuchetto*, a clerical skullcap, a red *mozzetta*, a shoulder cape with a buttoned-down collar trimmed in ermine, and matching red loafers, His Holiness carries a wreath of white roses decorated with a gold ribbon for the Madonna. The Spanish ambassador and several Spanish cardinals greet and invite him to sample tapas after the ceremony. The Embassy of Spain to the Holy See is conveniently located across the square. Gianni Alemanno—Rome's mayor at this date—looks stiff and sullen even in a tricolor sash. He bows and introduces to His Holiness the Prefect of the Department of Fire Watch, Public Rescue, and Protection.

Dressed in a visored cap with gold trim and a military jacket with starred epaulettes and chest badges, the Prefect puffs his chest and presents his own wreath. Bound in a red ribbon longer than a dragon's tail, it bears the motto *"Flammas domamus, donamus corda."* ("We tame flames, giving our hearts.") Pope Benedict frowns, but the crowd chuckles. I must admire the Prefect's cheek, which is perfectly justified. The *Vigili del Fuoco*, Rome's Fire Department, still resents the Vatican for coopting this ceremony some sixty years ago. After all, the *pumpieri,* the city's volunteer firefighters, had started the tradition in 1919 to honor comrades lost in World War I and to secure the Madonna's future protection. It was entirely their show until Pius XII took over in 1953 to boost his public image.

His Holiness and the dignitaries process to a waiting fire truck, which the Pope sprinkles with an aspergillum. He hands his wreath and the Prefect's wreath to a helmeted fireman in bunker gear, who mounts the truck and climbs to the top of a retracted aluminum ladder. The Pope flicks a switch, a motor whirs, and the ladder slowly rises.

The ascending fireman caresses the Corinthian column, sculpted in my day from Cippolino marble but unearthed in 1777 during the construction of the monastery of Santa Maria della Concezione on this very site. The fireman places the Prefect's wreath at the Virgin's feet and slips the Pope's wreath around her right arm, where it will remain until next December.

Everyone looks up, including me. I can't help but brood. Once, this column was topped by a helmeted Minerva, the Roman goddess of wisdom and war, brandishing a spear. Now it supports a simpering Madonna on a crescent and globe, stomping a serpent. The German historian Ferdinand Gregorius compared the effect to "a champagne cork mounted upside down." Virginity's fine. Diana, goddess of the hunt, and Vesta, goddess of the hearth, were also virgins, but they weren't neurotic about it. Lilies that fester stink worse than weeds.

When the column was first dedicated, Rome's leading statues were appalled but said nothing for fear of offending Jesus Christ. "Why don't you speak?" I asked Michelangelo's Moses. "I can't!" he replied. "My mouth is too small!" "Then whistle!" I suggested. "Yes, I'll whistle," Moses retorted, "at the Madonna on the Column!" But he didn't think Mary was sexy. Quite the opposite. In Rome, a loud whistle is not only a catcall but the equivalent of a Bronx cheer, and a chorus of them is the same as a round of booing.

While Pope Benedict gives a sermon on "the evils of possession," a group of ragged and unshaven men admire his *papamobile*: a brand-new, Mercedes-Benz M-class SUV, Polar White. Because his Holiness is German, Mercedes offered the Vatican a huge discount on a shipment of twelve. One for each apostle. Does this explain why Mercedes sponsors the Christmas decorations on Via dei Condotti?

The company logo hangs from the trees like Stars of Bethlehem. The papal license plate reads SCV: "*Status Civitatis Vaticanae*, Vatican City State." But the men claim it means "*Se Cristo Vedesse*. If Christ could see this!"

Two months later, Benedict XVI resigns, the first pontiff to abdicate since 1294. According to rumor, the cause was a two-volume, 300-page report bound in red documenting the Vatican's gay subculture. The news upsets Valentino Garavani, who comforts himself by staging an extravagant summer fashion show in Piazza Mignanelli. Beneath the Column of the Immaculate Conception, braless models wear see-through, saffron, taffeta blouses; one-shouldered toga-like velvet sheaths backed by starbursts of straps; and sleeveless gladiatorial gowns of silk crepe under embroidered gold leather.

Naturally, foreigners and Italian academics are shocked. Will Rome, they wonder, ever cure itself of its eternal Madonna-whore complex? Not my problem. Time has taught me to enjoy Rome's contradictions rather than denounce or resolve them.

25.

THE POPE OF PEACE:
Pasquino praises Benedict XV

Following tradition on this last Sunday of January 2014, Pope Francis releases two white doves from the balcony of the Apostolic Palace: an offering to God for world peace. The birds flutter and coo overhead. I smile with the other spectators in St. Peter's Square. But delight turns to horror when a pair of crows suddenly appears and attacks the doves.

One crow corners the larger dove near Bernini's colonnade, nipping a leg and plucking some feathers. The victim retreats to the Pope's balcony. The smaller dove, less lucky, is pecked until it bleeds. The marble saints on the colonnade watch helplessly as more crows join the melee. The caws and shrieks sicken me. Pope Francis grimaces.

His photo appears in next day's *La Repubblica*. The caption reads: "Blessed are the peacemakers?" The Audubon Society states that the Pope should better emulate his namesake, Francis of Assisi, and protect birds from "harmful rituals." The PR disaster reminds me of another humiliated pontiff, a peace dove harassed by human crows.

On December 24, 1914, a dejected Pope Benedict XV celebrated midnight mass in St. Peter's Basilica. His efforts to secure a Christmas truce had failed. Only four months after the start of World War I, a 400-mile trench stretched from the Belgian coast to the Swiss border. Some British and German troops near Ypres, Belgium, stopped killing each other long enough to play soccer in No Man's Land. Most soldiers, however, were quite willing to butcher one another on Christ's birthday, with the full blessing of flag-waving clerics.

"May the guns fall silent at least on the night the angels sang!" Benedict had pleaded. The backlash had been scathing. "Why not Easter?" asked the Italian press. The Commander-in-Chief of the French Army, who obviously had never gotten over the Dreyfus affair, scoffed: "Why not Yom Kippur?"

The ecclesiastical buzzards also circled. During Christmas Eve service, I noticed how the Curia—the judges and administrators of the Holy See—scrutinized the Pope's performance. Beneath Bernini's *baldacchino*, a bronze and gold canopy weighing seventy tons, Benedict was as gawky as a curate at his first mass. He sighed and fumbled at the altar. His shoulders slumped. His hands shook. The acolytes exchanged embarrassed glances. Never had His Holiness seemed so frail and small.

The faithful called Benedict "*Il Piccoletto*," the Little Guy. Tailors had had to prepare the smallest of the three papal cassocks at his September 7 election. Raised in a noble Genovese family, sixty-year-old Giacomo della Chiesa was dignified in bearing and courtly in manners, but his appearance was hardly pontifical. Sallow and stunted, he was cursed with matted hair and buck teeth. His eyes and nose, chin and neck were crooked. Doctors blamed childhood rickets, a weakening of the bones caused by calcium deficiency. Milk is full of calcium, so milkmen used flyers with Benedict's wizened face to push their wares in poor neighborhoods. Contractors compared the new pope to a carpenter's ruler: "You could fold him up in sections and put him in your pocket."

Whatever his physical defects, Benedict, it seemed to me, was the only world leader who realized the grim implications of the Guns of

August. In *Ad Beatissimi Apostolorum* (*Appealing for Peace*), his first encyclical published on All Saints Day, 1914, he called the Great War "the Suicide of Civilized Europe." The West's most powerful and prosperous nations had provided themselves with the most awful weapons modern military science had devised.

"They strive to destroy one another with refinements of horror," said Benedict. "There is no limit to the measure of ruin and slaughter. Day by day, the earth is drenched with newly shed blood and covered with the bodies of the wounded and the slain."

Secular authorities ignored him, particularly in Rome. Everyone had caught war fever. "Only violence," right-wing demagogues declared in Parliament, "will save our civilization from Communism!" Benito Mussolini, then a Socialist and editor of the left-wing daily *Avanti!*, urged workers to "join the battle in the name of revolution." Avant-gardists beat the war drum the loudest. "Peace," sneered Filippo Tomasso Marinetti, the founder of Futurism, "is more decadent than canned ravioli!" He threatened to kidnap Pope Benedict in an airplane and drop him in the Adriatic "like a piece of stinking black manure."

Less than four months after the Pope's first Christmas mass, Italy declared war on Austria-Hungary. Nearly 700,000 Italians would die on the Western Front, but first came horrors and portents that might have spewed from the Book of Revelation. The Ottomans launched the Armenian Genocide. The Madonna appeared at Fatima, uttering ominous prophecies and making the sun whirl in the sky. The Russian Revolution exploded. Before the disaster of Caporetto, a desperate Vatican issued a seven-point peace plan. Some editorials called it "quixotic," but I thought it was sensible and humane.

Benedict proposed an immediate ceasefire, a lowering of armament stocks, guaranteed safety on the seas, international arbitration, and compensation for confiscated property. I often assume the worst of people, simply to survive Rome politics, but the cynical reactions to the Pope's plan still shocked me. Italian liberals accused Benedict of conniving to restore the Papal States. Foreign leaders suspected his neutrality. Both the Allies and the Central Powers were convinced that he was biased towards the enemy.

When the war ended, American President Woodrow Wilson, whose Fourteen Points plagiarized Benedict's plan, kept the Pope away from Versailles. What place was there for a pacifist at a peace conference? For that matter, what place was there for a saint at the Vatican?

Isolated in the halls of power, Benedict relied on his friends in the streets of Rome. Milkmen, partly for commercial reasons, had made *Il Piccoletto* their mascot. They glued his photo to the side of their carts and delivered the freshest of their milk to the Apostolic Palace. This allowed the Pope's cook to prepare his favorite comfort food: *risotto al latte*, a creamy rice dish made with boiled milk, ground nutmeg, and grated Parmesan. Believe me, the little man needed comfort. Everyone thwarted him, from the Cardinal Secretary of State to the Papal Chamberlain, to "protect" His Holiness from what they called his "foolishness."

Benedict's generosity upset his aides. He often helped poor Roman families with cash gifts from his private revenues. When the money ran out, prelates instructed petitioners at papal audiences not to mention their financial woes. During the war, Benedict donated millions in church funds to the Save the Children Foundation. All that remained in the Vatican treasury was the equivalent of $19,000. The bankers would have poisoned him if he had not fallen ill.

On December 21, 1921, the forty-fourth anniversary of his ordination to the priesthood, Pope Benedict celebrated mass with the nuns at St. Martha Hospice. While awaiting his driver in the rain, he caught the flu. Pneumonia developed. A month of agony followed. To make their dying friend more comfortable, milkmen spread straw over the cobblestoned streets and squares of the Borgo, the neighborhood next to Vatican City, to muffle the clop of hoofs and the grinding of iron-rimmed wheels. At the time, Rome had few automobiles, so this traditional act of kindness was still practical.

Unfortunately, the straw also hid huge potholes. When a milk van loaded with heavy metal churns overturned in front of Palazzo Rusticucci, which faces St. Peter's Square, the clanging and gonging could be heard from the Apostolic Palace to the Castel Sant'Angelo. On hearing the news, *Il Piccoletto*, I am told, chuckled on his deathbed.

Pope Benedict XV died on January 22, 1922, and was interned in the Vatican grottos. If I could have, I would have nominated him for a posthumous Nobel Peace Prize. But since I couldn't, I settled for the monument to him that was erected six years later in St. Peter's Basilica. Whenever a blowhard autocrat threatens war in the latest news cycle, I visit it.

Benedict's statue prays in front of a bronze relief of the Madonna and Child. Wearing a simple skullcap rather than the triple tiara, the Pope of Peace kneels over the casket of a fallen soldier. His face is careworn but kind, just as I remember it. Baby Jesus waves an olive branch over a world gone up in flames.

ROYAL PAINS

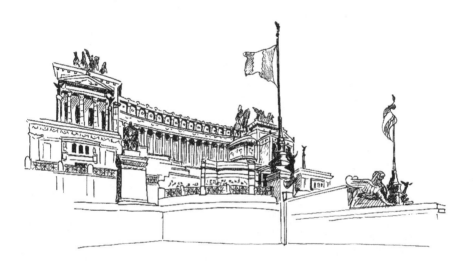

26.

A CITY DIVIDED:

Pasquino remembers the Breach of Porta Pia

Each year I dread September 20 because it always reopens an old wound in Rome's collective memory. On this day in 1870 Piedmontese artillery blasted a hole in Porta Pia, the stately fortified gate on the northeastern side of the Aurelian Wall. A battalion of Bersaglieri, the black-plumed sharpshooters of the Royal Italian Army, routed a company of Zouaves, the pantalooned French Algerian mercenaries of the Papal States. Thus ended a thousand years of pontifical rule. Romans called it the Great Breach (*La Grande Breccia*). Italy was finally united, but the city was divided between two squabbling factions: the Blacks, loyal to the deposed pope Pius IX, and the Whites, pledged to the new king Victor Emmanuel II.

The Blacks, comprised of Rome's oldest noble families, the Barberini and Odoleschi, Chigi and Borghese, detested the House of Savoy. I am told that Prince Alessandro Torlonia, the richest of these crusty reactionaries, changed his footmen's red livery so as not to share the same color with the royal grooms. After Pius operatically declared himself "a prisoner of the Vatican," a parade of grief and outrage followed. Lords hid in their shuttered *palazzi,* covered their gilded mirrors, and wore elegant mourning. Ladies ceased their daily carriage rides in the Corso, except in summer when the so-called "usurpers" left the capital for vacation. Both boycotted receptions at the Quirinal Palace, the Pope's former residence which had become the king's court.

They also stopped slumming for fried artichokes in Jewish *trattorias* because the Savoyards had demolished the walls of the Ghetto.

The Whites were Rome's less established but more politically liberal aristocrats, young fogies who had made strategic marriages with the rising middle class and owned banks and businesses. They were eager to help the new regime to modernize the city. Until now, Rome had been a bucolic provincial capital, two-thirds of it covered with lovely vineyards, orchards, and farmlands. Where the Via Veneto lies today, wood and bush grew then. The Palazzo Barberini was on the outskirts of town. The hovels and the shacks of the rural poor stood beside classical ruins. Cattle grazed in the Forum. "Very bucolic," progressives sneered, but I doubt that Italy would ever have taken its rightful place among the nations so long as its capital remained a squalid barnyard.

The Whites and their allies, local speculators, and transplanted bureaucrats from Turin, went to work. They shaved the ivy off the Coliseum and uprooted its wildflowers. They bought up the Prati district, dynamited churches and villas, and used the rubble to build administrative offices. I could hear the sound of hammering and falling masonry crashing to the streets. Plaster dust hung in the air like the ashes of Pompeii. Thousands of workers were injured in construction site collapses and landslides. What remained standing were ponderous stone monstrosities that soon turned blacker than the pillars of the Portico of Octavia, an ancient colonnade in the heart of the Ghetto used as the city's fish market. To cover up these blunders, the government splashed whitewash over everything—churches, convents, palaces—until Rome became a mausoleum.

Defying the architectural carnage, the Blacks compared themselves to the Spartans at Thermopylae. Prince Torlonia, a collector of Greco-Roman antiquities, quoted Thucydides: "*They have the numbers; we, the heights.*" In other words, let the Whites control urban development. The Blacks still dictated court protocol. The king's chaplain could not celebrate mass in the royal chapel because the Quirinal, along with the rest of the palace, fell under papal interdiction. The king and queen were forced to worship in Santa Maria Maggiore, where, on one occasion, Queen Margherita was given the ceremonial rituals reserved for foreign royalty. Whenever possible, the Blacks undermined the legitimacy of the Italian monarchy, sometimes with outside help. When the Spanish ambassador prevented the king and queen from passing through his anteroom to attend a benefit concert for Andalusian earthquake victims, masons had to carve an entry from the road into the embassy.

This feud, I regret to say, continued for almost sixty years, long after the Pope and the king had passed away. After the longest pontificate in modern history, Pius IX died on February 7, 1878. His body was buried temporarily in St. Peter's grotto but moved in a night procession three years later to the Basilica of San Lorenzo Outside the Walls. When the cortege approached the Tiber, a gang of anticlerical agitators threatened to throw the coffin into the river, but the militia prevented them. "Death to the Pope!" the protesters cried. "Long live Italy!"

Ironically, Victor Emmanuel had predeceased Pope Pius, succumbing to malaria on January 9, 1878. To honor the Father of the Fatherland, the government built the Vittoriano, a colossal mausoleum twice the size of St. Peter's Basilica between Piazza Venezia and the Capitoline Hill. Made of dazzling white Brescia marble, to distinguish it from Rome's ocher-colored travertine, the monument is a notorious eyesore. Like a glacier, it dominates the city's skyline, upstaging the Campidoglio and overshadowing the Forum. Romans call it the Wedding Cake or the Typewriter. Hollow to the core, it is also the largest and most expensive cenotaph in Italian history. Due to a botched embalming, the king's corpse had deteriorated too quickly to be interred here. What Rome truly buried, I believe, was any hope of unity.

No matter how many flags flew from the poles of the Vittoriano, no matter how many wreathes were laid at the Tomb of the Unknown Soldier, the breach between church and state never healed, not even after the Lateran Treaty of 1929 recognized the Vatican's political sovereignty and compensated it for the loss of the Papal States. To celebrate this agreement, Benito Mussolini, with his usual fascist finesse, bulldozed part of the Borgo district to construct the Via della Conzillazione, the Road of Conciliation, but no real conciliation was possible.

As I've witnessed for more than 90 years, civil strife continues. From the dueling editorials in *La Repubblica* and *L'Osservatore Romano* to the protests and counterprotests in Piazza San Giovanni in Laterano over abortion and same-sex unions, the political battlelines remain drawn. During the Sesquicentennial of the Risorgimento, radicals stoned the Vatican Secretary of State when he spoke at a ceremony in September of 2011. Across town, the Union of Christian and Center Democrats staged a maudlin memorial for the 19 Papal Zouaves killed at Porta Pia, complete with golden banners and stinking incense.

Time will resolve this conflict, my fellow statue Marforio assures me. Once Italy is completely secularized, the state finally will checkmate the church. Marforio reclines in a cozy fountain in the courtyard of Palazzo Nuova, so he can indulge in such facile optimism.

Fortunately, Romans have learned to treat the tragic rivalry between church and state as an intriguing pastime. I would compare it to the marathon chess matches in Piazza del Fico, a small square near my neighborhood. Beneath a large fig tree in front of a crowded bar, old men play for hours on checkered boards. Most of the delighted spectators know more about soccer than chess, so it really doesn't matter whether a white king takes a black bishop, or a black bishop checks a white king. As long as the game continues and the wine flows, Romans will laugh and argue about the outcome.

27.

THE LAST DANCE:

Pasquino attends the Quirinal Ball

During the 1880's, Rome's social season began with the lighting of the Christmas tree in the Quirinal Palace and ended six to eight weeks later with the carnival in the Piazza di Spagna. Between these events, King Umberto and Queen Margherita of Italy always gave three balls. Each was more lavish than the last. Why? Because our sovereigns wanted to proclaim three things to the world: their nation was united after decades of revolution; their subjects were blessed with peace and plenty; and their dynasty (the House of Savoy), which had made these accomplishments possible, was the greatest in Europe.

None of this was true, of course. But I still enjoyed their seasonal balls, especially the first on New Year's Eve. For eight hours on the dance floor, the only neutral territory in the capital, I could forget partisan politics, watch young couples waltz, and pretend the future was bright. Pathetic, I know, but hope was worse than malaria during Rome's Gilded Age. Almost everyone had caught the fever of progress and prosperity, even a professional cynic like me,

Perhaps the most memorable New Year's Eve Ball occurred on December 31, 1884. Rome badly needed the relief. For three weeks, a *scirocco,* an oppressive North African wind, had paralyzed the city. Everyone suffered from nervous exhaustion, from the humblest dustman to the proudest senator. I saw the signs everywhere. The unseasonably warm weather had caused a drop in grain prices, but brokers were too listless to buy beef and pork commodities. Instead, they fled the stifling trading hall to mope outside against the columns of the Stock Exchange.

Rome's busiest avenues were vacant, except for the occasional stray carriage clopping on the cobblestones. Veiled and caped in otter, socialites drowsed while their maids fanned them and complained about the pervasive grit. Wind-borne sand from the Libyan Desert settled everywhere. On fashionable streets, shopkeepers grumbled and wiped their show windows. From the belvedere on the Janiculum Hill, the city seemed covered in red soot. The Duke of Somosa, an amateur Dante scholar, compared the panorama to the Seventh Circle of Hell: a burning plain where ashes fell from the sky.

Naturally, the foul weather put everyone in a foul mood, but Romans already were inclined to quarrel. The Capital of United Italy was badly divided between the Blacks, the conservative aristocrats who had remained loyal to the Pope during the revolution, and the Whites, their liberal counterparts who had backed the new regime. Both factions detested the bourgeoisie, who they said were buying up Rome and treading on the heels of the nobility.

But class divisions were nothing compared to regional hatreds. The King and Queen, born and raised in the northern province of Piedmont, awarded major government ministries and minor bureaucratic positions to their *paesani*. Romans called these detested newcomers *buzzuri*, chestnut vendors. As the *scirocco* dragged on, brawls occurred in parliament and duels were fought in parks. I thought the hostility would never end. But around Christmas, a *ponentino*—a cool eastern sea breeze—blew in from Ostia and calmed the capital in time for the Quirinal Ball. I hired a cab and headed for the royal palace.

Built for popes and cardinals, the Quirinal wasn't ideal for midnight suppers and waltzes, despite its recent makeover. After the Wars of Unification, the new regime had replaced its austere images of saints and pontiffs with bigger-than-life paintings of revolutionary heroes. Decorators brightened the reception hall with yellow damask and hung a portrait of blue-eyed Princess Margherita in the ballroom. After eight centuries of Spartan austerity, the House of Savoy finally had acquired panache. Nevertheless, although the chic Margherita was now queen, public entertainments were still conducted like military drills.

It was a quarter-mile march down a cloistral corridor to the buffet table. Guarded by sabered guards, the Swiss Hall was more forbidding than the Vatican. The tight security was for the King. Nine months after his coronation, he was nearly assassinated by an unemployed cook. The frightening incident had left him insecure, but he compensated with bluff humor. At palace banquets, he always joked: "Be seated, ladies and gentlemen, and don't keep the cook waiting. I know from personal experience what they're capable of."

The poet Gabrielle D'Annunzio, bullet-headed and perfumed and wearing a sleek evening jacket, greeted me in the serving line. Then a society columnist for *La Tribuna,* he had arrived in time for what he called "the gladiatorial games." Rival ministers and parliamentarians stampeded to the banquet table and scuffled over canapés and champagne. The remaining twelve hundred guests grazed and milled about near the throne room. The small talk was excruciating.

"Is it true," asked an overstuffed grande dame, "that the Queen collects porcelain dinner sets from every province in Italy?"

"Yes," I replied. "A touching symbol of national unity, don't you think?"

The masters of ceremonies smiled, offered their arms and dance cards stamped with the Savoy crest, and escorted the ladies into the ballroom. D'Annunzio and I commented on the colorful frescoes on the vaulted ceiling. Dressed in Grecian tunics and gowns, nubile young women held hands in a festive circle-dance that resembled a game of ring of roses. Joyful cherubs hovered near a crowned woman, representing the Kingdom of United Italy. Seated on a throne, she held an Italian flag and guarded an urn full of ballots.

"If elections were staged as tableaux," said D'Annunzio, "I might bother to vote."

"Only if you were running for office," I said.

The ballroom was a scintillating interplay of lights and reflections. Everyone admired the crystal chandeliers, gilt mirrors, and scarlet curtains, but some guests were ambivalent about the huge fir tree in the room. Introduced to the palace five Christmases ago, this novelty still seemed, well, *too German*: a misplaced tribute to the Queen's Saxon mother. Still, its blazing candles confirmed that Rome's social season truly had begun.

At precisely eleven o'clock, one of the two doors on the opposite sides of the hall opened. The orchestra played the fanfare to the Royal March, and the King and Queen entered to gasps. Margherita's silk ball gown was embroidered with silver thread and crystal beads. Umberto wore tails, the Collar of the Annunziata, and the sash of the Military Order of Savoy. Their Majesties were followed by the foreign princes in Rome, the Knights and Dames of the Order of the Annunciation, and the English, Turkish, and Chinese ambassadors.

The chamberlain signaled for the quadrille of honor, and the couples, chosen in advance, took their places. The King stepped aside and let the Queen dance with the Prince of Sweden. The aristocratic leader of Italy's conservative opposition gave his hand to the wife of the liberal prime minister. The quadrille lasted fifteen minutes, and then everybody waltzed.

The ballroom was the only place in Rome where nobles and the burghers comfortably mingled. After the annexation of the Papal States in 1870, which was the last and most resisted step in the Unification of Italy, the old aristocracy could no longer remain aloof from the new bourgeoisie. The capitalist economy had driven prices upward, and only incomes tied to it rose accordingly. As feudal wealth diminished, crossing class lines became a necessity. Some resisted this change. For them, the wedding announcements read like obituaries: a timid young woman from the once powerful House of Borghese, whose ancestors included several popes and cardinals, was married to a fat parvenu shipping magnate; an impoverished young aristocrat from a bankrupt branch of the Buoncompagni family was engaged to the well-endowered but horse-faced daughter of a prosperous bicycle manufacturer.

Most aristos made peace with the new order. The nobles needed money; the burghers craved respectability. What could be simpler? The two sides might deplore each other, but the irresistible lure of power was openly pursued and often secretly enjoyed at the Quirinal Ball.

As the dancers whirled past D'Annunzio and me, I noticed one couple. The young man, the son of a liberal banker, looked stiff in his suit, but he was utterly charmed by his partner. The young woman, the daughter of a conservative marquis whose debts had forced him to sell their family vineyard in Frascati, was a swirl of crinoline and silk. I could tell that she had set her cap on this young man and was determined to impress his father, who smiled from the sidelines.

Her ball gown, perhaps her only one, had been dyed Savoy blue: an exquisite color between peacock blue and periwinkle. She wore a corsage of lilies, peonies, and rockfoils: flowers associated with the royal family. But the crowning touch was the Savoy knot on her waistband, which she boldly encouraged her partner to clasp. "*Stringe ma non constringe*," I thought, remembering the Savoy motto: "It tightens but does not constrain."

Older guests had trouble breathing. The body heat from the dancers, spectators, and servants, the perfume from the corsages, bouquets, and floral arrangements made the ballroom feel and smell like hothouse. Or a funeral parlor.

"The year is dying," D'Annunzio said. "But very sweetly."

My young couple left the dance floor and rejoined their parents. The lad's father bowed and presented the young woman with sugar-coated almonds wrapped in a small tulle bag.

Crowned Prince Victor Emanuel, growing older but not taller, saluted the dancers as he guarded the Christmas tree. He looked charming in his miniature dress uniform, but would his feet touch the floor, I wondered, when he sat on the throne of Italy? The Little Prince nodded, and liveried flunkeys threw chocolates and nougats at the ladies, who clapped and squealed. Umberto and Margherita beamed. At three in the morning, the orchestra began the *Die Fledermaus* suite, and Blacks and Whites, nobles and burghers waltzed until dawn.

"The last dance," I sighed, stifling a yawn. Such a glorious night amid so much social discord, but how long could this delicious détente last in Rome? Time was passing, and I thought about the future. The young would become old, the old would die, the dead would be forgotten. But the painted goddesses on the ceiling were literally above such cares. Joining hands in a spiral dance of their own, they rivaled the constellations twinkling over the Quirinal Palace.

28.

CHRYSANTHEMUMS:
Pasquino explains a floral taboo

During November, Americans often bring chrysanthemums to Roman social events. These New England and Midwestern transplants mean well, I suppose. What could brighten a fall engagement party at Cul de Sac, a popular wine bar here in Piazza Pasquino, better than a bouquet of Mums? But native Romans, including me, always greet these good intentions with gasps of horror.

Chrysanthemums are the flowers of the dead. That is why they are so plentiful in Rome. Trucks transport tons of chrysanthemums from Calabria's Crati Valley. Groceries, nurseries, and floral shops begin to fill in early October. Orange pompoms flood Campo de' Fori and other markets. On All Souls Day, prices quadruple, but Romans stuff their cars with chrysanthemums and decorate graves in the Cimitero Flamineo.

The post-holiday glut causes prices to fall, but vendors unload surplus stock on naive American tourists and students. Laden with chrysanthemums, they never realize that they are violating a taboo until their host orders them to leave the table, or their lover kicks them out of bed. Raised on FTD and plastic pink carnations, they do not know the legend of Prince Amedeo of Savoy, Duke of Aosta.

Like his father Victor Emmanuel II, the Duke was a notorious womanizer. When he became engaged to Donna Maria Vittoria del Pozzo, a spiteful mistress sent the couple a bouquet of chrysanthemums. Donna Maria swooned. Their marriage was doomed! Amedeo laughed, but the curse came true. On their wedding day (May 30, 1869), the Duke's best man shot himself. The palace gatekeeper slit his own throat. The king's aide died after falling from his horse. The bride's wardrobe mistress hung herself. The colonel leading the wedding procession collapsed and died from sunstroke. The stationmaster was crushed to death under the wheels of the honeymoon train. The only sensible thing to do was to whisk the groom to Spain.

The Cortes Generales, the Spanish Parliament, had recruited Amedeo to rule after Queen Isabella II was deposed in a military coup. The substitute monarch was detested by resentful subjects, who prayed for his assassination and pelted him with chrysanthemums at his first public appearance in Madrid. "*Flores!*" they brayed. "*Flores per los muertos!*"

I heard that as the state carriage clopped along the Calle del Pardo one day, a royal secretary pointed out the house of Miguel de Cervantes. "And who is this Cervantes?" Amedeo asked. Spain's most famous writer, the secretary replied. "Well, if he's so famous, I must visit him," Amedeo said, "even though he hasn't come to see me."

"Very gracious, Sire," the secretary said.

Amedeo smiled, too stupid to realize he had been insulted.

As king, he was a disaster. Unwilling to learn Spanish, he alienated his ministers, provoked uprisings in Basque and Catalonia, and mishandled a revolt in Cuba. Within two years, he abdicated and returned to Italy. Resuming the title Duke of Aosta, he planted chrysanthemums at il Borro, his country estate in Valdarno. The gardener burned sage leaves and resigned. After Amadeo's father died and his brother Umberto became king, he divided his time between Turin and Rome. People shunned him because his sunken eyes, blistered cheeks, and shovel beard made him look like a jinx.

When the flu broke out in Rome in December 1899, the superstitious blamed the Duke, then wintering in the capital. Palace spokespersons insisted that visiting boyars had brought the infection from St. Petersburg. Whatever the cause, the epidemic raged for two months and spared no one. Ettore Bertolè-Viale, Minister of War, was stricken. Several members of the royal household were quarantined, including Prince Amedeo.

The patient remained stable, until Miss Minerva Porter, daughter of the American ambassador, sent dried chrysanthemums to his sick room. When his condition worsened, King Umberto summoned Dr. Guido Baccelli, who ran the glorious but decayed Santo Spirito Hospital, between the Tiber and the Vatican. A stocky man with a walrus mustache and a mop of grey hair, Baccelli tossed the chrysanthemums out the window.

A pioneer of the stethoscope and intravenous therapy, Baccelli had prolonged Victor Emmanuel's life during his last illness by administering oxygen, but he could do nothing for Amedeo. The Duke died on Saturday, January 18, 1890, at 6:45 AM. He was only forty-four. After lying in state at the Quirinal Palace, the body was transported to Turin and interred in the Basilica of Superga. The crypt was smothered in chrysanthemums. Giacomo Puccini composed an elegy, a sobbing string quartet in C-sharp minor named after the flowers: *Crisantemi*.

Ever since, Romans have associated chrysanthemums with death, funerals, and bad luck. After Italy joined the Anti-Cominterm Pact in

November 1937, Emperor Hirohito presented Benito Mussolini with the Imperial Order of the Chrysanthemum. At a private induction ceremony, the dictator cringed. Making excuses, Mussolini snubbed the Japanese ambassador and commanded a white-gloved aide to lock the medal in a safe. Being superstitious myself, I was relieved when the newspapers refrained from publishing the name of the award. They described it merely as "Japan's highest order."

29.

KING FOR A MONTH:

Pasquino pays tribute to Italy's last monarch

Ever since the Burger King opened on Via Nazionale, teenagers have come to Piazza Pasquino to eat French fries and to place paper crowns on my head. These coronations never last long. A stray breeze or a conscientious tour guide always intervenes and deposes me. During my brief reign, however, I think of Umberto II, the last King of Italy, who ruled for only a month: specifically, May 1946. We Romans still call him *e' Re di Maggio*, the May King.

I always felt sorry for Umberto. He might have been a tragic hero if fate hadn't cast him as the amateur tenor in a rather seedy comic opera. Umberto was the only son of King Victor Emanuel III. Nicknamed Sciaboletta (Little Sabre), Victor Emanuel was barely five feet tall and needed a stepladder to mount a horse. A special sword had to be forged for him so that it would not scrape the ground when he carried it. Whenever the little king inspected troops in Piazza Venezia, Prince Umberto winced. I always laughed. His Majesty was like a beribboned mouse sniffing wooden soldiers in a toy shop.

Even if he had been a physical giant, the little king would have remained a moral pygmy because of his collusion with the Fascist regime. Determined to repair the House of Savoy's image after the fall of Benito Mussolini, Victor Emanuel had transferred power to his son while retaining his title. But on May 9, 1946, he abdicated his throne to Umberto, a desperate last stand against a referendum to abolish the monarchy. This will never work, I predicted.

King Umberto faced a hostile press. The newspapers had never forgiven the royal family for abandoning Rome in '43. "Bad kings make good subjects," editors reminded their staff. Cartoonists exploited Umberto's physical quirks. Tall (unlike his father), stiff, and balding, he had smooth, clean-shaven blue cheeks, thin lips, and a weak chin. Dressed in military uniform, decorated with the Supreme Order of the Most Holy Annunciation, he seemed more like a majordomo than a major general. Columnists capitalized on his peccadillos, but I could never blame him for these indiscretions. The men in his family had set such bad examples.

Umberto's paternal great-grandfather, Victor Emanuel II, the first King of Italy, was a louche boor. His maternal uncle, Prince Danilo of Montenegro, was the model for the dashing but brainless hero of Franz Lehrer's *The Merry Widow*, the most popular operetta of the Belle Époque. As a youth, therefore, Umberto was little more than a charming cad. Queen Margherita, his *nonna*, called him "a rascal, a true Savoy." During the Roaring Twenties, the Crowned Prince and his friends crashed the Marchesa Bertarelli's midnight jazz party at the Casino dell'Aurora Pallavicini. As the Asti Spumante bubbled and flowed, Umberto pinched the maids and danced the Charleston with a dozen flappers. His now drunken pals—before the terrified eyes of four liveried houseboys—launched from the salon window all the desserts on the buffet table. The king was billed for the damages.

Umberto's libido was as strong as his piety. In the words of a family chronicler, he was "forever rushing between chapel and brothel, confessional and steam bath." He courted Hollywood star Jeanette

McDonald on the Côte d'Azur, wearing a Canadian Mountie uniform and warbling "Indian Love Call" from the musical *Rose-Marie*. He encouraged the advances of Mexican spitfire Dolores del Río and seduced French actor Jean Marais and Italian director Luchino Visconti. The prince also had affairs with army officers, who received U-shaped jewels and diamond-studded fleurs-de-lis. One conquest flaunted a silver cigarette lighter inscribed with the words "*Dimmi di sì!*" ("Say yes to me!")

When Mussolini assembled a file on these indiscretions, Umberto married Princess Maria José of Belgium to prevent blackmail. The prince even designed her wedding dress. Gossips claimed that he also modeled it for her. Umberto doted on Maria José but soon resumed his philandering. When the royal couple began to sleep apart, however, the prince yearned to rekindle their love. He disguised himself as a hussar and snuck into her bedroom. The princess shrieked for the palace guards. Three of their four children, a gynecologist later confirmed, were conceived through artificial insemination.

Fatherhood, however, changed Umberto. He became thoughtful and responsible. Before and during World War II, he proved himself a disciplined military officer and a discrete critic of the Fascist regime. Whatever his private troubles, the prince always did what he considered his public duty, even if this meant kneeling to kiss his cold and emotionally distant father's hand before speaking. If the monarchy held any remaining dignity for the Italian public, it was only because of Umberto's conduct at state events.

As the national referendum approached, the young king won many supporters. Bookies were surprised, but not me. Southerners adored him. During his campaign in Sicily, he could name every village between Messina and Palermo, could describe every tower, fountain, and citrus grove. Neapolitans considered him a war hero. On the eve of the Battle of Monte Lungo in December 1943, when Italy finally joined the Allies, he volunteered for a dangerous air reconnaissance mission, flying with an American pilot over German defense lines under heavy fire from anti-aircraft artillery. Edwin Walker, Commander of the Third Regiment of the First Special Service Force, nominated Umberto for the American Bronze Star Medal. Six months later at Monte Cassino, the worst battle of the Liberation of Italy, Umberto risked his life to tend the wounded.

On June 2, 1946, voters went to the polls to decide whether Italy would remain a monarchy or become a republic. The outcome was closer than expected. The king won 47% of the national vote, primarily in the South. Reactionaries urged him to stage a coup before the new government formed. If he rejected the results of the referendum and withdrew to Naples, the army would support him in the ensuing civil war between the monarchists and the republicans. Umberto refused this plan.

"My house united Italy," he declared. "I will not divide it."

Prime Minister Alcide de Gasperi acknowledged the nobility of Umberto's sacrifice. "We must strive to understand," he said, "the tragedy of someone who, after inheriting a military defeat and a disastrous complicity with dictatorship, tried hard in recent months to work with patience and good will towards a better future. But this final act of the thousand-year-old House of Savoy must be seen as part of our national catastrophe. It is an expiation, an expiation forced upon all of us, even those who have not shared directly in the guilt of the dynasty."

At 3:00 PM on June 13, 1946, the king vacated the Quirinal. In the courtyard he passed in review of the palace coachmen. He wore a gray flannel suit and carried a fedora and a walking stick. The servants and gentlemen-in-waiting sobbed. Pale and drawn, Umberto looked much older than his forty-one years, but his head was held high, and now and then he managed a smile. At Ciampino Airport, as he stepped into the plane that was to carry him to Lisbon, a *carabiniero* squeezed his hand and said, "Your Majesty, we will never forget you!"

Umberto II spent the next 38 years in exile on the Portuguese Riviera. He never set foot in his native land again. The 1948 constitution of the Italian Republic not only forbade the restoration of the monarchy but barred all male heirs to the defunct throne from ever returning to Italian soil. Relations between Umberto and Marie José grew more strained until their marriage broke up. Marie José moved to Switzerland while Umberto remained in Portugal among a colony of deposed royals, fading pretenders, anemic bluebloods, and eccentric snobs who kept each other company in the fabled sea air of Estoril and Cascais.

When Umberto was dying of cancer, President Sandro Pertini wanted the Italian Parliament to allow the 78-year-old former king to return to Rome. Ultimately, however, Umberto died in Geneva on March 18, 1983. His last word was "Italia." He was interred in Hautecombe Abbey in France, for eight centuries the burial place of the House of Savoy. No representative of the Italian government attended his funeral.

Since then, Umberto's son (Vittorio Emanuele IV, Prince of Naples) has demanded that Italy pay 260 million Euros "to compensate for emotional damages suffered in exile," but to no avail. Umberto's grandson (Emanuele Filiberto, Prince of Venice) has appeared several times on *Ballando con le Stelle*, the Italian version of *Dancing with the Stars*. Now the property of curators and academicians, the throne of Italy stands in an old museum in Turin.

It saddens me to think of Umberto still planted in France when the bodies of his parents, disgraced and exiled to Egypt for supporting Mussolini, were allowed to be reburied in Italy in December 2017. Doesn't Umberto also deserve clemency? Whatever his faults, he wanted to redeem and to rebuild his country after the nightmare of dictatorship. Nothing in his brief reign, however, became him more than his leaving it.

30.

SOMEBODY AND NOBODY:

Pasquino eulogizes the Count of Ciampino

November is a month of wind and rain. Soaked in melancholy, Romans light candles on All Souls Day and sip *vino novello*, unaged new wine, on St. Martin's Day. If I had hands, I would lift a glass and toast the memory of the Count of Ciampino.

His real name was Mario Bianchi. Born illegitimate in Trastevere on April 1, 1902, he grew up on what is now the Lungotevere Raffaello Sanzio, the part of the boulevard running along the Tiber River between Piazza Trilussa and Piazza Giuseppe Gioachino Belli. Back then, this waterfront was littered with cigarette butts from careless pedestrians, slicked with droppings from gluttonous starlings, and prone to flooding despite the efforts of conscientious engineers.

Bianchi's childhood was squalid. I've heard that his father, a seminarian, visited his mother only on meatless Fridays for their extramarital trysts. Maybe this explains why their offspring sold fish. The boy caught eels and carps in the piss-colored Tiber and hawked them in the Campo dei Fiori. Later, he moved his stand to the west side of Piazza del Popolo, next to the Fountain of Neptune. Imitating one of the Tritons, he blew a conch to attract customers.

At twenty, Bianchi married and started a family. After bearing five boys in seven years, his wife became as armor-plated as a battleship. His sons dressed like scarecrows. He patched his shoes with cardboard from macaroni boxes. A plumber's bill for a ruptured faucet canceled a planned holiday to Rimini. Once, he spotted Mussolini on the Corso, driving his sports car back to Villa Torlonia in the late afternoon. Then the Depression ruined Bianchi's business, and the war drafted his sons. He would have died embittered if fate had not intervened.

On June 13, 1946, Bianchi was at Ciampino Airport, moonlighting as a baggage handler. This was the same day when King Umberto II went into exile after a national referendum narrowly voted to abolish the monarchy and establish a republic. At four in the afternoon, the king and his entourage arrived and were greeted by reporters and photographers. Curious, Bianchi joined a crowd of supporters, who were waving farewell. Umberto paused to wave back and gave final instructions to his staff.

"Make the accounts!" he told a financial attaché. But the royal appointments secretary, standing on the other side of him, misunderstood. He thought the king had said, "Make them all counts!" Before the secretary could question him, Umberto blew a kiss to the crowd, strode onto the tarmac, and boarded a military plane for Portugal. The secretary honored the king's "last wishes" and ennobled some 200 people, but only Mario Bianchi took his new rank seriously.

That night, Count Bianchi celebrated at Bar San Calisto near Piazza di Santa Maria. He drank five bottles of Marino and wobblily mounted a table. Henceforth, he proclaimed, anyone caught watering wine would be garroted. "Hear, hear!" cried the regulars. I heartedly concurred, though not as noisily, of course. Bianchi vowed to scrub the bird shit off the monument to the poet Giuseppe Belli, to prevent Vespa motor-scooters from backfiring at weddings and funerals, to endow a chair in soccerology at the American University of Rome. A notary took down his words, brought them to a print shop, and plastered his edicts all over Trastevere.

Count Bianchi adopted the Ciampino town seal as his crest (six silver darts and six golden grape clusters on a sky-blue field) and chose the motto: "*Absentem laedit cum ebrio qui litigat.*" (To quarrel with a drunk is to argue with a man who is not present.") The Libro d'Oro, the formal directory of Italian nobility, refused to recognize his title, but the Banca Nazionale di Lavoro loaned him money to start a new business. Bianchi opened a kiosk near the Spanish Steps and sold high quality bathroom fixtures to tourists. These included novelty soap dishes and jewel-encrusted toilet paper holders. His wife called him a genius. His sons impressed hookers by showing a snapshot of Papa posing with Alberto Sordi, the hangdog Italian movie star who specialized in playing little men with big dreams.

Despite celebrity customers, Count Bianchi still patronized Bar San Calisto. Sitting with a mug of Perroni beer, he watched TV and cheered his beloved football club, AS Roma. Sadly, His Lordship always drank more than beer—and always more than one mug. When he was a happy drunk, he recited dialect poetry and treated strangers to an *affogato,* a scoop of *fior di latte* gelato or vanilla ice cream drowned with a shot of hot espresso. When he was an angry drunk, he thrashed anyone who mocked his title or questioned what he called "his prerogative."

"*Io sò io,*" he roared, "*e vvoi nun zete un cazzo!*" All *Trasteverini,* inhabitants of Trastevere, know this line from Giuseppe Belli's sonnet, "*Li sovrani der monno vecchio*" ("The Sovereigns of the Old World"). Roughly translated, it means: "I am somebody, and you're fucking nobody!" Declared with such vehemence, the claim seemed irrefutable.

The patrons of the Bar San Calisto could only nod and say, "*È vvero, è vvero*! It's true, it's true!"

Of course, it wasn't true, and when he was sober, the Count of Ciampino knew it. "I know I'm ridiculous," he admitted to his wife. "But it's better to be a fake somebody than a real nobody."

Mario Bianchi died on March 24, 1971. Five days later came the historic meeting between Pope Paul VI and Marshall Tito at the Vatican. As the motorcade passed the Piazza di Spagna, Tito noticed a kiosk arrayed with gaily colored toilet paper holders draped in black crepe. Aides never told him that the mob in Via della Croce had not come to see him, but to attend the funeral of an ex-fishmonger.

Mourners showered the cortege with chrysanthemums. So profound was the hush over the Corso that the Princess Orietta Doria-Pamphilj appeared at her balcony and crossed herself. There would be no more Counts of Ciampino. Twenty years before, Italy had abolished the creation of new aristocratic titles and had instituted the Orders of the Republic. That was a bit harsh, I thought. True, Bianchi had been besotted with self-importance, but which of us doesn't have a strong head for status? Even real kings and aristocrats do, but that's because they're born drunk with power. For Mario Bianchi and the rest of us, the old Romanesco proverb applies: "*Anni, amori e bbicchieri de vino, nun se conteno mai!*"

("Years, lovers, and glasses of wine should never be counted—for dignity's sake!")

DREAMS OF GLORY

31.

ILLUSTRIOUS NOSES:

Pasquino tours the Pincian Gardens

"If Cleopatra's nose had been shorter," said the French philosopher Blaise Pascal, "the whole face of the earth would have been different." The same thought struck me at a reception held for the young Egyptian queen in November 46 BC at Julius Caesar's villa on Rome's Quirinal Hill.

Everyone admired Cleopatra's nose. Long and curved like the prow of a warship, it was bound to attract Caesar, nearly as good an admiral as he was a general. If she had been snub-nosed like her youngest brother and puppet co-ruler Ptolemy XIV, Caesar—whose aquiline profile was stamped on every silver denarius in the Mediterranean world—never would have made her his consort in Alexandria. Neither, I'll bet, would he have shown off her marble bust to appreciative guests here in Rome.

"A peninsula worthy of conquest!" Caesar said, kissing the tip of the statue's nose. Cleopatra, only twenty-two years old, could not refrain from nuzzling him. Even Cicero, whose bulbous nose was dented at the end like the cleft of a chickpea, laughed and applauded.

Roman history is a parade of noses. Scipio Nasica, the consul who enshrined the statue of Magna Mater on the Palantine Hill, was named after his enormous schnoz. So was the poet Ovid, surnamed Naso, who forlornly blew his exiled honker on the shores of the Black Sea. Sulla, the dictator who suffered from rhinophyma, executed anyone foolish enough to mock his proboscis, which resembled a mulberry encrusted with oatmeal.

Roman noses are still displayed all over the city, from the head of the shattered Colossus of Constantine in the Courtyard of the Palazzo dei Conservatori to the billboard for Lady Gaga's latest Europride Concert at the Circus Maximus. But the largest collection of illustrious noses can be found in the Pincian Gardens, overlooking the Piazza del Popolo. Let me show you.

Laid out by Giuseppe Valadier during the Napoleonic Wars, the Pincian Gardens are Rome's oldest public park and its Hall of Fame. Marble busts line its shady paths and the bridge connecting the gardens to Villa Borghese. Not part of Valadier's original design, these busts feature monarchs and statesmen, painters and sculptors, scientists and inventors, poets and novelists, historians, and philosophers, but no popes or cardinals.

After the Roman Republic overthrew Pope Pius IX in February 1849, Giuseppe Mazzini, eager to inspire patriotism, commissioned unemployed sculptors to carve 54 busts of famous Italians for the Pincian Gardens. I could have told him this quixotic project was bound to flop. Four months later, when the papal government was restored, only the busts of the most uncontroversial figures were set into place. The busts of secularists, heretics, and revolutionaries were removed and stored in Casina Valadier, the park's neoclassical villa.

Eventually, these busts were returned outdoors, but not before receiving drastic makeovers. Giacomo Leopardi, the nihilistic poet, became the Greek painter Zeuxis. Niccolò Machiavelli, the anticlerical political scientist, was turned into the mathematician Archimedes. Girolamo Savonarola, the radical Dominican friar, was recast as Guido of Arezzo, the Benedictine monk who invented musical notation. I admired the censor's ingenuity. Most visitors to the park, however, ignored the recast heroes and simply enjoyed the view.

After the Papal States fell in 1870, these and other historical figures altered for political reasons finally received recognition. New busts of them were carved and set side by side with the older ones already in the Pincian Gardens. Over the next ninety years, busts of other famous Italians were added to the pantheon until the total number reached 228.

As you see, they are a snooty bunch. Their upturned noses, whose blanched marble stands out in stark relief against the park's evergreens and palms, are often smashed or docked. The vandals include disgruntled art critics, who consider the statues Risorgimento kitsch; angry feminists, who resent that only three women (Catherine of Siena, Vittoria Colonna, and Grazia Deledda) are among the immortals; spiteful anarchists, who hate all governments; and selfish tourists, who want souvenirs.

Ten to twenty busts are defaced each month, so the Ministry of Cultural Heritage and Activities keeps an expert restorer on the payroll and a depository of casts of the Pincian's illustrious noses: hooked noses and cocked noses, sharp noses and flat noses, round noses and square noses, pinched noses and wide noses. Each nose job, City Hall estimates, costs 800 euros (about $900). This expense drains funds from other restoration projects.

Since I am a noseless statue, whose features have been eroded by time, I could complain. But all things, whether stone or flesh, are subject to the cruelty of fortune and the absurdity of politics. No one is exempt, not even the Queen of Egypt, whose mutilated bust is relegated to a corner of the Museo Greogoriano Profano at the Vatican.

After Julius Caesar's assassination in March 44 BC, conspirators broke into Caesar's villa and snapped the nose off Cleopatra's bust, but the lady herself had long fled. Thirteen years later, when her new lover Mark Antony angrily recalled this outrage, Cleopatra shrugged and smiled.

"What do you expect?" she asked. "Eternal glory?" She shook her head and sighed, thinking of the coming Battle of Actium. Possibly she foresaw that she and Antony would lose it. "When the great die," she said, "they don't go to Elysium but to Rhinokoloura."

The allusion, I'm told, perplexed Antony, a hunk with a chiseled nose but no genius like Caesar, so Cleopatra explained. Rhinokoloura was a place of banishment in the Sinai desert for criminals whose noses had been sliced off.

32.

LAST OF THE TRIBUNES:
Pasquino invokes Cola Rienzi

At the foot of Rome's Capitoline Hill, by the staircase leading to the Piazza del Campidoglio, I exchange grim nods with a statue of a hooded man waving a sword. Often overlooked by tourists, this bronze monument commemorates a crime that occurred seven centuries ago on this very spot. Here on October 8, 1354, a mob murdered Nicola di Rienzo.

Known to history as Cola Rienzi, Last of the Tribunes, this charismatic young dictator briefly resurrected the Roman Republic and almost united Italy before his terrible fall. Why did he lose the love of the people? The question baffles me. In his rage and his resentment, his dreams of the past and his fantasies of glory, Cola was so clearly one of them.

Nicola di Rienzo was born in the spring of 1313 in Rome's Regola district, then a remote slum. Cola's house, located below the Church of San Tommaso in Piazza delle Cinque Scole at the entrance to the Jewish Ghetto, faced the water mills on the Tiber. His father, Lorenzo Gabrini, ran a riverside tavern. His mother Maddalena washed laundry. Cola, however, boasted that he was actually the bastard son of Henry VII, the Holy Roman Emperor, who once spent a night at Lorenzo's inn. Didn't he have the same cleft chin and noble high-bridged nose as the Emperor? Such fantasies allowed Cola to endure Rome's squalor and misery.

Eight years before Cola came bawling into this world, a feud between the French king Philip IV and Pope Boniface VIII had ended in the disaster. Philip deposed Boniface, forced the College of Cardinals to elect his friend Bertrand de Got pope, and moved the papacy to Avignon, France. Bereft of temporal and spiritual leadership, Rome collapsed like Jerusalem during the Babylonian Captivity. Churches were desecrated, murder and rape were rampant. Marauders roamed the streets. Monuments were ruined not by vandals but by robber barons, who plundered forums and temples for materials to build and adorn their palazzi. As rapacious nobles carved up Rome like a capon, gang warfare spread everywhere. When his younger brother was killed in a brawl, Cola blamed the barons.

Brooding, he wandered the ruined city. The Lateran Basilica was roofless, the Milvian Bridge shattered, the belfry of Saint Peter's split by lightning. Cola vowed to repair these landmarks, and his eyes blazed. He possessed—I should say, was possessed by—an almost hallucinatory imagination. Having taught himself Latin, he deciphered the inscriptions on derelict buildings. "Where are those good Romans?" he exclaimed. "Where is their high justice? If only I could live in such times!"

Whenever he muttered and tossed pebbles into the Forum, the superstitious crossed themselves. I can see why. The lad seemed to practice *sortilegio*, casting lots to tell his fortune.

Now a successful notary, Cola joined a delegation to Pope Clement VI at Avignon. His report on the barons' abuses antagonized the powerful but captivated the poet Petrarch, who admired the young man's smooth tongue and rugged features. The Pope, equally impressed, appointed Cola Apostolic Notary and authorized him to return to Rome and reform civil law. Power emboldened him to settle scores. By confiscating weapons, imposing heavy fines, and imprisoning and exiling ringleaders, he subdued the barons and established popular rule.

On May 19, 1347, heralds invited citizens to a special parliament on Pentecost Sunday. Dressed in full armor and attended by the papal vicar, Cola headed a procession to the Capitol, where he addressed the assembled crowd from the balcony of the Palazzo dei Conservatori. Henceforth, he declared, everyone would be equal under the law. Proclaiming himself Tribune of the People, Cola announced that he had restored the Roman Republic. Laws would be ratified by the people, and Roman citizenship would be offered to everyone in Italy. All cheered.

Soon the streets were safe, crimes swiftly punished, and buildings repaired. But when Cola awarded himself lordly titles, when he seized estates, silenced dissent, and executed enemies without trial, even his supporters balked.

The nobles revolted. Pope Clement issued a bull denouncing Cola as a pagan, heretic, and rebel. Driven out of Rome, he became a hermit in the Maiella Mountains before going to Prague to offer his services to Charles IV, who handed him over to the Pope. Imprisoned and pardoned, Cola returned to Rome in August 1354 and resumed the office of Tribune, but he had changed.

Gluttony had swollen his once limber body to the size of a heldentenor's. He wore foppish clothes and flashy rings. His balcony speeches were empty bombast, his edicts pretexts for graft and extortion. Some say prison had warped his character, but I think the explanation is simpler. After fighting tyrants for so long, Cola had turned into one. Well, don't we always become what we hate? Whatever the reason, his cruelty alienated the people, and his extravagances bankrupted the city. Severe taxes on salt and wine sparked an insurrection.

On October 8, a mob stormed the Capitol. During the raid on the palace, Cola disguised himself as a humble gardener, but his fancy rings gave him away. He was seized and dragged to the square. For an hour, nobody touched him, so great was the memory of his former glory. Finally, an incensed nobleman drew his dagger and plunged it into Cola's gut. A fellow notary struck the next blow. The plebs utterly butchered him.

Cola's mangled body was dragged by the feet to Piazza San Marcello and strung upside down from a balcony. For two days, it hung there, its guts dangling, like the carcass of an ox. Urchins threw stones and jeered: "Now make a speech!"

Over the centuries, Cola's life has inspired poets, painters, and composers, but his death, I regret to say, has never impressed other dictators. Aldo Parini vainly warned Benito Mussolini on the eve of World War II. "This regime of yours will end badly" said Parini, an old Socialist who had been Il Duce's friend in their youth. "Such things always do. Benito, you'll die like Cola Rienzi."

Mussolini grimaced in mock horror, then laughed and spread his fingers for Parini's inspection. "You see?" he said. "I wear no rings. It will never happen to me."

33.

MASQUERADE:

Pasquino relives the March on Rome

Halloween is becoming more popular in Rome than Carnival, thanks to American TV. Teenaged zombies right out of *The Walking Dead*, which streams daily on Netflix Italia, startle tourists in the piazzas and frighten seniors in the alleys.

"*Dolcetto o scherzetto!*" groan the fake ghouls. "Trick or treat!" With a nervous smile, the victims surrender their cigarettes or spare change. The pranksters laugh, get back into character, and shuffle off menacingly. Harmless enough, I suppose, but the spectacle reminds me of a more sinister masquerade: Benito Mussolini's March on Rome.

October 1922, when *real* ghouls overran Italy, was one long Witches' Sabbath. After a general strike had touched off riots, thousands of law-and-order college students joined the *squadristi*, the paramilitary squads of the rising Fascist Party. Called the Voluntary Militia for National Security, these young vigilantes ruled the streets.

Waving banners with the skull and crossbones, the *squadristi* wore black shirts and military insignias and carried pistols, rifles, and grenades. The guns rarely were loaded, though, and the grenades almost always were duds. Instead, daggers, truncheons, and clubs intimidated and injured opponents. For show, baby-faced goons carried torches and chanted slogans. They also forced journalists and professors to drink castor oil until they shat themselves, presumably to purge the body politic of leftist ideas.

Nobody could control the *squadristi*, not even Mussolini, who watched events unfold in Milan. Safe in his headquarters, he wrote incendiary articles, abused bespectacled parliamentarians, challenged enemies to duels, and forecast a national bloodbath, but he never once participated in a street brawl. Even as he egged on followers to march on Rome, Mussolini negotiated with officials and planned his escape to Zurich.

This waffling exasperated his second-in-command. "We're going," Italo Balbo declared on Tuesday evening, October 24, "either with you or without you! Make up your mind!" Mussolini pursed his lips, jutted his chin, and folded his arms across his chest. He was resolved. He would remain behind in Milan, a short drive to the Swiss border, while his henchmen slogged to the capital through heavy rain.

The marchers, some 26,000 men, seized telephone exchanges, telegraph offices, town halls, and prefectures in Tuscany and Emilia-Romagna. Only 16,000 reached Rome. Lacking food and ammunition, this sodden and demoralized crew was no match against the army. Nevertheless, Victor Emmanuel III refused to declare martial law. The king detested the Fascists but dreaded the Communists, who wished to abolish the monarchy. He also dreaded his mother, Margherita of Savoy.

Occupying the state room like an overstuffed divan, the dowager queen considered Mussolini the greatest *condottiero* (commander of mercenary troops) since Bartolomeo Colleoni, the Captain General of the Republic of Venice in the late 15th century. The young Fascist leader even resembled Andrea del Verrocchio's equestrian statue of Colleoni. Mussolini had the same flashing eyes, the same granite jaw, the same broad shoulders. Wasn't this proof, the queen mother asked, that he was fated to lead the country?

Apparently so. On Sunday morning, October 29, the king bowed to political and domestic pressure. He telegrammed Mussolini and asked him to form a new cabinet. Prime Minister Luigi Facta had resigned. Recording the event in his calendar, the king wrote: "*I order Mussolini.*" As if Il Duce was a pizza.

The pie arrived the next day, with all the toppings. Mussolini had intended to travel by plane and scatter leaflets and confetti in his wake. Much to his chagrin, he could not even catch an early train. This humiliation strengthened his resolve to make the railroads run on time. Obliged to depart on a luxury sleeper, Mussolini compared the comfy nine-hour ride to Caesar's crossing the Rubicon.

At the stroke of eleven, Italy's new prime minister presented himself to the king in a shabby morning coat, borrowed spats, and a Fascist black shirt. "Please excuse my appearance, Your Majesty" he said, "but I have just returned from the battle which we had to fight. Fortunately, without shedding blood."

Mussolini declared allegiance to the House of Savoy. The monarchy, he said, had provided Italy with a splendid constitution and had won the greatest victory in the recent world war at Vittorio Veneto. It deserved to be protected and glorified. The king basked in the glow of these words. Mussolini smiled. Like a seasoned courtier, he bowed, clicked his heels, and left. His shoes squeaked on the parquet floor. Visibly relieved, the king turned to his palace crony, Vittorio Solaro del Borgo, and said: "The nightmare is over."

Few realized that it had only begun. Blame the regalia. Mussolini's black shirts, party ministers explained, were modeled after machinists' uniforms, just as Garibaldi's red shirts had been glorified butchers' smocks. Historians scoffed at the analogy, but Garibaldi's grandsons, Ezio and Peppino, supported the new regime. Didn't their *nonno* also march on Rome? Didn't his followers also beg him to seize power?

Du-ce! Du-ce! Du-ce!

The Fascists held a victory parade. Fifty thousand marched before the Altar of the Fatherland, singing "*Giovinezza*" and Risorgimento hymns. Bands blared and orators spieled in Piazza Navona. Propaganda films were shown. When *garibaldini* and *squadristi* exchanged Roman salutes on screen, the mob cheered. I shook my head, sickened and ashamed. From red shirts to black shirts in sixty years. History, I thought, is a tawdry costume party.

Trick or treat!

34.

STARLINGS:

Pasquino interprets signs in the sky

At dusk, I watch millions of starlings invade Rome. After feasting all day on ripening olives, they fly south from the Sabine Hills and fill the sky. A cyclone of feathers swallows the sun. The birds scatter and regroup, form a living tidal wave, surge and drown an archipelago of tiles and chimneys, garrets and loggias, domes and spires.

I dread this sight, particularly near the Ides of March. Starlings, after all, foretold Julius Caesar's death. The day before, a gold-crowned kinglet flew into the Theatre of Pompey, a sprig of laurel in its beak. It was pursued by a flock of starlings and torn to pieces. When the augurs warned Caesar, he laughed. That night he dreamt he flew above Rome, clasping the talon of Jove's eagle. The next day, he was murdered on the very spot where the kinglet had perished.

Ever since, starlings have harbingered disaster. But as old Communists note, the birds did not conquer Rome until 1926, the year Benito Mussolini assumed total control of Italy. Avian phalanxes occupied the stone pines at Villa Ada and menaced the picnickers in the Giardino degli Aranci. Squadrons dive-bombed the cars parked along the Lungotevere and disrupted flights at Ciampino Airport. These incidents peaked in March, but Mussolini ignored the omens.

On Wednesday April 7, Il Duce delivered the keynote address at the International Congress of Surgeons. After finishing a paean to science, he paused to salute an ecstatic crowd in the Piazza del

Campidoglio. As he strode to his Lancia Astura limo, he failed to notice a shabby, bespectacled woman wearing a feathered hat and a hideous black dress. She was the Honorable Violet Gibson, the 50-year-old daughter of Edward Gibson, 1st Baron of Ashbourne and Lord Chancellor of Ireland. This small, birdlike spinster was determined to kill the dictator.

Ever since moving to Rome, Gibson had become obsessed with Mussolini. Like most Anglo-Irish aristocrats, she revered Mazzini and Garibaldi. Mussolini, she believed, had betrayed the Risorgimento, the campaign to unify Italy in the late nineteenth century. Nevertheless, Great Britain lionized this tyrant. George V awarded him the Order of the Garter. Winston Churchill hailed him as Italy's savior. British journalists praised "his trim handsome black-shirted lads" for doing such a fine job of keeping down the Bolshies. For Gibson, an Irish nationalist and parlor Socialist, this must have been the last straw.

Once Mussolini was in his car, Gibson removed a revolver from her pocket. She raised and pointed the gun at the dictator's head and fired at point-blank range. At that moment, a band started playing "*Giovinezza,*" the Fascist anthem. Mussolini turned to face the flag and snapped to attention, bringing his head back just enough for Gibson's bullet to miss him. Rather than pierce his skull, it passed through his nostrils. Burn marks were left on both cheeks, but these wounds proved superficial.

Within minutes, Mussolini continued his parade on the Capitoline. Photographers ignored his bandaged nose, while reporters wished him luck on his coming trip to Libya. Surrounded by guards, Il Duce addressed spectators: "*If I advance, follow me! If I retreat, kill me! If I die, avenge me!*" But despite the roaring adulation, he remained shaken. An Irish hag had nearly dispatched him. "A woman!" he murmured. "Fancy—a woman!"

After the shooting, the mob beat and nearly lynched Gibson, but plainclothesmen rescued and dragged her into the Palazzo dei Conservatori. Unconscious and badly bleeding, she resembled a mauled crow. Police revived her with brandy and interrogated her in a room containing the colossal marble foot of the Emperor Constantine. As she was carted away to Mantellate Prison, a cloud of starlings swirled over the Campidoglio.

Gibson's was the first of four assassination attempts between April and October 1926. Declaring a state of emergency, Mussolini abolished parliament, replaced it with a junta, established a special police force, and instituted secret tribunals. He also introduced capital punishment for treason, insurrection, incitement to civil war, and attempted assassination. He did not, however, demand the death penalty for Violet Gibson.

Diagnosed as a paranoid schizophrenic, Gibson was deported back to Britain, where she spent the next thirty years in St. Andrew's Sanatorium in Northamptonshire. Shapeless in an old mackintosh, she wandered the asylum grounds and fed sparrows. She may have posed like St. Francis, but she behaved like the mad sorceress Fata Morgana. She attacked orderlies with a broom and invoked thunder and lightning against the doctors. Whenever she flapped her arms and squawked, claimed the groundskeeper, starlings would roost in the trees. A refugee from Fascist Rome, he always crossed himself in her presence.

35.

JUBILEE:

Pasquino greets his liberators

Before midnight on June 4, 1944, the news reached Piazza di Pasquino: *The Americans have liberated Rome!* At first, I was reluctant to believe it. I was too exhausted from the bread riots in April, too shaken by the more recent and senseless atrocities the Germans committed before they abandoned the city to the Allies. But when a roar of jubilation rose from the Baths of Caracalla to the Quirinal Palace, I knew it was true—we had been freed from those Fascist bastards at last! If I had had legs, I would have jumped up and down for joy.

Old men in nightshirts and slippers poured into the streets, braying whatever English they knew. "Weekend!" one coot repeatedly shouted. "Weekend!" Not to be outdone, young men clapped in time, spun on their heels, and performed a swing tune: *"Singa, singa, singa, sing! Ever'body starta sing!"*

During the wee hours, everyone prepared for the arrival of our heroes. A translation of the American Declaration of Independence was pasted on my pediment. The Stars and Stripes were raised above Piazza Venezia. A huge banner draped the Pantheon: *"WELCOME TO OUR LIBERATORS!"*

At dawn on June 5, a Yankee convoy rolled through Porta San Giovanni, carrying a detachment of scouts and engineers. As the column advanced, squads peeled off to secure telegraph offices, power plants, and pumping stations. Sergeant John Vita, however, a reconnaissance photographer from Port Chester, New York, went alone on a special mission.

Vita had promised to phone his immigrant mother from Benito Mussolini's office in Palazzo Venezia. After putting his feet up on the dictator's desk and lighting a cigarillo to make the call, he got another idea. Vita strutted onto Il Duce's balcony and gave a speech.

"*Vittoria!*" he declaimed, imitating Mussolini's salute to amused spectators below. "Not for Il Duce but for the Allies!"

The U.S. Fifth Army entered Rome at ten-hundred hours. People gathered at Porta Maggiore to throw confetti at Sherman tanks that were covered with the dust of Highway 6. Young women ransacked flower stands on the Spanish Steps to weave garlands for the Jeeps. Old women showered baby-faced infantrymen with irises and roses.

As Piper Cubs flew over the Vittoriano, the iceberg-shaped memorial to the first king of United Italy, Lieutenant General Mark Wayne Clark climbed a broad flight of steps to the top of Capitoline Hill. Nicknamed the American Eagle because of his aquiline nose, Clark surveyed his conquest from between the massive statues of Castor and Pollux. The general, I later learned, had disobeyed his superiors to rescue us. Compared to neutralizing the retreating German army, Allied command considered liberating Rome "strategically unimportant."

"Tell that to the Romans," Clark said.

"*Vivano gli Americani!*" cheered the crowd. "*Viva Italia Libera!*"

Regrettably, the next morning's headlines about the Allied invasion of Normandy ("D- DAY!") upstaged Clark's triumph. *Che peccato,* I thought. What pity. As a consolation prize, however, Pius XII gave an audience at the Vatican to American officers and journalists. Some reporters carried sidearms, others wielded cameras. One—an enormously fat woman who flirted with Eric Sevareid of CBS—wore pleated slacks printed with cabbage roses.

As flashbulbs exploded, photographers shouted: "Hold it, Pope! Attaboy!"

"Just another changing of the guard," said Monsignor Enrico Pucci, the Pope's press secretary. I knew what he meant. It was the second time in a year and at least the fiftieth time in twenty-seven centuries that Rome had been taken, but it had never fallen before to Americans. Not to mention Italian Americans.

Colonel Charles Poletti, Regional Commissioner of the Allied Military Government, who had served briefly as Governor of New York before becoming a U.S. Civil Affairs officer in Italy, was determined to restore order and faith in democracy. Romans instantly disliked him.

A jovial, talkative man, Poletti provided K rations but little pasta for the starving populace. He also broadcast obnoxious pep talks, suggesting among other things that Romans ought to use more soap than, according to him, they were doing. Someone retaliated with this pasquinade:

Charlie Poletti, Charlie Poletti,
Meno ciarla e più spaghetti.

"Get it?" crowed a dogface in the 88th Infantry. "Less talk, more spaghetti!"

He was sharing a meal with two buddies at La Matriciana, a no-frills restaurant on the Esquiline Hill, while I eavesdropped from a corner table. All came from Bensonhurst but had never met until the war. Waiters called them the Brooklyn Triumvirate. But although their

194

last names were Cesare, Crasso, and Pompeo, these G.I.s knew nothing about Rome. When their platoon first entered the city and strode past the Coliseum, Pompeo had muttered: "Christ, the Krauts bombed that, too!"

The celebration lasted a week, but it wasn't a carnival so much as a jubilee: a giddy time of emancipation and restoration. The Vatican granted a dispensation to baptize all the illegitimate *bambini* in the working-class Testaccio district at a somewhat scandalous ceremony in the Church of Santa Maria di Liberazione. Convicts released from the cells of Regina Coeli Prison blinked like owls at a midday block party honoring them in their old neighborhood. Most remarkable of all, beneath my very nose here in Piazza di Pasquino, a loan shark impetuously tore up his little black accounts book and showered his bewildered debtors with silver coins.

We were drunk on liberty, but the inevitable problems caused by any foreign military presence somewhat sobered us. The Fifth Army, camped at Villa Borghese, turned Rome's loveliest park into a barracks. The black market, which flourished under the Nazis, still thrived, despite irksome and ineffective regulations and restrictions. Buildings were graffitied with parodies of official slogans and staff cars were requisitioned for drunken joy rides.

Some American officials flouted the rules they sought to impose, and American soldiers, despite their pressed uniforms and a patina of shoe polish and brilliantine, were less disciplined than the Germans had been. Within a month, they were infected by Rome's corrupt, lackadaisical attitude. They gorged on spaghetti, got shit-faced on cheap wine, fell all over the wrong girls and boys, and paid for these and other vices with Hershey chocolate bars, Camel cigarettes, and Zippo lighters.

The conquered always conquer their conqueror, said Horace. Hustlers and opportunists might have complained, but unprejudiced Romans admitted that they enjoyed great freedom of expression and movement under the U.S. occupation. They were elated that the Nazi oppression, which had overshadowed Rome, had been permanently lifted. They were relieved that the occupiers were eager to hand back the government of the city and the county to us Italians as soon as possible.

When the Americans left, Villa Borghese retained the marks of their youthful enthusiasm. The tracks of the jeeps, the ruts of the trucks and tanks, the trash from refuse pits spoiled the paths among the myrtle bushes and scarred the meadows and flower beds, but nobody truly minded. Eventually, the nannies and toddlers, pensioners and lovers ventured back to the park.

The Americans had left an indelible blessing. They had forever reminded us of what it truly means to be Romans. Two years after our liberation, we voted to make Italy a Republic. With Rome as its capital! This miracle never would have happened, I think, if the Americans hadn't reawakened our thirst for freedom. It was a tangy freedom buried for centuries under the rubbish of kings and dictators, popes and emperors—like the musky wine cellars deep in the grottoes of Monte Testaccio, an ancient waste mound in the historic district.

Liber, the Roman god of liberty and free speech, was also a god of the grape. At the Festival of Liberalia, we honored him with solemn processions and ribald drinking bouts. Freedom is a heady wine, but it never gives you a hangover. I say to you: *Drink deep, my fellow citizens! There is no liberty without joy.*

36.

WITH CHALK:

Pasquino billets a troop of toy soldiers

As the sun shone on the octagonal dome of Sant'Agnese in Agone, Piazza Navona teemed with life. Another Sunday afternoon, I thought, at the Befana Christmas Market. By the Fountain of the Four Rivers, puppeteers performed a knock-down, drag-out Punch and Judy show. Couples rode a 19th-century carousel. Pushcart vendors hawked salted flatbread, chestnuts, and *supplì,* deep-fried rice balls stuffed with mozzarella. Kiosks sold trinkets, ornaments, and dolls of the good witch, La Befana, who, kerchiefed and riding a broom, delivers presents to Roman children on the morning of January 6, the Feast of the Epiphany. In the evening of that same day, her papier-mâché effigy explodes in a burst of fireworks here in Piazza Navona.

From the northern edge of the square, a sound system played canned battle music from Tchaikovsky's *The Nutcracker.* The Nutcracker himself and the Mouse King dueled in front of Al Sogno, Piazza Navona's deluxe toy store. Since 1960, Al Sogno has sponsored the Balleto di Roma's annual Christmas production of Tchaikovsky's fairy tale, and members of the company were promoting this year's performance at the Teatro Constanzi.

The store's interior had been transformed into the Land of Sweets. From the show window, I admired figurines based on characters from the ballet. A display case contained porcelain dancers, costumed as Spanish chocolate, Arabian coffee, Chinese tea, and Russian candy canes. The shelves were stocked with wooden nutcracker men at attention. How fierce and silly they looked, with their bright uniforms and bristling moustaches! The sight of their wild hair and huge teeth packed the shop with unruly children.

Ignoring both the pitiful glances of the neglected Pinocchios in the corner and the stern frowns of their parents, who were ordering takeout from Bernini Ristorante on Just Eat Italia, boys and girls fought over the hideous little soldiers. A grim-faced nun glared from behind steel-rimmed glasses, confiscated the toys, and scolded the children. She wore a Celtic cross and a starched white habit, so she might have been one of the Irish Dominican sisters who run the Villa Rosa convent hotel in the Trastevere district.

The kids hung their heads. The nun relented and returned the nutcracker men but continued wagging her finger. The good sister should forgive them, I thought. Don't we adults adore toy monsters, too? I recalled how a mob hailed another nutcracker man: Charles VIII, the grotesque French king who captured Rome more than 425 Christmases ago.

"Providence," observed John Addington Symonds, the British cultural historian, "frequently uses for the most momentous purpose some pantaloon or puppet, environing with special protection and with the prayers and aspirations of whole peoples a mere mannikin.

"Such a puppet was Charles VIII."

He was nicknamed *L'Affable*, the Affable, but, believe me, there was nothing affable about him. A series of childhood illnesses had left him stunted and half blind. Hook-nosed and slack-jawed, he slobbered and drooled from thick, fleshy lips, constantly open but partially concealed by a wispy reddish beard. His hands and feet twitched. The few words that ever escaped him were muttered rather than spoken. His limbs were so disproportionate and his posture so stooped that he seemed more like a crab than a man. He walked with a crouch and a limp, and he always wore big boots to conceal the fact that he had six toes.

Now I'm no beauty myself. A faceless, limbless statue, I never judge people by their appearance. Despite his physical quirks, I might have sympathized with Charles, if he hadn't been so ugly and twisted inside. The lout yearned to be great but was unfit to rule.

Not only was the king a glutton and a lecher but he was also an ignoramus, barely capable of writing his name. Sycophants and counsellors told him what to do. Ambassadors flattered and manipulated him. When Ludovico Sforza, the Duke of Milan, enticed Charles to help him settle a dispute with the King of Naples, Charles, who craved the Neapolitan throne for himself, never realized he was being played. Instead, he mustered 25,000 men and marched into Italy in early September 1494.

Over the next ten weeks, Charles took Genoa, Pavia, Pisa, and Florence, virtually unopposed. This amused Rodrigo Borgia, the Spanish prelate recently elevated to the Chair of St. Peter as Pope Alexander VI. "The King of France," he joked, "conquers Italy with chalk," implying that, to seize the country, Charles merely needed to send quartermasters to mark the houses in which his troops would be billeted.

The Pope stopped laughing when Friar Girolamo Savanarola, a fanatic preaching apocalyptic sermons from the pulpit of Santa Maria del Fiore, hailed Charles as a messiah, chosen to liberate Florence from the Medici family and to purify the church from corruption. This Borgia pope, the friar said, was guilty of simony. He bought and sold ecclesiastical offices to enrich a brood of bastard children. To chasten him, heaven had appointed Charles *flagellum dei*, the scourge of God. Convinced of his newfound destiny, the French king continued marching south and reached the outskirts of Rome by Christmas week.

Fearing he would be deposed, Pope Alexander retreated to the Castel Sant'Angelo. When the French fired a salvo, the Pope mounted the battlements and held above his head a gold monstrance, a transparent receptacle containing a consecrated host. Seen from a distance through a spyglass, the monstrance flashed like a sunburst. Charles, pious to the point of superstition, ceased fire. Through a messenger, he assured His Holiness that "not a hen, not even an egg" would be disturbed when his troops entered the city on New Year's Eve.

Despite sleet and mud, Romans mobbed the Porta del Popolo to see the miliary parade. The procession amused me. First came the gigantic Swiss mercenaries, flaunting their plumes and emblazoned surcoats; then the French chevaliers with their silk-draped armor and gilded corselets: then the king's Scottish guards in their strange tartan uniforms; then the German *landsknechte* with their scythe-like halberds; and finally, the king himself, looking as drenched and woebegone as a monkfish dragged from the bottom of the Tyrrhenian Sea.

The commoners cheered themselves hoarse. "*Francia, Francia!*" they cried, hoping Charles would rid them of the Borgias. To dissuade him from tossing His Holiness into the Tiber, Johann Burchard, the owlish Protonotary Apostolic and Master of Ceremonies, feted Charles in the Papal Palace. Gorging on pork roast and basking in the light of flambeaux, the mighty warrior justified his clemency.

"How could I shoot the Pope?" he asked a simpering courtesan. "Whatever his faults, he is the Vicar of Christ! I'm no Turk or heretic.

So, I hit the brothels and let my boys loot the city. Wasn't that the Christian thing to do?"

Burchard peered through his spectacles and smirked. "*Si non caste tamen caute,*" he murmured. (If you can't be chaste, at least be careful.) Charles understood no Latin, but for Vatican gold and a few fortresses, he agreed to abandon Rome after three weeks: enough time for his men to gather supplies and break some hearts. Then he marched to Naples, where dreams of glory ended in disaster.

Two and a half years later, while on his way to a tennis match, he struck his head on the lintel of a door. "Don't worry," Charles said. "I have a thick skull." While returning from the game, he collapsed in a heap, a marionette whose strings had been cut. He died that evening. If he is remembered today, it is for bringing syphilis to Italy.

Charles's Spanish mercenaries had served with Columbus and had contracted the disease in the New World. During the siege of Naples, they infected the city brothels frequented by the French troops. The French, in turn, transmitted the virus throughout the peninsula—but the pox never stopped them from whoring. Their persistence, I think, would have pleased Charles. He always urged his men to take risks, whether on the field of Mars or in the courts of Venus.

A fanfare of toy trumpets returned me to Piazza Navona. The Nutcracker led a platoon of tin soldiers in a march around the Fountain of Neptune. I chuckled ruefully. That's not what happens in Tchaikovsky's ballet, I thought. After killing the Mouse King, the Nutcracker turns into a prince and wins the young heroine, Clara Stahlbaum. But in real life a puppet rarely becomes a prince, even after capturing Rome.

LAST JUDGMENTS

37.

GRAVE THOUGHTS:

Pasquino books a tomb at the Campo Verano

Even in Rome, people die. Some can't wait, and I don't blame them. In this town, all thoughts and prayers, all Christian charity go to the dead. The living can lump it. Romans will abuse our friends and relatives while they still breathe, but if a casual acquaintance drops dead in the street, we will parade our grief and spare no expense. The litter, the candles, the incense! The holy water, the music, the bells! For the departed, a sung requiem and a marble headstone. For the survivors, a laminated mass card and onerous gratuities. If you want a send-off to impress the neighbors, comp the undertaker two tickets to the next A.S. Roma soccer game.

Even so, funerals are not what they used to be. Most people blame the pandemic, when public mourning was suspended and army trucks escorted coffins to mass graves, crematoriums, and abandoned warehouses. Long before the lockdown, however, I noticed that standards had fallen from what they were sixty, seventy years ago.

Like the seating in Alitalia, Italy's now defunct national airline, funerals then came in three classes. Third class (*classe economica*) was modestly decorous. Chrysanthemums were few but fresh and tastefully arranged. Second class (*classe commerciale*) was fancier. Attendants wore double-pleated cuffed trousers, and the hearse—a Pilato Mercedes-Benz station wagon—was double waxed and buffed. But first class (*classe magnifica*), reserved for statesmen, prelates, and celebrities, turned heads and stopped traffic.

The hearse, a gigantic coach of ebony and crystal, came with two black-and-gold liveried coachmen in front and two similarly dressed footmen in back. All wore black, gold-trimmed bicorn hats. Four glossy black horses in black-plumed harness pulled the hearse. Its huge steel-rimmed wheels rumbled on the cobblestones. The hearse was followed by another equally impressive coach, smothered in wreaths and flowers, and a long shuffling line of elegant mourners. Such solemnity occasionally drew hoots of derision.

I recall a state service held at the Church of Santa Maria degli Angeli e dei Martiri. As the funeral coach circled the Fountain of the Naiads in Piazza della Repubblica, the women crossed themselves, but the men scratched their crotches and made the "horns" sign with their fingers to ward off bad luck. This upset the coachman, who snapped his long, red-and-blue tasseled whip at the crowd. A pimply kid from the Trastevere district, who must have seen the latest Western at the Alcazar Cinema, shouted: "Wells Fargo!"

Nothing that colorful happens anymore, not even when a pope dies. But just because funerals have become more generic doesn't mean that death has become more democratic. Quite the opposite, believe me. Rome remains a bastion of privilege, and the dead, far more than the living, settle in neighborhoods based on class standing.

At the Campo Verano, Rome's most exclusive cemetery, the dead keep office hours. Although the grounds are open between 7:30 AM and 6:00 PM, formal mourning is allowed only at set times. Visitors must enter on foot, unless obtaining a permit for age or handicap.

Limited access and strict protocol reflect the cemetery's cachet, which explains why tourists flock here.

Tour guides call the Verano Rome's "ultimate district." People are dying to belong. Located on the Via Tiburtina near the Church of San Lorenzo outside the city's eastern wall, the necropolis resembles a gated community. It features unified streets and avenues, neoclassical statues and monuments, and perfectly manicured lawns. Cypresses guard and shade its twenty-foot-high walls.

Rome did not always segregate the dead from the living. For most of its history, the two mingled. Ancient pagans buried relatives in the kitchen or cremated and kept their ashes in the parlor. Early Christians used catacombs only when they were an underground sect. Once their faith had triumphed, they converted houses of worship into family crypts. Basilicas were for the affluent and important, simple chapels for the *hoi polloi*. Marble floor slabs in old churches are usually tombstones, the inscription smoothed and made illegible by the footsteps of time.

Napoleon abolished this custom, for olfactory and hygienic reasons. On September 5, 1806, the French emperor implemented the Edict of Saint-Cloud in Italy. All burials, the law stated, must occur outside city walls. Furthermore, to promote democracy, all monuments for the dead must be the same size and their inscriptions regulated by a special committee. This fiat overturned centuries of tradition. Ugo Foscolo, in a celebrated ode (*"Dei Sepolcri"*), protested the violation of Italy's sepulchers: *"Today's new law sets tombs apart from reverent glances, and denies the dead their glorious name."*

Pius VII, a much prosier man, sought a practical solution for the Papal States. To comply with Napoleon's ordinance, he proposed designating and blessing a field outside Rome. The church would consecrate the ground, but the civil authorities would administer the burials. But where, asked city prefects and canon lawyers, should this holy field, this *camposanto*, be? As former Bishop of Tivoli, Pius suggested a tract beside the ancient consular road leading to his old diocese. Containing catacombs, this field once belonged the Verani, a senatorial family from the time of the Republic; hence its name Campo Verano.

Giuseppe Valadier drafted the blueprints and broke ground between 1807 and 1812. The cemetery, however, was not consecrated until 1835. Work continued during the papacies of Gregory XVI and Pius IX, under the supervision of Virginio Vespignani. Further construction was performed, even after Rome became the capital of United Italy, but the wall surrounding the cemetery was left unfinished. Cows, goats, and sheep snuck through the gaps and pastured among the dead. Scandalized relatives unburied them at night and smuggled the remains back to their neighborhood churches.

Respectability came in the late 19th century. King Umberto, an incorrigible Philistine, praised the Verano's kitschy monuments. A simpering angel, chin on hand, rests against a memorial bench. A reclining soldier seems to have perished in a brothel, not a battle. The cemetery's architecture is equally bathetic. The main entrance with its three openings, rendered even more imposing by four large statues depicting Meditation, Hope, Charity, and Silence, precedes a large, four-sided portico. The mausoleums, some built like Art Nouveau villas, are decorated with climbing ivy, truncated pillars, bronze flower urns, and stained glass.

Everyone wants to be buried here, if only to socialize with celebrities. Silvio Spaventa, the great statesman, clears his throat and resumes a petition on behalf of Bomba, his home district in the Chieti province of Abruzzo. Alessandro Moreschi, the last surviving castrato, squeaks Gounod's "Ave Maria." Marcello Mastroianni, who needs no introduction, smooths his dinner jacket, lights a cigarette, and traces circles of smoke in the air.

But the round-shouldered ghost of Giulio Andreotti, Prime Minister, President of the Republic, Senator for Life, is nowhere to be found. How disappointing, I think, for who is better qualified than Andreotti to welcome visitors to the Verano? Here he courted and proposed to his wife, Livia Danese, and defeated and buried his many rivals and enemies. The press called this crooked politician the Hunchback, the Black Pope, and Beelzebub, and accused him of everything that has gone wrong in Italy apart from the Punic Wars. But the old fox survived every scandal and made his final den under a marble slab.

Before he died, Andreotti, for whatever reason, expressed a desire to be forgotten. Most Romans, however, long to be remembered, which is why the waiting list for the Campo Verano is thicker than a phone book. Unfortunately, demand has caused overcrowding. To accommodate new generations of the dead, management must evict old tenants. From time to time, the tombs are opened. Workmen enter, remove the cadavers (now rags and bones) from their coffins, place them in much smaller zinc containers, and then label and stack them in ranks along the walls. Once the coffins are gone, space is free for new arrivals, provided the Department of Antiquities and Fine Arts approves.

From what I can see, these indignities do not disturb the dead. Their ceramic images, embedded beside their chiseled names on vertical slabs of shiny black Carrara, are as resigned as passport photos. The living, however, sigh and shake their heads. Is the sleep of death less heavy, they ask, beneath the shade of cypresses or within a sculptured urn?

Not at all, I assure you, and I speak from experience. As a statue, I should desire silence and tranquility, but I much prefer the streets of Rome to the groves of the Verano. God knows, the living endure much in this city: fumes and traffic, fines and taxes, swinish bureaucrats and wild pigs rooting through trash. Yet in the end, the living—good or bad, beautiful or ugly, lucky or unlucky—are still better off than the dead.

For one thing, they can still laugh.

38.

VANITY OF VANITIES:
Pasquino picks a bone with mortality

Via Veneto, an elegant but now unfashionable street in Rome's historic district, was once the center of *la dolce vita*, the sweet life. During the 1950s and 1960s, movie stars, supermodels, and jet setters congregated here. Most are dead now, I'm sad to say, but their ghosts still order cocktails at Harry's Bar or book the cupola suite at the Westin Excelsior. At the other end of the street, the accommodations are less cushy in the basement of Santa Maria della Consezione, a Capuchin church dedicated to *la dolce morte*, sweet death.

Nicknamed the "Bone Church" by irreverent young Romans, this grim building stands near Piazza Barberini, where for centuries I weekly saw anonymous corpses publicly displayed for identification. A *memento mori* for the sophisticates on Via Veneto, Santa Maria is also a mecca for Goths everywhere. Its ghastly crypt—a popular attraction in November, the Month of the Dead—proclaims the vanity of human wishes and laments the fate of Antonio Barberini, a member of the arrogant family associated with the church. His misfortunes prove that no one escapes judgment, not even in the tomb.

If you don't believe me, visit Santa Maria yourself. Go early to avoid the crowds. At the entrance, poke your head into the nave to admire the altarpiece in the first side chapel, Guido Reni's *St Michael the Archangel Conquers Satan*. Then turn to the left and take the narrow, steep stairway down to the vault. But brace yourself. Unless you're made of stone like me, the sight will shock you.

Six small rooms teem with the bones of four thousand monks arranged into decorative patterns: arches of femurs, pyramids of skulls, frescoes of vertebrae. Ribs and clavicles, joints and teeth form crosses, hearts, and crowns. On the walls are trellised vines of knotted backbones. The curving tendrils are made of sinews and tendons, the blooming flowers from kneecaps and toenails. The effect is weirdly rustic. I might be tempted to picnic here, if weren't for the gruesome company.

Beneath a flickering chandelier of wired humerus bones, skeletons attired in hooded robes grin in their niches. Wisps of tendons and cartilage hold together limbs and torsos, skulls and jaws, barely hidden under disintegrating brown habits. Until the 19th century, these alcoves also included mummies. The bodies of dead monks were cured upon beds of human bones like *baccalà,* dried cod: shriveled hands clasped on their breasts, tufts of hair stuck to their skulls, parchment-colored skin stretched over their cheekbones, flaccid eyes sunk into their sockets.

Miraculously, this process was odorless. "There is no disagreeable scent," marveled Nathanael Hawthorne, during a visit to Rome in 1858, "such as might have been expected from the decay of so many holy persons, in whatever odor of sanctity they may have taken their departure. The same number of living monks," he added, "would not smell half so unexceptionably."

Mark Twain, who toured the crypt ten years later, agreed but still wondered why the Capuchins were "cheered by the prospect of being taken apart like a clock and turned into a diorama fit for the Barnum Museum." I could have told him that the monks were less eager to honor their Heavenly Father than to please their earthly patron, Antonio Marcello Barberini.

This illustrious man built the Church of Santa Maria della Cosezione in 1626, under orders from his brother Maffeo Barberini, Pope Urban VII. Grain merchants and minor nobility from Florence, their family had moved to Rome a century earlier and had hurled themselves into church affairs. Their coat of arms featured three busy bees. "They'll gather the honey," I predicted, "and sting the city." I was right.

Like most parvenus, the Barberini aggrandized themselves through public works. Maffeo plundered the bronze beams from the portico of the Pantheon for the *baldacchino*, the sculpted canopy for the high altar of St. Peter's Basilica. When the leftover bronze went to the papal cannon foundry, somebody posted this epigram on my pedestal: "*Quod non fecerunt barbari, fecerunt Barberini.*" ("What the barbarians did not do, the Barberini did.")

Antonio, however, seemed the opposite of Maffeo. As a young man, he had rejected rank and wealth to join the Capuchins, the most austere branch of the Franciscans; but when his brother was elected Pope in 1623, Fra Antonio—against his will—was made a cardinal and appointed Grand Inquisitor of Rome, Director of the Vatican Library, and the Major Penitentiary. His first assignment was to build a new headquarters for his order.

Its old convent, San Bonaventura on Via dei Lucchesi, had become too cramped, so His Eminence picked a spacious suburban lot occupied by vineyards and owned by his brother. After construction, the Capuchins moved into the friary, along with the skeletons of three hundred dead monks. Pope Urban donated cartloads of earth from the Holy Land, so that the deceased brethren might be properly buried in the convent's crypt. A great boon. Since the Resurrection will begin in Jerusalem, according to tradition, the dead monks would be among the first to receive their reward at the Last Judgment. Unfortunately, they must spend the rest of eternity sorting and reassembling their jumbled bones.

To prevent overcrowding, the Capuchins laid their dead in Holy Land soil for only thirty years, enough time for the bodies to completely decompose. As the bell tolled the passing centuries, the longest-buried monks were exhumed to make room for the recently departed, who were buried without coffins, and the newly reclaimed bones were added to the ossuary. This practice ended in 1870, but by then, the convent's underground chapel had become a famous tourist destination.

The crypt still attracts the glib and the morbid. Randy young bucks come here to make their dates squeal. Horror fans prefer it to streaming slasher films by Dario Argento at home. As the basement's sound system pipes in a Palestrina *Kyrie,* a Billie Eilish wannabe takes a selfie beside a plaque that proclaims: "WHAT YOU ARE NOW, WE USED TO BE. WHAT WE ARE NOW, YOU WILL BE." The *padre guardiano,* the friar custodian, shakes his head. Thank God, the church's founder never witnessed such indecencies.

Cardinal Antonio Barberini died on September 11, 1646, two years after his brother Pope Urban VIII. He had hoped to resign his offices and resume the life of a simple monk, but relatives pressured him to participate in the conclave that elected his brother's old nemesis, Giovanni Battista Pamphili, who took the name Innocent X.

Pope Innocent nursed a grudge against the Barberini family. You may laugh when you learn why. Remember the altarpiece upstairs in the main church, Guido Reni's painting of St. Michael vanquishing Satan? When unveiled in 1636, this work scandalized Rome. Crushed under the Archangel's foot, the Devil resembled Giovanni Battista Pamphili, then only a cardinal. But Pope Innocent also blamed the Barberini for a costly war between the Papal States and the Duchy of Parma. When he exiled Cardinal Barberini's three nephews, the grief and shame killed poor Antonio, 77 years old and in failing health.

Because he had lived too long in the world and had never renounced his power, despite a solemn vow, Cardinal Barberini felt unworthy to be placed in the ossuary of Santa Maria della Concezione. Instead, he asked to be buried near the church altar, not in a grand marble sarcophagus, like most cardinals, but beneath a simple flagstone with no name or date, only this bleak Latin epitaph: "HIC IACET PVLVIS CINIS ET NIHIL." ("HERE LIES DUST, ASHES, AND NOTHING.")

Very moving, but I'm still disappointed. If he truly had craved eternal anonymity, Barberini would have chosen the boneyard. But that's Rome for you. Here the dead steal attention from the living, and humility is a pretext for ostentation.

39.

GOD AND MASTRO TITTA:

Pasquino indulges in some gallows humor

Located north of the Piazza Bocca della Verità, where public executions were held until 1868, the Church of San Giovanni Decollato is the headquarters of the Confraternity of Mercy, a voluntary association founded in 1488 to serve condemned criminals. Members administered the last rites, accompanied prisoners to the scaffold, and buried their bodies. Whenever those robed and hooded figures passed me, I shuddered. They acted like angels but looked like ghouls.

Now dedicated to penal reform, the Confraternity's members no longer wear penitential black. Rome's night traffic laws prohibit dark clothing for pedestrians. But the Confraternity's emblem remains carved in a circular relief above the cornice of the church door: a severed head on a platter. Due to its wealth and influence, the Confraternity had the right on August 29, the Feast of John the Baptist's Martyrdom, to free one convict sentenced to death. But only one prisoner and only on this one day. Further clemency would have interfered with the duties of Mastro Titta, the *boia* or executioner for the Papal States. I knew him well.

His real name was Giovanni Battista Bugatti. Mastro Titta was his nickname, a Romanesco corruption of his official title: *Maestro di Giustizia*, Master of Justice. Between 1796 and 1864, he dispatched 514 prisoners and recorded their deaths in a meticulous notebook. But there was nothing sinister, I assure you, about this tubby, frog-faced man with the rolling gait and the hearty grin. He would have preferred to support his adoring wife by making, painting, and repairing umbrellas for the curio shops around St. Peter's. The couple was childless, but their straitened circumstances forced Giovanni Battista to moonlight as a headsman.

Bugatti lived near the Vatican. For his safety, he was confined to the Borgo district on the west bank of the Tiber. If he had shown his face anywhere else, believe me, he would have been torn to pieces, so he patiently waited for his assignments at his compulsory residence in Vicolo del Campanile, decorating parasols with papal portraits and Roman scenes until his other services were required. Executions occurred about every other month. For each one, he was paid three cents a head: half the price of a cabbage sold in Campo de' Fiori.

Whenever a summons came from the Vatican, Bugatti removed the clothes of his humble trade and like a comic book superhero transformed himself into his powerful alter ego. He didn't wear a mask, but he did wear a hooded, calf-length scarlet cloak. Because of his girth, the cloak had an elastic section around the belly that expanded with its wearer. After going to confession and receiving communion at Santa Maria in Traspontina, he strode across the Castel Sant'Angelo Bridge with great pomp and ceremony. Urchins yelled: "*Mastro Titta passa ponte!*"

Mastro Titta was crossing the bridge. Heads would roll, and people would cheer.

Executions were held in several piazzas, where the shows always drew huge crowds. Papal dragoons provided security, to the frustration of whores and pickpockets. Cigarmakers and pastry chefs hawked their wares. Vendors sold memorabilia. Gamblers bet on how long it would take for a criminal's head to drop into the basket. Children chanted a nursey rhyme: "*Sega, sega, Mastro Titta!* Saw, saw, Mastro Titta, a sausage and a loaf of bread! The juicy sausage we will eat! The loaf of bread we will keep!"

For the spectators at this street fair, the victim (almost always a man) was the Ace of Spades and Lord of the Feast; but for Mastro Titta, the people's surgeon, the criminal was a suffering patient whose headache must be cured as quickly and painlessly as possible. Whether the condemned prisoner's crime was murder, sodomy, or sedition made no difference. Mastro Titta always offered a pinch of snuff and a word of encouragement: it would all be over soon.

Bugatti's skill always impressed me. As a bull-necked young buck, he preferred the *mazzatello*. He would swing a large mallet through the air to gather momentum and then bring it crashing down on a prisoner's skull. This was exactly how cattle were killed in the stockyards. When this method proved too taxing, he switched to the axe and reserved drawing and quartering for more heinous crimes. Eventually, he used the guillotine. Even though this device was invented by the godless French, it was still efficient and humane, not to mention simple. Place the prisoner's head in the lunette, release the cord, and *swish*!

The severed heads were hung along both sides of the Castel Sant'Angelo Bridge. It was the perfect place for the Master of Justice to display his handwork and to remind sinners about Judgment Day. The bridge's marble angels presented the instruments of Christ's torture and crucifixion like exhibits at a trial. When the practice of showing off Mastro Titta's gruesome trophies was discontinued, they remained enshrined in a popular saying: "*Ce so' più teste a ponte che cocomeri al mercato.*" (There are more heads on the bridge than watermelons in the market.)

Mastro Titta's was always busy. Executions were as common as weddings in the Papal States. During the reigns of Popes Gregory XVI and Pius IX, a period lasting from 1830 to 1870, even petty theft was a capital offense. Since Mastro Titta could not process all these convicted criminals alone, he asked the churches in Rome's historic center for help. Every month, they performed special rites for death-row inmates.

For these occasions, Mastro Titta supplied two notices, which the sacristan nailed to the church door. The first notice announced the name and offense of the condemned. The second advertised the following: "A plenary indulgence will be granted to the faithful who make a good confession and adore the Blessed Sacrament displayed in this church on behalf of all sinners sentenced to death." No good Catholic could turn down an offer to serve less time in Purgatory. Not in my neighborhood, anyway.

The Church of the Nativity of Jesus, opposite me here on Piazza di Pasquino, regularly held masses for condemned prisoners. I remember one service from March or April 1835. I can picture every detail of the scene because the Roman artist Achille Pinelli captured the moment in a sardonic sketch now hanging in the Museo di Roma.

At the church entrance, parish officials prepared for a death march. Hooded figures called *sacconi* began forming a procession. As protocol required, one *saccono* held a cloth-covered crucifix perfectly straight. A *mannataro*, a beadle in a cocked hat and a caped coat, tapped his mace on the cobblestoned pavement. Inside, some poor wretch was receiving the last rites and would soon be escorted to the block.

His plight did not bother a middle-class family that had paused beside my pedestal during their Sunday promenade. They were the sort of respectable folk whose favor Mastro Titta curried on his days off as Giovanni Battista Buggati. Perhaps they even bought his handmade umbrellas. The young wife wore a bonnet and a mutton-sleeved dress and chatted with her dowdy mother- and sister-in-law. Her older husband, quite spruce in his top hat, cravat, frock coat, and striped trousers, peered at me through opera glasses.

Was he surveying my eroded features or deciphering the papal insignia carved above me on the wall of Palazzo Braschi? I couldn't tell, but the gentleman was completely absorbed and never reacted to his surroundings. Not when the *sacconi* groaned a miserere, not when the prisoner emerged from the church with a black bag over his head, not when the beadle bawled his name and pronounced his death sentence to spectators in the square, not when the procession headed up Via del Governo Vecchio to keep his appointment with Mastro Titta. The gentleman remained impassive and peered through his opera glasses.

And people say *I'm* made of stone. But I've always maintained that indifference is worse than cruelty. Compared to this bourgeois, Giovanni Battista Bugatti was a saint, which is why I never resented his professional success. As Mastro Titta, he skillfully plied his trade until he was eight-five years old. One day, however, things went horribly wrong.

As usual, fathers, who had dragged their sons to the execution as a warning against wickedness, clouted them on the neck just as the blade came down. "*Pijja!*" they said. "Take that and know that the same fate awaits a thousand others who are better than you!" But this time the lesson was drowned in a geyser of blood that astonished even

Mastro Titta. While displaying the severed head to the crowd, the old executioner slipped in a puddle and fell flat on his face. The head tumbled off the platform and landed in the lap of a wealthy matron.

"What is this masher's head doing in my lap?" she demanded. "He has accosted me! Arrest him!" The police were perplexed, and the blood-spattered crowd began to mutter. Slowly, Bugatti struggled to his feet, approached the quivering matron, and bowed.

"*Scusi, signora,*" he said gallantry. "He meant no harm. To you, I mean!"

Everybody laughed, including the matron, and the police breathed a sigh of relief. Mastro Titta's wit had restored order and decorum; but after this near fiasco, he retired. The Vatican awarded him a gold medal and a monthly pension of thirty *scudi* (roughly $470 in today's money). Five years later, shortly after his death, capital punishment was abolished in Rome when the Kingdom of Italy annexed the Papal States.

Today, Mastro Titta's cloak, axe, and guillotine are preserved in the Museum of Criminology on Via del Gonfalone, but his legend looms even larger in our imagination. Whenever the axe is about to fall at work, employees announce: "Mastro Titta is crossing the bridge!" Children impersonate him. Restaurants are named after him. He even provided comic relief as a character in the musical *Rugantino*.

At the show's premiere on December 15, 1962, I was among those who mobbed the back of the Teatro Sistina baying for Aldo Fabrizi's autograph. With his bulging eyes and carp lips, the Roman actor looked so much like Mastro Titta that for a moment I was convinced that the old ruffian had come back to life. People shouted as if they were at a beheading.

"You are a legend playing a legend!" a woman cried.

Others repeated her words: "*You are a legend playing a legend!*"

Fabrizi tried to smile but managed only a grimace. He clearly feared for his life. With a chopping gesture, he alerted security, who hustled the fans out of the theater.

Mastro Titta's enduring fame is only fitting, I think, in a city that worships the Cross. To quote an old proverb: "*Roma è santa, ma er su popolo boja.*" ("Rome is holy, but her people are executioners.")

40.

A CITY DESERTED:

Pasquino endures another plague

*H*ow lonely she is now, the once crowded city! Widowed is she, who was mistress over nations.

These lines from the Book of Lamentations, the Old Testament dirge attributed to the prophet Jeremiah, were pasted on my pedestal at the height of the coronavirus pandemic. By a priest, perhaps. When the laity comment on current events, they quote Beppe Grillo, the comedian turned politician, not the ancient Hebrews. Maybe it was a modern Hebrew from the Roman Ghetto. Seriously, nobody understands desolation better than Roman Jews. They never walk under the Arch of Titus because its sculpted relief depicts the sack of Jerusalem.

But whoever posted that quotation was right. During its two-month lockdown in spring 2020, Rome felt abandoned and unreal. Only the painter Giorgio de Chirico—whose urban dreamscapes of monuments and arcades were all the rage before the First World War, but who never sketched me until 1968, long after he had become unfashionable and had moved into that poky palazzo near the Spanish Steps—could capture the mystery and melancholy of its empty streets.

Piazza Navona, normally mobbed with pedestrians and alfresco diners, was deserted in 2020, except for bare tables and stacked chairs. Only the gurgle of the Fountain of the Four Rivers broke the eerie silence. Two Jeep Wranglers, turreted with machine guns and stationed between the twin churches of Santa Maria in Monte Santo and Santa Maria dei Miracoli, enforced the curfew in Piazza del Popolo. A defiant but masked jogger sprinted past the Coliseum. Floodlights cast a weird glow on its tiered arcades, as if the stadium somehow had survived an atomic blast.

Isolated in Piazza di Pasquino, I would have perished from boredom and despair, if I couldn't rely on the Angelus bell from the Church of Sant'Agnese in Agone. Every day, precisely at 6:00 AM, twelve noon, and 6:00 PM, it chimed a series of three strokes, each followed by a pause, to mark the three verses of the Angelus prayer; then a peal of nine bells as the nine choirs of angels rejoiced at the Incarnation: Jesus Christ's taking on human flesh to redeem the world. For this blessed distraction, I must thank Cardinal Angelo De Donatis, Vicar General for the Diocese of Rome.

Good church administrators are rarer than saints, so Cardinal De Donatis's efforts to maintain order during a plague-ridden Lent earned my respect, even if the results were not entirely satisfactory. Despite strict rules for social distancing, baptisms continued, but using a squirt gun instead of a font made the ceremonies ludicrous. For the benefit of shut-ins, all weekly masses were streamed, but the video was often blurred and choppy.

Romans might tolerate unanswered prayers but not lousy broadband. The people were irate. Nevertheless, when De Donatis announced at a press conference in the Lateran Apostolic Palace that he had tested positive for COVID-19, everyone sympathized. Well, almost everyone.

"I live this moment as an opportunity that Providence has given me to share in the sufferings of so many brothers and sisters," the cardinal told reporters assembled in the Hall of Conciliation. "I offer my prayer for them, for the whole diocesan community, and for the people of the City of Rome."

"Is this guy being fitted for a crown of thorns?" scoffed a correspondent from *Il Manifesto*. But the joke fell flat. De Donatis might be a powerful churchman, but nobody thought his rank would protect him from the virus. When he was sent to Gemelli University Hospital, I kept tabs on him. The orderlies and janitors proved reliable and often entertaining sources.

Despite a painful convalescence, the Cardinal Vicar insisted on Zooming with his staff, who were quarantined in the Lateran Palace after being exposed to him before his hospitalization. When doctors objected, the Cardinal Vicar reminded them that hundreds of priests had perished: six in Bergamo alone. Most died while anointing the sick or comforting the dying. Surely, Rome's acting bishop can hold a briefing, despite a slight fever? His aides popped up on the MacBook screen and reported the following:

When His Eminence was admitted to the clinic on March 30, 2020, the Monday before Palm Sunday, Rome had been locked down for three straight weeks, but people still ventured into the streets. On this Easter Monday, the city was as empty as Christ's tomb, its silence broken only by the plash of fountains, the chirps of sparrows, the sporadic tolling of bells, and, late at night, the rumble of military trucks policing the streets and gathering the dead. Old women had stopped singing to each other from their balconies. Male teens, sullen because they were forbidden to gather in groups, refused to rev their Vespas in solidarity with the shut-ins.

The Cardinal Vicar crossed himself. Morale was worse than he had thought. Well, I wondered, what did he expect, after that dismal Good

Friday service on Facebook? *Mi ha depresso.* Or, as you Americans would say, it bummed me out. Beneath a waning gibbous moon, Pope Francis performed the Stations of the Cross, completely alone in St. Peter's Square. His amplified voice echoed against Bernini's colonnade. "*Daughters of Jerusalem,*" he intoned, repeating Christ's admonishment to a group of keening women on his way to Calvary, "*do not weep for me. Weep for yourselves and your children.*"

In his Easter Vigil homily, livestreamed the next evening from the Basilica of St. Peter, the Holy Father compared the suffering from the pandemic to the silence of Holy Saturday, a silence of transition and travail, when Christ harrowed Hell to rescue the souls trapped in Limbo. But I disagreed, and so did Cardinal De Donatis. The silence oppressing Rome was completely different. It was the silence of the Apocalypse, after the Lamb opens the seventh seal: the expectant hush before a verdict.

And Rome itself was in the dock.

Before the plague surfaced in Italy on January 31, 2020, the city was blasé. The news from China was distant thunder on a humid summer evening, a frisson to liven drowsy gossip and tepid Campari and sodas on one's balcony. But things changed when COVID-19 invaded Milan as boldly as the French king Charles VIII did in 1494. While Charles cut a swathe through the Italian peninsula to claim the Kingdom of Naples, his troops spread the pox.

Like that French army long ago, the coronavirus advanced across Lombardy and Veneto, turned south into Tuscany and Umbria, marched into Emilia Romagna, and headed straight for Rome. Dreading its arrival, the city developed a siege mentality. Black marketeers sold illicit rice and toilet paper. Children syphoned gas for their families' cars. Matrons disinfected their kitchens until even fried garlic tasted like lye disinfectant. Racists, of course, scapegoated foreign tourists and immigrants. Their hatred proved more contagious than the virus.

Hotels canceled reservations for Chinese guests. Restaurants refused to serve Chinese diners. Universities banned Chinese students from classes. Barflies asked Chinese women if they had a cousin named Ah Choo. Punks vandalized Chinese shops in the Esquilino district. Graffitists spray-painted the Pu Tuo Shan Temple on Via Ferruccio. Beneath a crudely drawn mouse with slanted eyes, some jerk wrote: "The Year of the Plague Rat!"

Chinese-Italian business leaders protested. They had transformed the seedy neighborhood near Termini Station into a prosperous enclave of upscale boutiques and laughing Buddhas. Was this their reward? Sonia Zhou Fenxia, owner of the popular restaurant Hang Zhou, shamed the city in an exposé in *Il Messaggero*. "An epidemic of ignorance is going 'round," she said, "and we must protect ourselves!" The President of the Rome Chamber of Commerce and Industry pledged his support to her, but far-right politicians stoked the bigotry.

When the lockdown began, Romans repented, if only because they had nothing else to do. Cardinal De Angelis was ambivalent about this. Contrition is good for the soul, particularly at Lent, but penance without limits leads to despair. How much longer, he asked, must laymen sanitize their hands with Amuchina? Even Pontius Pilate, the Roman governor who unjustly condemned Christ to death, washed his hands only once after committing that terrible sin.

Unrest was growing, warned the papal secretary on WhatsApp. What if millions of Catholics, now unable to attend Sunday mass, got in the habit of not showing up and never returned? People will abandon the Church if they feel the Church has abandoned them.

Perhaps audacity is required, the Cardinal's aides suggested. During the Plague of Justinian, when the dead clogged the streets, Pope Gregory the Great gambled. On April 25, 560 AD, he led a procession through Rome, begging God to spare the city. Looking up at the Emperor Hadrian's tomb, he saw the Archangel Michael brandishing a flaming sword. As the procession approached, Michael lowered and sheathed his weapon. "The plague is over!" Gregory proclaimed. "God's wrath has been appeased!"

The faithful cheered and sang *Regina Caeli*.

"A bold publicity stunt," His Eminence conceded. "Unfortunately, if I recall correctly, eighty people also dropped dead. It might be prudent, therefore, to maintain social distancing at church services until this current plague ends."

With these dry remarks, the Cardinal Vicar ended the Zoom conference and lay back in bed. Time must undo this knot, not men. He reached for his missal and caressed its leather cover. Bookstores might reopen as early as next Monday, April 20, 2020, according to a bulletin from the City Council. If I recover, he thought, I will browse at the San Paolo bookshop near the Vatican, and Easter Sunday finally may dawn. Until then, it is Holy Saturday. Rome is Christ's tomb, and we souls in Limbo must await our salvation.

But not for long, thank God. Slowly, warily, the city returned to life, and its squares once again rang with laughter by early May.

While sunning myself in Piazza di Pasquino, I overheard Maurizio, the waiter at the pizzeria named after me, serve two coltish young women delicious gossip along with a platter of prosciutto, salami, dried cured beef, artichokes, and olives. The Vatican Museums Gift Shop, they said, had added face masks to its line of clothing and accessories. Made of silk with adjustable bands, they showed a detail from *The Last Judgment*, Michelangelo's fresco in the Sistine Chapel: With a sweep of his hand, Christ condemns the damned as the Madonna looks away. Agitated saints clutch the instruments of their martyrdom.

These face masks, Maurizio said, were "selling like fritters." Naturally, I wanted one for myself. After what happened in Rome during the pandemic, they were the ultimate fashion statement.

AN APPETITE FOR LIFE

41.

FLESH AND FLOWERS:

Pasquino visits the Campo de' Fiori Market

R ome's Campo de' Fiori district features the city's most spectacular flower market. For me, it is the beating heart of the city, pulsing with sights and sounds. Wassily Kandinsky, the Russian painter whose name adorns a plaque on an orange apartment house in the neighborhood, called the market "a symphony of color." Each season strikes a different keynote: chrysanthemums in fall, poinsettias in winter, lilies in spring, roses in summer.

Campo de' Fiori literally means Field of Flowers. At least twice in the past twenty-two centuries, this market has been a meadow. Even now, I feel, it is a country fair in the middle of the city. We Romans always enjoy this bucolic retreat but never let its fragrance cloud our judgment. The piazza's notorious history complicates its beauty. Blood, not fertilizer, has made its roses bloom.

Until the Late Republic, the district between the Tiber and the Temple of Venus remained underdeveloped due to frequent flooding. Fortunately, as I have learned over the centuries, politicians always pursue public works to buy votes. When Pompey the Great built a sports complex in the Lago di Torre Argentina, he converted the scrub and muck into a proper lot for spectators and vendors. At the dedication, Rome's most glamourous prostitutes (*meretrices*) tossed red roses to the cheering crowd. Their diaphanous gowns and jeweled anklets made my heart bloom, among other things.

Pompey called the site Campus Floralis after Flora Primavera, the Roman goddess of spring and flowers. That, at least, is what Victorian classicists claimed. More likely, Pompey was honoring Flora Meretrix, Rome's greatest courtesan, who never allowed Pompey to leave her bed without showering him with petals and biting his ear.

Until the Vandals sacked Rome in 455 AD, florists and butchers, prostitutes and loan sharks plied their trades in this open-air market. After the city fell, the fairgrounds reverted to a field. Borage and yarrow ran amok. For a thousand years, the poor planted vegetable and flower gardens and fought a losing battle with hares and badgers.

Then, in the mid-1400s, Pope Callistus III reorganized and paved the entire district. During this renovation, many elegant buildings were constructed, such as the Palazzo Orsini and the Palazzo della Cancelleria. Once the area was restored, cardinals and ambassadors socialized here. The rich established a thriving horse market, held every Monday and Saturday. Hotels and inns, taverns and restaurants, studios and workshops sprung up overnight. Sometimes I sent my secretary, Antonio Di Renzo, to shop for me. He bargained surprisingly well.

As Rome's only churchless piazza, Campo de' Fiori was consecrated to commerce. Its surrounding streets honored various trades: Via dei Balestrari (crossbow-makers), Via dei Baullari (coffer-makers), Via dei Cappellari (hatters), Via dei Chiavari (locksmiths), and Via dei Giubbonari (tailors). However, there was never a Via dei Fiorai dedicated to florists. A grave injustice, I think. After all, it was florists who gave this square its distinct character.

Business was brisk. Visitors bought wreaths for the jockeys in the *palio*, the annual municipal horse race, garlands for the dancers and musicians in the street fairs, and bouquets for the Swiss Guards in the papal parades. They also bought posies for condemned prisoners. For centuries, criminals and heretics were tortured and executed here. Some were hung. Others were drawn and quartered or thrown into kettles of boiling oil. Most perished at the stake.

The most famous victim was Giordano Bruno, condemned in 1600 for denying the Trinity and the divinity of Christ. The Dominican friar also taught that stars are other suns in the universe. Proud and sarcastic, he accused opponents at a debate in Oxford of "farting out of [their] mouths." The authorities were determined to muzzle him.

After the death sentence was passed, Bruno's jaw was clamped shut with a metal gag. His tongue was pierced with an iron spike, and another iron spike was driven into his palate. With his mouth padlocked, Bruno was driven through the streets, stripped naked, and burned at Campo de' Fiori. Spectators stopped their noses with rose petals or threw lavender sprigs on the flames to kill the stench.

Nineteenth-century liberals made a martyr of Bruno. When Pope Leo XIII denounced Freemasonry, the Grande Oriente d'Italia decided to honor Bruno with a bronze statue. The monument was unveiled, to defiant applause, on June 9, 1889, in Campo de'Fiori. The inscription reads: "A BRUNO—IL SECOLO LUI DIVINATO—QUI DOVE IL ROGO ARSE." ("TO BRUNO—FROM THE CENTURY HE FORETOLD—HERE WHERE THE STAKE BURNED.")

The quickest way to get there is across the Piazza di Trevi. Bruno's statue stands in the center of the square on the exact spot of his execution. It faces a popular restaurant called La Carbonara. The house specialty is *maialino arrosto*, roast pork. I wince but also laugh.

Meanwhile, smiling couples continue to shop at a flower stand beside the statue's pediment. That's life.

Moralists complain because people flirted and haggled as Bruno's ashes fell like charred petals on Campo dei Fiori. Historians sigh because all glory passes away like a meadow. But poets rejoice because, despite a cruel heritage, Roman lovers still buy roses. Breathe deep, my friends, and savor their scent. The dead are pollen in the wind.

42.

FRIED ARTICHOKES:

Pasquino prepares a classic Roman dish

As another Passover approaches, I see Jewish housewives stroll up Via Portico d'Ottavia, beside the faded arches and Corinthian columns of the Theater of Marcellus and beneath the gleaming aluminum dome of the Great Synagogue, to buy artichokes in Campo de' Fiori. Armed with wicker baskets, leather purses, and iPads, they haggle with the *carciofàre*, the market's artichoke cleaners. Seated among tubs of lemony water, these cackling old women with stained but nimble fingers quickly pare the outside leaves, turning the globes as if they were on a lathe.

Artichokes, which come into season in late February and grace the pantry until early summer, emblazon the signs and decorate the tables of the restaurants in Rome's Ghetto district. The most popular menu item is *carciofi alla giudia*, Jewish-style artichokes. Whether served as a snack, an appetizer, or a side, this deep-fried dish is the ultimate soul food. I can't get enough, perhaps because for twenty-one centuries I have witnessed the passionate love affair between Roman Jews and *carciofi alla guidia*. A totem of cultural identity, fried artichokes symbolize the Jewish community's appetite for life and its endurance in the face of oppression.

Jews have lived in the Eternal City since the Late Republic. The first contact came in 161 BC, when Judas Maccabeus, the Jewish military leader, sent two envoys to Rome to secure an alliance against the Seleucid dynasty in Asia Minor. By 69 BC, when Pompey the Great conquered Palestine and incorporated it into Roman province of Syria, several thousand Jews had moved to Seven Hills. Added immigration from the Levant and Egypt swelled the colony until it reached thirty to forty thousand people.

The immigrants settled in a riverside district east of Tiber Island, where they ran shops, leased warehouses, and cultivated artichokes in urban gardens. The edible thistles, neighbors joked, suited the newcomers' prickly temperament. As I recall, pagan Romans accepted the Jews' stubborn monotheism but were flabbergasted by their prohibition against pork.

Life was good until an uprising occurred in Roman-occupied Palestine in 67 AD. This revolt took the empire three years to crush, during which a million people died and Jerusalem was sacked. Back in the imperial capital, Romans became less tolerant of their Jewish neighbors and suspected them of sedition. The Arch of Titus, erected in 81 AD, commemorated the Roman victory over the Jews and showed the prisoners and booty brought back into the city by the legions commanded by the Emperor Vespasian's son Titus. Vespasian imposed a punitive tax against the Jewish colony called the *fisca judaicus*.

"You can pay in cash" the Emperor said, "or in artichokes."

After that, the Jews of Rome dropped out of recorded history, surfacing only occasionally in the Middle Ages as victims of restrictive laws or mob violence. For the most part, Roman Jews, whose population had shrunk dramatically, minded their business and ate their artichokes. Most considered themselves lucky. Unlike the Jews of Venice and other Italian city states, the Jews of Rome had the freedom to come and go as they pleased, thanks to the money they lent to worldly Renaissance popes. But everything changed during the Counter-Reformation.

On July 14, 1555, Pope Paul IV issued a bull confining Rome's thousand Jews to a small area along the bank of the Tiber across from the Trastevere district. This ghetto was walled and its gates were locked at night. If residents ventured outside during the day, they were required to identify themselves by dress. Men wore a *sciamanno,* a yellow badge as big as an artichoke, on their vest. Women wore a yellow veil, the same color worn by prostitutes.

On the Jewish Sabbath, the entire community was forced to attend compulsory sermons in front of San Gregorietto, a tiny church outside the wall of the Ghetto, but people put wax in their ears to avoid hearing the words. Over the church portal, this inscription was written in Latin and Hebrew, a quotation from the prophet Isaiah: "*All day long, I have stretched out my hands to a rebellious people, who walk in the wrong path and follow their own crooked thoughts.*"

On Catholic feast days, Roman Jews entertained their Christians neighbors by competing in cruel games. They were forced to run naked through the streets, with a rope around the neck or their legs encased in burlap sacks, or they were ridden by booted and spurred soldiers as spectators pelted them with artichokes. But these humiliations were nothing compared to an awful ceremony that occurred every spring. Whenever I think about it, I grind my teeth.

The ceremony had two parts. First, at the Arch of Titus, commemorating the sack of Jerusalem in 70 AD, all Roman Jews swore allegiance to the Pope. Then, at the public square crowning Capitoline Hill, the Chief Rabbi paid homage to Caporione, the Chief City Councilor. In exchange, the Chief Rabbi received a kick to his bottom.

This meant that the Jews could remain another year in Rome as second-class citizens. Somehow, over the next few centuries, they managed to survive under their Gentile oppressors.

Which reminds me of a story still told in the Ghetto.

Once upon a time, the Pope (never mind which one) decreed that all Jews must become Catholics or leave Rome. Because of the outcry, the Pope offered a deal. He would debate the Chief Rabbi in Piazza Gerusalemme, the square in front of the Church of San Gregorietto. If the Rabbi won, the Jews could stay in Rome. If the Pope won, they must convert or leave. But since the Chief Rabbi spoke no Latin and the Pope spoke no Hebrew, both sides agreed that the contest would be a silent debate.

On the chosen day the Pope and the Chief Rabbi sat opposite each other.

The Pope raised his hand and showed three fingers. The Rabbi raised one finger and shook it at the Pope. The Pope swept his hand across the sky. The Rabbi pointed to the ground and stamped his foot. Then the Pope snapped his fingers, and a clean-shaven seminarian with soup-bowl haircut brought a plate of roasted lamb with bread and wine. The Rabbi also snapped his fingers, and a bearded Talmudical scholar with sidelocks brought an artichoke heart salad.

The Pope stood, declared himself beaten, and said that the Jews could stay in Rome.

Later, the cardinals met with His Holiness and asked him what had happened.

"That Rabbi is a brilliant theologian!" the Pope said. "First, I held up three fingers to represent the Trinity. He responded by holding up a single finger, shaking it to remind me there is still only one God common to both our faiths. Then, I waved at the sky to say that the heavens declare the glory of God. He pointed to the ground to show that the earth is God's footstool. Finally, I presented roasted lamb with bread and wine to proclaim that Christ has redeemed the world. He presented an artichoke salad to suggest that God of Israel will restore the Garden of Eden at the end of the time. He trounced me at every move, so I admitted defeat."

Meanwhile, the Jewish community gathered to ask the Chief Rabbi how he had won.

"I haven't a clue," the Rabbi said. "First, he told me that we had three days to get out of Rome, so I shook my finger and said no. Then he waved to tell me that the whole city would be cleared of Jews, but I stomped my foot told him that we were staying put."

"And then what?" asked a woman.

"And then what?" said the Rabbi. "He ordered his lunch, so I ordered mine."

The Jews not only resisted conversion but also partly converted their Christian enemies through alchemical cooking. Despite being a persecuted minority, they utterly transformed Roman cuisine. The reason is easy to explain.

When Pope Paul IV confined Jews to the Ghetto, he banned them from most professions. Since food vending was one of the few permitted activities, many Jews operated *friggitorie*, stalls selling *fritti*, or fritters. Unlike other local fried foods, prepared with pork fat, Jewish *fritti* were cooked with olive oil, due to kosher rules and to the influence of Spanish and Sicilian Jews, who came to Rome after being expelled from Castile and Aragon in 1492. Experts at deep frying, these refugees perfecting a series of skillet dishes that have become Roman staples: fried stuffed zucchini flowers, fried sweet-and-sour cod, and, of course, deep-friend artichokes.

The ingredients are simple—artichokes, oil, and salt—but the prep is complicated. Benvenuto Cellini, the sixteenth century sculptor and goldsmith who often dined in the Ghetto, said it was easier to smelt and cast his bronze statue of Perseus than to cook *carciofi alla giudia*.

The trick, Cellini told me, is to fry the artichokes twice: the first time in hot oil; the second time, after a brief cooling, in scalding oil. The thermal shock of the second frying causes the artichokes to bloom. When served, they resemble chrysanthemums sculpted in gold: the outside leaves crisp as chips, the inside soft and flavorful. Almost no trace of frying oil remains. What could be more satisfying or delicious?

Ever since Cellini's day, *carciofi alla giudia* have been a Roman delicacy. Nevertheless, this traditional dish ignited a war that rivaled the Great Jewish Revolt of the first century AD. This time, however, the conflict wasn't between Roman legionnaires and Jewish zealots but between the Jews of Rome and the religious authorities of Jerusalem.

Before Passover 2018, the Chief Rabbinate of Israel declared artichokes non-kosher and banned all imports. While not distinguishing artichokes grown in Israel and other Middle Eastern countries from those grown for the Italian market, the Rabbinate specifically referred to the way cooks prepare the vegetable for Rome's Jewish community, the oldest one in Europe.

"An artichoke heart is full of worms," said Rabbi Yitzhak Arazi, Director of Imports. "There's no way you can clean it." The Roman Jewish style of frying artichokes, he pontificated, makes it even more difficult to remove the pests. And because worms, along with reptiles, amphibians, and most other insects (except certain types of locusts), are *treyf*—forbidden—eating *carciofi alla guidia* was now prohibited.

Roman Jews objected. Generations of Jews have been eating *carciofi alla guidia* with no spiritual or other problems. A kosher food can't lose its certificate. It doesn't work that way! Besides, Roman artichokes are superior to Jerusalem artichokes. Their stems are tighter, their leaves more compact, making them impenetrable to insects. These arguments failed to persuade Arazi. The dish can't be kosher, he insisted. This wasn't politics; it was Jewish religious law.

Yeshivas petitioned the Rabbinate. Demonstrators picketed the Israeli embassy on the Pincio. Social media was flooded with thousands of posts, from angry diatribes against the diktat to tender love poems about *carciofi all guidia*. Political memes were recycled. "*Je suis Charlie*," which went viral after the 2015 attacks on the French satirical magazine, *Charlie Hebdo*, became "*Je suis Carciofo.*"

Despite the ban, *carciofi alla giudia* remained on the menu when I visited Nonna Betta, my favorite kosher restaurant in the Ghetto. "Romans Jews have prepared this dish the same way for five centuries," explained Umberto Pavoncello, the restaurant's manager and a pal of mine. "We're not going listen to those ignorant killjoys in Jerusalem."

Still, Umberto worried about the souls of all those pious Jews who had eaten deep-fried artichokes for half a millennium. Would something bad happen to them after death? The living, however, could eat fried artichokes with a clear conscience. Both Rome's Chief Rabbi and the President of the Jewish Community had posted photos on Facebook showing them thoroughly washing and preparing *carciofi alla giudia* to celebrate Passover. Look—no worms!

With a wink and a toss of the head, Umberto directed my attention to the table across from ours. A young waiter delivered a plate of fried artichokes to an Orthodox Jewish family from Lakewood, New Jersey. The matriarch, a statuesque woman wearing a knitted snood, gasped in delight when she saw them. Catching the light, the largest artichoke gleamed like the dome of the Great Synagogue of Rome.

43.

EASTER LAMB:

Pasquino discusses a tender subject

A mile and a half from the Circus Maximus, sheep graze in Caffarella Park. This dreamy pastoral, worthy of the landscape painter Giovanni Paolo Panini, makes me sigh. Warming themselves in the April sun, the sheep are indifferent to the ruins of towers and mausoleums and oblivious to an annual rite of spring. Shepherds gather and transport the youngest of the flock for slaughter and sale at Piazza San Cosimato and Piazza Testaccio. As Easter approaches, Rome once again craves *abbacchio*, suckling lamb. I lick my lips, albeit guiltily.

Abbacchio was a delicacy before the city's founding. During this bucolic period, sheep were Latium's basic monetary unit, called a *pecus*. Their skin and wool provided clothing. Their milk, cheese. Their meat supplied protein. When Roman law was codified, *peculium* (the Latin root for "pecuniary") came to mean transferable property, sometimes in the form of pasturage or livestock. The Divino Amore district, between the Alban Hills and central Rome, was the finest grazing range in classical times. The best *abbacchio* still comes from here.

According to Juvenal, who satirized Rome's imperial appetites, true suckling lamb should be "more milk than blood," killed before the animal tastes its first grass. The tender-hearted may weep, but the tough-minded shrug. Believe me, lambs are not harmless. They nibble everything in sight and compact and erode the soil. Dairy ewes live about a decade, producing up to four lambs a year. When too many threaten to deplete a pasture, ranchers whisk them away. With their hooves twined over a long stick called a *bacchio*, the lambs are carried from their pens, clubbed to death, and tossed into a pickup truck.

An overabundance of lamb usually beats down spring prices. But during the fourth century, butchers gouged customers. Because the growing number of Christians craved *abbacchio* at Easter, demand always exceeded supply. This annoyed Aurelius Augustinus, the future St. Augustine, who had moved to Rome in 398 AD to teach rhetoric to spoiled preppies but couldn't afford lamb for his own family table. Not long ago, he complained, Christians were fed to the lions in the area. Now they were being devoured by wolves in the market, but only because their own gluttony made them easy prey.

I can see Augustine's point. Unlike the Christians in his native North Africa, Christians in Rome rarely fasted or observed such dietary restrictions as avoiding meat used in pagan sacrifices. The daily temptations were too strong and pervasive. Although Christianity was made the official religion of the Roman Empire in 313 AD, Rome itself remained defiantly pagan. For Augustine, the city's insatiable appetite for food and cruelty was symbolized by the Colosseum, whose gaping arcades resembled tier upon tier of hungry mouths.

The extravaganzas of munching and crunching shocked even me. While spectators snacked on hot rolls and pickled lupini beans, a feeding frenzy exploded in the arena. Wild animals fought each other to the death and were forced to eat their victims. The leftovers were offered to the ravenous crowd, who snatched raw chunks of boar, deer, bull, or bear, surged through the *vomitoria*, the stadium's exit passages, and dashed back to the Aventine Hill to cook their supper and honor the gods.

Could the Christians truly convert such people? I wondered. These carnivores would never fast during Lent, unless they also could feast on a delicious sacrificial victim. I'm sure that's how Jesus Christ, the Lamb of God, became a blue-plate special.

For ages, Roman Jews had cooked lamb for Passover. Having co-opted this culinary tradition for Easter, the Church now permitted the city's plebs to eat such greasy street food as grilled lamb chops and deep-fried lamb spleen. Patricians were allowed to serve more refined dishes, such as Parthian sweet-and-sour lamb, lamb stew with green beans and croutons, and poached lamb brains with parsley and lemon sauce, but nothing was more coveted than *particum* (suckling lamb), the ancestor of *abbaccchio*. Such excess kept the economy humming.

Lamb remained a reliable commodity, even after the Sack of Rome. Medieval popes, the self-styled "shepherds of the church," profited the most. They turned huge tracts of land into pastures extending from the gates of Rome to the borders of Tuscany and Umbria. To replenish its treasury, the Church established a *dogana dei pastorizie*. This customs act allowed the Vatican to tax all sheep farms within its purview and to collect rent on all pasturage.

Rome also promoted sheep-keeping in the Campagna, which belonged to its most powerful families. The Orsini and Colonnas, the Caffarelli and Torlonias converted wheat fields into grazing land. Over time this land became marshy and covered with *macchia*, maquis brush. Poor drainage bred mosquitoes. Even after quinine became available, most Roman shepherds suffered from malaria. Sallow and shivering, they drove Easter lambs to market. The men looked more dead than alive, but the lambs bleated and skipped and wiggled their tails.

Tough luck makes tender flesh. Despite its unsavory history, *abbacchio* is too succulent to resist. Unlike grass-fed lamb, suckling lamb is pale, buttery soft, and sweet. Slaughtered at one or two months old and weighing between 15 to 20 pounds, *abbacchio* has burned off most of its baby fat but has not developed muscle. Every ounce of the animal is consumed with relish, from legs to ribs, organ meats to intestines. This thrift can salve even the tenderest conscience. As Eugenio Pacelli, the Secretary of State of Vatican City who would become Pope Pius XII, told his fellow cardinals as they settled down for a lamb dinner at Ristorante del Colonnato near St. Peter's: "If there is no waste, there is no guilt."

Well, everyone deserves a little papal indulgence, even the most self-denying saint. Let me treat you to dinner on this Saturday before Holy Week.

At a *trattoria* near Campo de' Fiori, a waiter recites a litany of mouthwatering dishes to Maryknoll nuns on pilgrimage. Would the good sisters like *abbacchio al forno con le patate*, roast baby lamb with potatoes? For something slurpier, try *abbacchio brodettato*, braised lamb in broth with white wine and scrambled egg yolks. Would you prefer a simpler meal? We recommend *abbacchio scottadito*. These grilled lamb chops will singe your fingertips. For the more daring, there is *coratella con carciofi*, sauté lamb's offal with slivers of artichoke hearts.

Such guilty pleasures! The waiter winks. The nuns blush and stare at their menus.

The Mother Superior, raised on a Nebraskan sheep farm, orders *pajata d'abbacchio*: lamb chitterlings stewed in tomatoes and served with rigatoni. A baby-faced novice wonders whether it is right to eat lamb before Easter but swallows her scruples with the first bite. That's human nature for you, don't you think? We beat our breasts and lick our fingers.

44.

THE TASTE OF SPRING:
Pasquino craves his favorite greens

Early on the first Sunday in May 2020—at the end of a COVID-19 lockdown that in Rome had lasted for two months, one week, and two days—the goddess Flora returned to us. At her tender smile, the plane trees budded along the Tiber River. The swifts responded with cries of joy as a demoralized city slowly awakened to spring.

Standing in Piazza di Pasquino, I imagined the transformation: a promenade of Japanese cherries blossoming around the artificial lake of a business complex, the trees' graceful outlines softening the harshness of the district's Fascist architecture. I heard the goddess's laughter float on the morning breeze until it reached an elliptical park—a chariot racetrack back in my day—between two hills in the heart of the city. Here, opposite the ruins of the Temple of Flora, roses bloomed on the menorah-shaped paths of what was once a Jewish community garden.

These sights, however, were only a prelude to the marvelous smells that engulfed Rome.

The scent of the wisteria draped over the Aurelian Wall, surged through the city's northern gate, and flooded the historic city center. I swooned on my pedestal and nearly drowned in the fragrance. Virginia creeper and bougainvillea cascaded down the façade of a nearby terraced hotel. Jasmine and honeysuckle poured from the roofs, splashed over the decks, and trickled down the lintels of the weathered houses in the working-class district.

I watched my fellow Romans react. The differences between the sexes were striking. From their windows and balconies, the men squinted and sniffed the air warily. It was if they feared being tricked by a perfumed but treacherous courtesan. After so many disappointments, so many crushed hopes during the quarantine, they didn't want to risk feeling joy. In contrast, the women—the cyclist tracing figure eights around Giordano Bruno's statue in Campo de' Fiori, the student sunbathing on the rooftop of her dorm, the matron in a Versace bathrobe reading an Elena Ferrante novel on her flagstone patio, the tattered widow sneaking into the Forum to feed the stray cats—all savored the bouquet and surrendered to bliss.

That is why I admire Roman women. They have the courage to be happy. They also have a feral appetite for pleasure. It wasn't enough to *smell* spring. They wanted to *taste* it, too. After weeks of strict curfew, during which they couldn't venture more than 200 meters from home except to walk dogs or do the groceries, these daughters of La Lupa—the She Wolf that suckled Romulus and Remus—craved *misticanza*: a Roman salad of wild mixed greens. The next day, when the curfew finally lifted, they flocked to the city's parks and foraged for ingredients.

This is a traditional rite of spring in Rome. Borage and chicory, dandelion and endive, sorrel and lamb's lettuce grow everywhere, from the clipped hedges of Villa Doria Pamphili to the unmown lawns Caffarella Park. But *agretti*, more precious than truffles, is found only in the ditches near the city's sprawling artichoke fields. Also called *barbe di frate*, because its fronds resemble a monk's beard, this elusive but succulent green is prized by Benedictine herbalists, Michelin chefs, and working-class Roman housewives.

A salt-water plant that once flourished on the beaches of Ostia and the marshes of Anzio, *agretti* was originally cultivated for industrial purposes. Until the nineteenth century, tons of this compact shrub were burned to form soda ash, crucial in the manufacture of soap and glass. When more efficient methods were developed, *agretti* was no longer harvested.

For the bourgeoisie, the now useless weed served no practical purpose, but the proletariat, clinging to rural customs even in factory neighborhoods, employed it in their kitchens. The chive-like stems, sold for pennies in open-air markets, were so highly versatile. They could garnish poached or brined fish or season stewed artichokes or boiled potatoes.

Agretti can be steamed and dressed with olive oil and lemon, sautéed with pancetta and poured on capellini, whisked with eggs and Parmesan and baked into a frittata, topped on white pizza with mozzarella and cherry tomatoes, or tossed with arugula, escarole, and radicchio and drizzled with vinaigrette for a tangy salad.

British and American gourmets, who turned this once marginalized green into a trendy delicacy, struggle to describe its flavor. I do, too, because it is so fickle and elusive. Raw *agretti* tastes like samphire or sea fennel but is chewier and grassier. Its chlorophyll bursts in the mouth, leaving a slightly sour, slightly acid residue that reminds me of pickled capers. Cooked *agretti* is more like spinach, but its minerality is more pronounced. It also tastes livelier, crackling with the electric power of spring. Glaucus became a sea god by eating a magical herb. Roman women rejuvenate themselves by eating *agretti*.

Such were my thoughts as members of Trastevere's Urban Foraging Club, eager to get down to work, gathered in front of a brick church with spires like asparagus tips. Despite the still-required medical masks, the ladies looked lovely in their bright spring dresses. Each carried a wicker basket with a digging fork, kitchen scissors, and a mesh bag. As swifts cried and swooped overhead, they marched up the street single file, crossed a stone bridge, and combed the overgrown ancient racetrack between the Aventine and Palatine Hills. After finding and cleaning some tasty treats, they spread a checkered tablecloth on the grass, prepared a mixed salad in a large wooden bowl, and picnicked by the ruins of the Temple of Flora.

Lunch finished, the friends returned home along the Tiber, gossiping and laughing, and spent the late afternoon at a villa that was once the gardens of Gaius Julius Caesar. The women admired the park's crumbling grandeur: the abandoned aviary, the statues of the muses, the crowded turtle pond. They imagined Furrina, the Roman water goddess, reclining on its plush lawn or Caesar himself cavorting with Cleopatra on the stone benches.

If we are to believe Shakespeare's play about her last days, Cleopatra regretted her youthful dalliance with Caesar. "My salad days," she sighs, "when I was green in judgment." Her words puzzle me. Does Cleopatra mean that youth, like salad, is raw? That salad is highly flavored and appeals only to youthful palates? Or that herbs are the food of youth just as milk is the food of babes and meat is the food of men?

The Bard never explains. But for these women of Rome, who had survived a pandemic to stand here at sunset with their appetites intact,

Cleopatra's meaning was clear enough: *All flesh is grass, so enjoy wild greens for as long as you can!*

EPILOGUE

45.

ARRIVEDERCI, ROMA:
Pasquino says goodbye

Thanks for spending time with me in Rome. I enjoyed your company. But before we part, let me treat you to a gelato. Bet you've never tasted anything like it! Because it contains so little milk fat and is churned so slowly, gelato is thicker, richer, and smoother than ice cream. The intense flavor, I guarantee, will sear the memory of Rome on your tongue.

Rome has many splendid gelaterias. Where shall we go? Fassi's, next to the train station, is a palace of Palladian windows, decorative wrought iron, and plaster arches. Giolitti's, near the Pantheon, is a café with marble counters, oak panels, and brass chandeliers. But Cecere's, a tiny shop on a side street in the heart of Baroque Rome, serves the best handmade gelato in the city. The quickest way to get there is to cross the Piazza di Trevi.

The square's famous fountain, the largest in Rome, towers ninety feet before us. Beneath a triumphal arch, Oceanus, father of all river gods, is being pulled in a shell-shaped chariot by seahorses and mermen as water cascades down rockwork. Tourists turn their backs and toss a coin over their left shoulders into the fountain's basin. This spare change, they think, will bribe Fate into bringing them back to Rome. It won't, of course, but it contributes to the fountain's upkeep and helps to feed the city's poor, who dream of the gelato at Cecere's.

As I expected, the glass counter is crowded, so grab a menu and follow me outside into the cobblestone courtyard. Someone will take our orders soon enough. Meanwhile, let us lounge in the shade of this cozy umbrella table, smelling the fragrance of the potted rosemary, boxwood, and olive trees and listening to the distant roar of the fountain.

What shall we order? I recommend the seasonal fruit gelatos; the ingredients are always fresh. With more than a dozen on the menu, it's difficult to choose, so let's play a game. Which flavor best captures our time together in Rome: Sweet pear, sour lemon, or tart raspberry? If you can't decide, I will order something that tastes like all three. Here's our waiter.

"*Cameriere,* two bowls of pomegranate gelato, *per favore*! If possible, garnished with pomegranate seeds. This is my guest's last day in Rome, so let us try to make it memorable."

Friend, I will miss you. But not half as much as you will miss Rome. Wherever you go, you will constantly think of her. Because Rome is your true home, the city of your soul. As soon as you arrived, you realized this is the one place on earth where you are free to be yourself.

I don't mean your best self. Rome delights in bringing out the worst in us. And I don't mean your whole self. Rome rarely provides a safe space for our inner healing. No, I mean your *true* self—with all your imperfections and illusions, contradictions and confusions, unhealed wounds and unresolved conflicts. Only Rome accepts us for who we are. She knows we are incorrigible, but she loves us anyway. Human nature, even at its worst, never scandalizes her.

And that is why you will return to Rome. Like the swifts every March on the Feast of San Benedetto, like the pilgrims every fifty years for the Great Jubilee, when all debts are canceled and all sins are forgiven, you will come back to be reborn. That is the secret to happiness.

Johann Wolfgang von Goethe learned this lesson while cultivating a taste for Italian ices. When he arrived in Rome on October 29, 1786, the thirty-seven-year-old poet was suffering from a midlife crisis. Tired of his court duties at Weimar, sick of German Romanticism, and frustrated by an affair with a married woman, he rented a ground-floor apartment on the Corso, the city's main thoroughfare, took up drawing, and pretended to be a struggling artist.

Because local bookstores displayed his face in their shop windows, I easily recognized the author of *The Sorrows of Young Werther*. This best-selling novel had inspired a generation of lovesick teens to blow their brains out. But Goethe, I could tell, was made of sterner stuff. When he strode into my piazza with his marble brow and chiseled features, he was already posing for his future monument in the Villa Borghese Gardens.

Wearing a broad-brimmed sunhat and wrapped in a white cloak resembling a toga, Goethe introduced himself to me. He doffed his hat, bowed low, and sang a tune from Mozart's *Don Giovanni*: "*O statua gentilissima del gran Commendatore!*" Charmed, I pledged to show him a good time in Rome, but Goethe only wanted to visit churches and museums—ideally, when they were deserted. He preferred the Coliseum at midnight to the Spanish Steps at noon.

We sat in Antico Caffè Greco, the coffeehouse off the Piazza di Spagna, and planned our itinerary. Because of the scirocco, the sultry North African wind, it was unusually warm, so I offered to treat him to a refreshing raspberry sorbet. Goethe wrinkled his nose and grimaced.

"Am I Nero?" he asked. Slaves would fetch snow from the mountains, mix it with honey, wine, and fruit, and serve the dessert to quench the emperor's thirst.

"No," I said, "but a little decadence would do you good."

Goethe solemnly shook his head. "Nothing," he said, "must come between me and the sun of the sublime. I am too old now for anything but truth."

What could I do with such a pompous ass? Nothing pleased him! Rites, operas, processions, ballets: they were merely "distractions and vanities." He ignored the living Rome, the Rome I loved and longed to share with him, to explore some imaginary Rome in his head. Rather than converse with monks and beggars, whores and buskers, who would have taught him the wisdom of its streets, he communed with the illustrious ghosts who haunted its ruins.

Goethe could sketch a broken column or ruined aqueduct for hours. Other times he became abstracted and lost himself in thought. This made it impossible to enjoy his company.

"*Che pensa!*" I said. "Why do you think so much? A man should never think. Thinking only ages you. And stop concentrating on only one thing! You'll go crazy. A man should have a thousand things, a great confusion, whirling about in his head."

Goethe did not understand me, until he participated in the Roman Carnival.

Unlike Rome's other religious and civic holidays, the Carnival was not an official feast. The people organized it for themselves each year. Shortly after twelve noon on *Giovedi Grasso*, the Thursday before Ash Wednesday, a bell rang on the Capitoline Hill. This signal gave Romans of all ranks and ages, most already in costume, permission to be as crazy and foolish as they liked. Everything was allowed, except punching and stabbing. Goethe, whose apartment house was at the center of the festival, put on a domino mask and surrendered himself to madness.

For six days, he was swept away. I couldn't believe my eyes. He mocked a procession of magistrates in full regalia. He threw flowers at an open carriage of masked clowns in conical hats and blouses decorated with fluffy pom-poms. He flirted with women dressed as men and men dressed as women. He bet and lost his rent money on a Berber horse race in the Corso. He even joined a melee of revelers pelting each other with powdered plaster.

Carnival ended at sunset on Fat Tuesday with the *Festa dei Moccoletti*, the Festival of Candles. A flickering parade flowed along the Corso and adjacent streets. All Rome was there. Like the rest of the crowd, Goethe and I carried a lighted candle representing the flame of our individual life. "*Sia amazzato chi nun porta er moccolo!*" we roared. "Death to anyone who doesn't carry a candle!"

With this bloodthirsty cry, everyone tried to blow out his neighbor's candle. Goethe and I saw a little boy snuff his father's flame. "*Sia amazzato er Signor Padre!*" he yelled. "Death to you, Signor Father!" Goethe's was delighted but became distracted by a spotted moth, fluttering around a streetlamp. Suddenly, it immolated itself on a torch! Goethe gasped. Seeing my chance, I snuck beside him and yelled:

"*Sia amazzato er Signor Poeta!* Death to you, Signor Poet!" and blew out his candle.

Goethe stiffened and glared. Then he relaxed, threw back his head, and laughed.

After the Carnival, Goethe gossiped with barbers and tobacconists, allowed his landlady's cat to mark his antique bust of Jupiter, and began an affair with an innkeeper's daughter named Faustina. He tapped Latin hexameters on her thigh and took her for dessert after sex. At Caffé Greco, they devoured raspberry sorbets. Faustina spooned the fruited ice into Goethe's mouth, letting it drip down his chin and stain his white cloak.

"But here's *our* gelato! Freshly made and generously sprinkled with pomegranate seeds. Dig in, my friend, and don't be ashamed!" There's nothing sinful about gelato, whatever Goethe's Lutheran ancestors might have thought. Why, even the early Christians craved iced desserts—cool foretastes of heaven, they said. If you don't believe me, read the epitaphs in the catacombs: "*In refrigerio dulcis anima tuam.*" ("May your soul enjoy sweet, cool refreshment.")

And nothing is more refreshing than pomegranate gelato! Provided you eat it right.

First, pop the biggest pomegranate seed into your mouth and bite hard. Let the juice spurt from your lips and the taste explode on your tongue. It's so intense that it burns, doesn't it? Now scoop a spoonful of gelato into your mouth and freeze the flavor. Feel the sparkles of sweet and sour and tart crystalize on your palate. Then close your eyes and empty your mind.

Like Goethe, you may think too much, my friend! Now you can stop trying to straighten yourself out. You can forget about saving the world. Instead, practice *la gaia scienza*, the joyful science. Cherish your contradictions and satisfy your desires. Never fret over private failures or public tragedies—and carry on! That is the Roman way. It will keep you happy and sane. The greatest pleasure of living in this city is to accept life on its own terms.

If we had more time, I'd show you the bronze pomegranate by the Coliseum. It must be twenty feet tall, at least. Seeds burst from its husk. Well, we'll save that for your next visit. Maybe next year, maybe next millennium. It doesn't really matter. Time doesn't exist here. A century is like a day in the Eternal City, and a day is like a century. So let's not say *addio*, or farewell, but *arrivederci*. We'll see each other again, I promise.

Now take a last look at this little corner of Rome. Say goodbye to the young honeymooners sharing a cone of strawberry ice cream, to the lovely mother fretting over the chocolate syrup her little boy has spilled on his sailor's suit, to the natty widower toasting them with a cappuccino, to the invalid in the wheelchair being fed a waffle cookie as if it were his last communion.

Enjoy these moments but don't try to save them. Let them melt in your heart like this gelato on your tongue. Nothing lasts forever, despite what they say about Heaven. But you don't need Heaven, do you?

Today, you have been happy in Rome.

ACKNOWLEGEMENTS

Earlier version of these essays appeared as bilingual columns in *L'Italo Americano*, America's oldest surviving Italian-American newspaper, between August 2013 and December 2020. Four were also previously published in *Forktales*, *Ovunque Siamo*, and *We the Italians*. I am grateful to editor Simone Schiavinato, who commissioned the original pieces, for permitting me to revise, expand, and collect them here.

I am also grateful to Edward Hower, my editor at Cayuga Lake Books, who believed in this book from the start and guided and encouraged its completion. If these essays now appeal to a wider, English-speaking audience, it is only because of Edward's coaching. I hope that our readers are pleased with the results.

Others supported me in different ways. My father, Philip Di Renzo, shared his intimate knowledge of Rome with me. My wife, Sharon Ahlers kept me sane and focused throughout a global pandemic. In addition, friends and colleagues provided feedback on this collection during its long gestation. If I could, I would chisel their names in marble:

Barbara Adams, Francesca Bezzone, Cory Brown, Patti Capaldi, Susan Adams Delaney, Julia della Croce, Peter D'Epiro, Maria DiFrancesco, Rhian Ellis, Marella Feltrin-Morris, Peter Fortunato, Christopher Gilbert, Andrei Guruianu, Lisa Harris, Rajpreet Heir, Eleanor Henderson, Eric Machan Howd, Tom Kerr, Katharyn Howd Machan, Jack Hopper, Jeanne Mackin, Joan Marcus, Katie Marks, Jerry

Mirskin, Umberto Mucci, Stacey Murphy, Patricia Ober, Raul Palma, Kristin Park, Shona Ramaya, Catherine Rankovic, Michelle Messina Reale, Tiziana Rinaldi, Kenneth Scambray, Robert Sullivan, Jack Wang, and Jaime Warburton.

I thank Claire Gleitman, Dean of the School of Humanities and Sciences, and Melanie Stein, Provost and Senior Vice President of Academic Affairs, who granted me a sabbatical leave from Ithaca College to work on this project. I urge them to throw a coin in the Dillingham Fountains and wish for a fellowship at the American Academy in Rome.

Finally, I am indebted to Giuseppe Gioachino Belli, Cesare Pascarella, and Trilussa, whose delightful sonnets in the Roman dialect inspired these pasquinades. I don't deserve to be included in their august company, but when I die, I hope to dine with them in the afterlife at La Cisterna, their favorite *trattoria* in the Trastevere district. Open for business since 1600, it serves the best *saltimbocca* in the city.

ANTHONY DI RENZO

ABOUT THE AUTHOR

Anthony Di Renzo, a fugitive from advertising, teaches writing at Ithaca College. His previous books include *Bitter Greens; Essays on Food, Politics, and Ethnicity from the Imperial Kitchen* (State University of New York Press, 2010), *Trinàcria: A Tale of Bourbon Sicily* (Guernica Editions, 2013), and *Dead Reckoning: Transatlantic Passages on Europe and America* (State University of New York Press, 2016), cowritten with Andrei Guruianu. These works satirize the ongoing culture war between Italian humanism and American capitalism. Italy usually loses.

A scholar of twentieth-century American literature, Di Renzo also has published two critical studies: *American Gargoyles: Flannery O'Connor and the Medieval Grotesque* (Southern Illinois University Press, 1993) and *If I Were Boss: The Early Business Stories of Sinclair Lewis* (Southern Illinois University Press, 1999). As Pasquino, Rome's talking statue, he contributed monthly humor columns to *L'Italo Americano* between 2013 and 2020.

He lives in Ithaca, New York: an Old World man in a New Age town.

Made in the USA
Monee, IL
10 October 2023

44259501R00173